Visitor

Book 1
Crocodile Dreaming Series

Novel by

Graham Wilson

VISITOR   GRAHAM WILSON

Contents

Acknowledgements

Thank you to my family and close friends, particularly my wife, Mary, who supported me on my writing journey.

Thank you also to the many backpackers and other travellers I met while living in the Northern Territory. Some of you came with me on my travels; many shared your experiences of the world from which you came and of journeying through this land. From you came many ideas for this story.

Special thanks to the aboriginal peoples of the NT, with many aboriginal friends giving me insights for parts of this story.

Most significantly, thank you to a large unseen crocodile, probably still living in a remote Arnhem Land billabong, who almost had me for dinner. Teeth marks, visible on my leg today, remind me of my own real-life encounter. This actual creature sits at the centre of this book's imagined story. I am often asked to tell the true story in outback bars.

My sense of the silent power of this predator remains with me yet. Along with aboriginal mythology and other people's stories, it feeds my fascination for these huge ancient creatures, barely changed since the time of the dinosaurs. Some of the largest crocodiles I have seen, which live in very remote parts of the Northern Territory, rival those in this created story.

Also thank you to readers of earlier versions of this story. Your comments, mostly positive, encouraged me to keep going with improving this series. Reviews, both the good and bad, give great insight into how to improve the telling of a story.

Along with the excellent professional editing advice provided by Kathryn Moore, these reviews were very valuable in helping me see areas where both the plot and the way it is told needed to be improved. As a result, it is hoped readers will find this is an even better version of the original story that has captivated many of you over the years since it was first written.

VISITOR   GRAHAM WILSON

Author's Note

This is a novel set in Australia's Northern Territory, a place where I lived and worked for four decades. Settings used are the places I know, including small towns, aboriginal communities, cattle stations and many remote, rugged and beautiful natural locations for which it is famous, places with names like Uluru and Kakadu. These give an authentic backdrop to this story.

This is a work of fiction. The characters are not real people. However, elements of the story have a real basis, as experienced by me, or as tales of the bush, spoken around campfires or over bars, somewhere in the Australian Outback. While the general locations described around the Northern Territory exist, many finer details are not accurate; they are created as a canvas on which to paint the story.

Backpackers are part of Outback Australia. Occasional horror stories occur and gain wide coverage. Some, like those of Joanna Lees, Josef Schwab, or the awful deeds of Ivan Milat, contributed ideas to this novel. However, these are rare events, as likely to happen in big cities or in other countries. They do not typify most people's experiences of these remote places.

The setting of this novel is an external frame for the story. It tells of the journey of two people both through real locations and within themselves. In bad situations they do awful things, despite desiring goodness. This reflects human experience. Each of us has an ability to make terrible choices and do evil if we cease to value life, but even the worst people may have parts that are good and decent. This book is also an impossible love story, with love destined for destructive failure.

Alongside this story of people's lives, this book seeks to capture the essence of the Northern Territory of Australia, the centre and north of the Australian continent. This land remains alive in my imagination from when I lived and worked in it.

Despite the coming of modern civilisation with roads, air transport, communication and modern comforts, the intrinsic character of this place, the 'Territory', remains little altered. Ernestine Hill, in her famous book of that name, called it 'a land too vast for human imagination'. It remains so to this day.

Wildlife is abundant. Stations still muster cattle and buffalo for a living. Aboriginal people live off the land and know it with an intricate understanding, as they have done for millennia past. Stockmen tell tales around campfires, gazing in awe at immense star filled skies.

This is a place where life moves slowly, as befits a land where time is driven by nature. Brilliant desert colours, huge tropical storms and endless emptiness live on, as they have from the dawn of time.

My thanks to the innumerable real characters of the Northern Territory who contributed to this story by lighting creative fires in my mind through the sharing of their own stories and memories.

Visitor is Book 1 of the Crocodile Dreaming Series. Other books in this series are:

Book 2 – Victim
Book 3 – Void
Book 4 – Vanished
Book 5 – inVisible
Book 6 – Vertigo (Vengeance Part 1)
Book 7 – Vortex (Vengeance Part 2)

For those who wish to read these books in eBook form they will be released progressively over 2021-23 from major eBook retailers. Print books will become available from online sources and selected bookshops on a slightly slower timetable.

If you wish to contact the author directly in relation to these books or other writing information please email the address

grahamwilsonbooks@gmail.com

Prologue – The Watchers

I watch him as he watches her.

I am an ancient being set apart from time. Before today I have seen him many times, both from close and afar. Part of him is twinned with me. He glimpses but knows not. We share the spirit of a dreamtime ancestor of this ancient land, one which calls us to him. Soon I will reclaim him. I will never release him, no matter what comes to pass.

And he will bring with him another. She neither knows nor sees what approaches. She thinks the future is her own. But she is as linked to him as he is to me. She will think she is free, but the links will hold her fast. When it is time I will claim her too.

***

A man stands alone above the shoreline, partly hidden by the foliage of a tree. He watches her. He desires her.

He wants to know who she is and all about her.

He came to Cairns early today, a week after hunting down a man. His end came far out in the Arabian Desert. It was fitting.

He remembers that day. What little remains of that man, once the birds and jackals finish their pickings, will soon be bleached white, matching the shade of the sand, then fast covered and hidden from sight within ever-shifting dunes.

He feels no remorse, only a small satisfaction that it is done. It was a kinder end than what this man offered to some he hurt. Where justice fails, vengeance is his part.

Now he is back in his homeland, this vast empty sweep of the familiar. It is a harsh land with odd fingers of civilisation like this tourist mecca on the beach. Here is a place of visitors, many visitors, some beautiful. He has known and sampled others alike to this one he watches now. Some have gone on their way, returned to their own lands. Some never left this land but are become a permanent part of its substance. For some it was from misfortune. For others it was due to his actions.

He feels faint regret at their passing, but it is now separated from him by layers of far distance, the distances of time and loss, and, moving beyond that, the distance of new experience.

Now he seeks another. He has just seen her standing on the beach. She appears like some he has known before, breathtaking in her beauty and vitality. He senses her wanton abandon as he watches, distant, through the tree. She dips toes in wavelets, dark hair flowing back. She sweeps hands above her head and arches her body backwards, goddess like, as if embracing the sun. He senses she is ripe for taking, hungry for the many new experiences and adventures he can offer; that she will come willingly if he but asks.

He must be more careful this time, lest some new bad thing happens to her. He senses she is both courageous and breakable.

***

Susan relaxes into her seat as the aeroplane levels out. She is going home, still alive. She glances at her hands. One tightly clutches her passport and boarding pass—her tickets to freedom—the other grips the armrest of her seat. She forces herself to loosen her grasp and pack her travel documents away. She prays to God to let it all be over. She has escaped; the evil is gone from her life. Soon she will be home free.

As these thoughts flow through her awareness she senses another is there, watching her, waiting and biding its time.

She shudders and pushes the idea out of her mind.

***

I am the watcher – she thinks she is free.
My time will come – she will return to me.

Chapter 1 – Safe Home – Day 31

Susan awakes with a jolt, feeling wrenched back into consciousness. Her head has been slumped into an uncomfortable position. Now her neck aches. There is a large woman squashed into the seat next to her. It seems this person has given a nudge to stop Susan falling onto her, not exactly friendly. But then Susan has barely spoken to this woman in the last fourteen hours.

Since she boarded this plane in Singapore, her sole stop after leaving Darwin, Australia, Susan has retreated into a cocoon, sleeping the hours away, with the barest of interludes for loo breaks and food, before returning to her slumbering respite. It's as if she has spent a whole day and night of her life locked away in a sealed time capsule.

Now she's totally disorientated. Here she is, approaching London; a month of her life has vanished into nothingness.

Gradually her mind pulls back fragments of those last awful days in Australia; a man's smiling, almost handsome face, devoid of normal emotions, memories of crocodiles, blood and torn body parts, images of a white four-wheel drive with a big cooler box on the back. The images wash over her.

She suppresses them with a shudder and looks around. London cannot be far now; people are waking and preparing for their 6.00 am touchdown at Heathrow. Some have raised slide windows. Early grey daylight squeezes through the gaps.

Breakfast is being served. The smell makes her ravenous. She eats the offered croissant and scrambled egg with relish. Afterwards, there is urgency as stewards remove breakfast trays and clear away.

The plane slows and drops into its final descent. She raises her own plastic slide. It is mostly grey outside. They are flying under a blanket of cloud, but with lighter sky to her left and behind her. It must be southeast England, somewhere over

Kent. They are scooting over farmlands, roads and villages, lush green in early dawn light. Further away are glimpses of busy roads and large towns. The gloomy sky matches an unquiet anxiety within her. Is it really over? Is she safely home? Or will the police be waiting for her at the arrival gate?

Suddenly a shaft of sunlight pierces through the cloud. It lights the countryside with glowing golden light.

Her mood soars as her eyes follow the path of the light. It's as if her connection to horror is broken. She smiles, unable to suppress infectious joy. Everything will be all right. She is alive! She knows life will be good again.

How great it will be to see her family and friends. None of them need ever know. She made a visit to Australia, travelled far and wide, saw interesting and beautiful places; that's her story. If anyone asks where she's planning to travel to next, she'll tell them she loved her trip to Australia, but her travel bug has been sated. She's happy to be back home.

The woman sitting alongside her must catch something of her happy mood. She catches Susan's eye and smiles. Susan smiles back; joy is a contagious thing.

The woman introduces herself as Annabel. She seems friendly. Susan knows it's her, not this woman's demeanour that's changed. She lets herself be drawn into a conversation about trips and travel. She explains that she was really exhausted from her trip, but now she feels ever so much better, after that long, long sleep.

Soon they are making a final approach. There's a slight jolt and body push as the airliner brakes on the black tarmac.

As they pull up at the terminal Susan feels amazingly refreshed and confident. A bad dream ended with the morning's sunshine—her anxieties belong to a far distant place and time. She gathers her minimal possessions—an overnight bag, book, cardigan, purse—and follows the slow procession of departing passengers down the aisle and out to the concourse. She hopes her mum and dad will be here to meet her. Perhaps also her gawky brother, Tim, and her Gran, Elizabeth.

She skips baggage collection, as she only has hand luggage, and is quickly in the customs line of nothing to declare. She says a silent prayer they don't want to pull out and check all her hand luggage. There's nothing obvious, but she doesn't want them to look too hard. What she has is minimal and, with a British passport, they quickly wave her through customs.

Now she's almost at the front of the passport queue. Anxiety bubbles up. Will they pull her aside? She glances up quickly, looking around for security. There's no obvious sign of police waiting. Her tension eases a notch. She holds up her passport and is through before she has time to think.

Suddenly there they are, all her family members as expected. Her mum and dad are together in the centre, with Gran and Tim to each side. She rushes into a group hug, feeling her dad's grizzled face brush her cheek and inhaling the familiar scent of her mother's perfume. She feels her Gran's light touch on one shoulder and a firm, almost punch from Tim on the other, as they all come together.

The familiar sameness of these people, one's that she thought she'd never see again, takes her words away. She stares at them all in breathless silence.

"How brown you are!" her Gran says.

Her dad smiles. "How's my girl?"

"Hi, sis, no new Aussie boyfriends in tow?"

"You look drawn around the eyes dear, all the bright sun and late nights," her mum adds.

When her dad asks her where's her big bag of luggage Susan already has this story worked out. She feigns an annoyed expression. "It went missing on the last leg of my trip. I only noticed getting off the bus, arriving in Darwin. Didn't have time

15

to try and find it before my plane left. I'll have to make some calls when I get the chance."

They drive home to Reading, following the familiar M4 motorway through increasingly lumpy morning traffic. Views of green fields and distant water have a soft surreal feel in the early morning light, so different from the barren harshness of what she left behind. Signs for Windsor Castle and Eton flash past with wonderful familiarity.

A couple times random thoughts jump into her mind, memories of that other place of nightmares, but she resolutely pushes them away.

Once home, she leaves her overnight bag in her room. Everything is just as she left it—was it only four weeks ago?

The smell of food draws her to the kitchen. Her dad has bacon and eggs sizzling. They sit around over coffee and chat. She tells stories of her first two weeks—the Barrier Reef, Sydney, Melbourne, but not much about the trip through the outback. It doesn't matter. She's done and seen enough in her first two weeks to fill the conversation and satisfy their curiosity. They're none the wiser.

Tim stands. "Must go, sis, or I'll miss my first lecture, you know that boring anatomy subject you almost failed."

Mum stands to go with him. "Sorry, darling, me too, I must go with Tim. See you tonight for the rest of the news."

As they walk out Susan is struck by the unreality of it all. Routines have continued unchanged in her absence, life in a parallel universe.

Dad and Gran chat with her for another minute as they finish cups of coffee. Dad puts his empty cup down, scoffs the last bit of bacon and says, "We'd better go too. I'll drop Gran home on the way. There's a Paddington train in twenty minutes, which I should be on. Will you be okay on your own? I imagine you'll want to stretch out for a good sleep."

"Yes, I'll be fine. Bed sounds so good." She stands and hugs each in turn before they leave, another layer of disjunct reality.

As she watches their car turn out of the drive onto the suburban road, her forced gaiety drains away. She goes to her room, sits on her bed and picks up her favourite childhood teddy. Its worn fabric is so soft, so same, so stable. She pushes her face into it.

Her body shakes as creeping horror and loss wash over her. Then tears come, streaming silently down her face. Soon her whole body is convulsing in wracking sobs. She hugs her teddy and sits there. After ten minutes the emotion subsides.

She goes to the bathroom and runs a hot shower, shampoos her hair and washes herself all over, then does it a second time for good measure. She slips on a bathrobe and dries her hair, makes up her face and finds her sassiest outfit: tight jeans and a sparkling top.

She opens the overnight bag she brought back from Australia. She removes a book, wrapped in a hankie. Then she takes out her toiletries bag. A small heavy cloth pouch which clinks is tightly packed in its bottom, buried under deodorant, shampoo and makeup. She takes it out and, avoiding looking at either thing, puts both items under jumpers, in the bottom drawer of her dresser.

The last item in the bag is her underwater camera; it's the only item she still cares about. It holds a handful of photos on the memory card from this trip, as well as some from other trips and dives. She feels she should throw it out, but this camera holds a big chunk of her past life before Australia. Memories she wants to fondly treasure.

After a moment of hesitation, she clicks open the cover and removes the memory card. She'll copy the photos she wants and then destroy the card. She slips it in her purse and puts the camera back in its normal place in a drawer.

In the kitchen she finds a large rubbish bag and places her overnight bag and its remaining contents into it. She ties the top shut, goes to the garage where her Ford Fiesta is parked, and puts this rubbish bag into the boot. Tomorrow it will go in an industrial bin at her work, the place where lab samples go for incineration. That will bring an end to any last fragments linking her to the past month of her life on the other side of the world.

She looks around and realises she's okay; today's a glorious English summer day. She will go out into it and enjoy the first day of the rest of her life. Yesterday and before is in the past, a finished time when she was a visitor to another place.

She will close that memory book, put it away behind other stories of her past life, at the back of the highest shelf, unseen and forgotten. She intends to leave it there, never to be taken out or opened again.

Chapter 2 - Holiday Alone – Day 1

Susan pushes back into her airline seat and stretches. There's a delight in being airborne and on her way across the world. She feels like a kitten, unwinding her body in golden sunshine, after having drunk a bowl of warm milk. The gin and tonics she had in the departure lounge might have something to do with the euphoric feeling too.

Now, at last, she's really on a holiday and going to a fantastic, exciting, unknown new place—all by herself. Something about taking this trip totally on her own seems especially important. It's like a growing up ritual. Not that she's a child. She's twenty-four and hasn't lived at home for over two years until just recently.

For six years it was as if Susan's life was taken over by Edward, her former boyfriend. They'd met in first year university and studied history and archaeology together. Edward with his languid manner, tousled blond hair and slightly posh accent—as if he'd gone to Eton—and she, the well-read, exuberant daughter of professional working parents.

Edward's father was a stockbroker in financial London. He had followed his family's business flair with an Arts-Commerce Degree, focused on finance, with some psychology and archaeology thrown in.

Susan had done a Science Degree, focusing on medical technology, but with an anthropology and archaeology sideline. She'd always been fascinated with early human history and civilisations, learning about the way these societies had adapted to diseases and environmental catastrophes. As a child, she'd been captured by the David Attenborough and Richard Leakey 'Out of Africa' stories of how early humans moved across and colonised the world.

Really, she'd have loved to go to Africa, perhaps Kenya or South Africa, but with the many stories of crime and violence, and with it being her first solo trip abroad, she knew her mum and dad would worry, and she didn't want to be the cause of that kind of stress for them.

So, she'd turned to Australia, a country of almost equal fascination for her—the strange animals, over 50,000 years of aboriginal history, the Great Barrier Reef, diving, rainforests. And, not least, those fabulous New Year TV pictures of Sydney Harbour Bridge, alive with fireworks.

She knew it was a safe place to visit. The people spoke English, and she'd always enjoyed the laid-back laconic humour of the Aussies who frequented London pubs. Sure, there were occasional stories of backpacker murders, but she knew she was too smart to get suckered like that. Visiting Australia felt right.

She thinks of Edward again, their lives together in their small north London flat, half an hour from her work. Living together had seemed the natural thing to do after graduation. They hadn't really discussed their future, but it seemed unsaid their lives would go on linked together, that one day marriage, children and a settled future would probably come.

She could see how she'd convinced herself she loved that image, but, deep inside, there was always a restless streak in her. Perhaps it was that Edward was a bit of a snob. He didn't like it when friends called him Ted or Eddie. He was attractive, but not with the rugged man look she'd normally go for. Edward was quick-witted with clever words. He was smart around money and had impeccable taste. What he wasn't was adventurous. He never seemed curious to experience life out beyond normal bounds. At first it did feel really good together: nights in pubs, dinners with good wine and food, talk of success in their investments, trips to Europe and enjoying the good things of

London. Their sex life had been great for the first year they lived together, lots of it and wild.

But then, as each started to forge their careers—she as a medical technologist in a large hospital and then in a commercial testing lab, and he as a rising business man who looked likely to follow his father's stockbroking career—they seemed to drift apart. They were often both working late. While there was still sex, plenty of it, there was less real tender lovemaking. She'd pushed aside growing niggles that came from their mutual friends and families with different interests.

She hadn't thought there was a major problem. Then she found a slip of paper lying on the bedroom floor. It said Eva, followed by a mobile phone number. Edward had never mentioned an Eva before. But he worked in an office with lots of women, so she supposed that was to be expected.

What really pissed her off though was that he was such a good liar. She'd asked him the next day who Eva was. Without batting an eyelid, he told her a story about someone in another group he'd worked with on a couple of business deals, how he needed her number to hand in their final stage negotiations. It all sounded totally innocent.

But then Susan was ambushed by a different reality. It came totally out of the blue. She'd been to a meeting at Cambridge and told Edward she thought she'd be late home. But the meeting was over soon after lunch so she'd caught an early train. Rather than going back to work for a couple hours she'd detoured to shop and surprise Edward with a special dinner.

She'd walked in their door just after three and felt surprise to see Edward's jacket on the coat stand but did not think further on it. She put her shopping on the kitchen counter and heard a noise in the bedroom. It sounded like Edward was home early too, a double surprise.

Then she met the real Eva. She was lying on her back, in their bed, with Edward's naked body on top of her, moaning as Edward said, "Eva, God this is so good, Eva," in between passionate grunts.

Susan had stood, open mouthed, too stunned to say anything. Finally, Eva's eyes turned her way and she gave a little scream. No introductions were needed, the identity was obvious.

Edward had climbed off her, silent, looking almost proud of his erect member. Eva at least had the good grace to seem embarrassed, trying to cover her blond bimbo dolly face and small, full-breasted body. After a few seconds of stunned silence, Susan turned, closed the door and walked out of the flat.

She'd tried not to cry as she stumbled down the stairs, but it was such a kick in the guts with the added ultimate duplicity of using their own bed.

That was the last time she'd seen Edward. She'd stayed in a hotel in Central London that night and thought of going out, getting drunk and laid, but decided she would not stoop to his level. Instead she'd distracted herself with TV movies and wine until she'd fallen asleep.

When she woke her hurt had hardened into cold anger. While he was at work she collected her things from the flat and left him a note on the table. *Don't ever come near me again.*

She visited the bank, closed their joint account and cancelled their combined credit cards. She bought a new phone, with a new number, and changed all her web logins and passwords. That was that: six years of their life together finished in a day.

Susan didn't go into details with her parents, only said they'd split up. Her parents accepted her back with a minimum of fuss. She took back her old room, which was now the spare. She found all her forgotten soft toys in the cupboard—best of all was her big soft teddy who, from her earliest memory, sat on her pillow. She'd returned him to his rightful place. When Susan left home she'd left him behind, neglected. Now, back at home, he'd seemed to give her a genuine welcome each day.

Mum and Dad had been busy with their own lives, Mum as a senior lecturer in the medical school at Reading University, where her brother, Tim, was a student. Her dad was a top-level public servant to the government, in No 10, with a daily city trip on the fast train to Paddington or, sometimes, for big occasions, a chauffeur. Despite his high role, he preferred ordinary things: a train to work, a beer at the local pub and the great outdoors.

Some of her best childhood memories were hunting or fishing with him in Scotland, where her cousins lived on a farm in The Highlands. They would almost always take a two-week summer trip and also visit at other times throughout the year.

Her father particularly loved to take her with him in the autumn when the leaves were golden. They would head off, his gun in hand, hunting pheasants, grouse, rabbits and sometimes deer. They would walk for miles across the high heather, plunging into glens, dark and mysterious. Sometimes they made a big fire out of turf and almost-dry branches, which smoked then burned brightly, while they roasted a rabbit or pheasant and ate it with their hands. Those were warm memories.

Edward made a few attempts to contact her, but Susan told her parents she wouldn't take his calls and didn't want to see him. When he came to the door with a bunch of roses she heard her father say, "Lad, are you a bit thick? Can't you tell she doesn't want to see you?"

Some smart arsed reply came back.

"If you ever come here again I'll wipe that smile of your pretty boy face."

Susan hugged her father fiercely when he closed the door.

His normally mild manner was gone. His face creased in a scowl as he muttered, "Fucking wanker. Good riddance."

He returned her hug, and she realised her father never really thought Edward deserved her but had refrained from saying so.

After this she got one letter from Edward. She burned it, unopened. That was that; so much for a relationship that consumed a large part of her adult life. Looking back now she's glad it's over. Despite the shock of the moment, she can see they were on a path to nowhere.

With Edward gone her life felt hollowed out. It was the middle of winter, a time of dreary English weather. She'd felt cold to her bones outside and roasted in the overheated labs and family house.

She'd buried herself in work and reconnected with old friends. Then, just as spring was beginning, the idea for a holiday came. It was like a light turned on in her brain, something to look forward to and focus her daydreams on. She looked at a couple magazines, one with pictures of an African safari, the other with sunlit photos of the Great Barrier Reef. That night, after hours of Googling, she made her plans, and the next night she booked her flights.

It took another three months of hard work, endless hours getting reports up to date and cross-checking thousands of laboratory sample tests results, until she was free to leave. Computers were fine, but real human brainwork was required to interpret decisions on many findings. There was no one she could delegate to, to review all these reports. Not to mention the mountain of validation and quality control for the laboratory, done behind the scenes.

As she ground her way through this work Susan longed to be in the outdoors, relaxing in comfort. She pictured herself walking along deserted beaches, sand and warm water squelching between her toes, blue sea, gentle waves and shady palms along the edge. It was a delightful, romantic and exotic mind space that fed her motivation.

Now, at last, she's on her way, four glorious weeks in Australia: first stop the reef, then on to Sydney and Melbourne, and lastly exploring the outback. Deep down, she knows this is something she's wanted to do all her life. When she returns, she hopes she'll have moved on and left those bad memories of Edward behind. Perhaps this shock to her love life was needed to make her fully grow up and find her own self. She thinks of her mum and dad and their relationship, built on solid trust and shared enjoyment, not some fickle glamour. That's the sort of future she wants.

She decides that, while she's away, she wants to meet a real man, perhaps an Aussie bloke, maybe someone tough from the far outback. She's missed the sex and intimacy over the last few months. She needs someone to bring this part of her alive again. She indulges herself with thoughts of having a new man in her life, even if only temporarily.

The aeroplane levels out. They're flying over a vast ocean somewhere between England and Norway. Soon they'll head across the Arctic tundra to Japan. She's looking forward to a short Tokyo stopover before flying south to Australia. Susan stretches out once more. She runs her fingers through her thick hair, then down her thighs, all warm inside at thoughts of her adventure ahead.

Susan loves her day in the air. It is a total chill out to have nothing to do for all those hours. She watches movies, flicks through magazines of holiday destination pictures, reads cheap trashy novels of others' lurid romances and chats to fellow passengers. Most are heading off and away for similar adventures to what she feels sure will come her way. At times she just sits in solitude, enjoying the splendid isolation of being herself, fully alone, nothing to do, no one else to answer to.

Chapter 3 – Cairns and the Barrier Reef – Days 2-4

As the plane descends, Susan presses her nose to the window and marvels at the white sands, little islets and the multi-coloured waters they pass over, starting as tiny dots in a picture book image then, as height strips away, they become clear and sharp. She's able to make out tiny waves and occasional boats.

Now the intercom crackles. "Ladies and Gentlemen, we are commencing our descent into Cairns, Australia and are due to land in thirty minutes. Our route south from Japan has brought us over the Great Barrier Reef, and you may see its coral atolls on view below. You'll shortly be asked you to resume your seats and fasten your seat belts."

The plane banks hard and turns into its final approach. Now she's looking at dark green forest-covered mountains and flashes of water in streams and waterfalls. This view falls away as they settle into their final descent. Glimpses of roads and ordinary houses flash past as they come over the tarmac, level out and land with barely a bump.

Cairns isn't as hot as she expects, but then it is winter here. She steps out of the airport building, wearing a short sleeved top and light skirt, and feels warm breeze caress her skin. It's good to be here, almost dreamy good. A light buzz and thrill of anticipation washes over her.

She surveys the scene around; people of all shapes, shades and nationalities move about, some hurried, others drifting through their day. Some are oblivious to her, a few appraise her with interest, some as if to sell her something. A couple of men stare at her with an obvious attraction, as if seeking to her catch her gaze. Her body responds with an electric charge of anticipation, even though neither of them draw her real interest or a desire to respond. Another man looks at her with intense interest as she clears customs. She barely looks his way, distracted with the process. She smiles with delight as her passport is stamped: *Australian Visitor Visa*. When she searches for a glimpse of this man again, he's gone.

There are innumerable backpacker buses, all touting their wares, along with taxis and regular shuttle busses to the city, but the day has only just begun, so she's in no hurry. Doing the backpacker thing will save her money, but the idea of an extra night or two of solitude is more appealing than saving money, and she can afford a hotel. Because it's barely 11.00 am she still has the whole day to sightsee and look around before she needs to find a place to stay.

She catches a shuttle bus to the city centre, and books herself into a mid-range hotel for two nights. The discount is good, two nights with breakfast thrown in for only $200. That's all she needs—her base.

Susan leaves her bags and sets out walking barefoot, with sandals in hand, along the fringing beach promenade past the city. Before long a side path leads to the sea. Clear water froths and bubbles as it spills over white sand. She walks to the shore and stands at the edge letting wavelets wash around her ankles and little fish nibble her toes.

She soaks it in for some time. Then, as she feels the sun start to burn her skin, she decides it is time to go uptown for ice cream, sun cream, reef tour booking and lunch, in that order.

Her gaze sweeps out across the low sea horizon one final time. She arches back, sweeping her hands up in homage to the sun, and looks skywards, before again running her fingers through her abundant cascades of hair. She feels in her bag for a hair tie, but then decides she'll let her hair be as free and relaxed as she feels right now.

Back on the promenade, a solitary man gazes out to the sea through a filter of green leaves. Susan sees him and feels unspoken kinship, stranger to stranger.

Walking slowly along the shore she passes an ice cream stall. She stops to buy a double mango and cream in a cone, then walks on, licking the ice cream as it melts over her fingers.

A big gaudy poster in a tour shop window catches her attention. 'Green Island Underwater Coral Viewing'. There are also posters for 'Jet Cat Outer Reef Tours', 'Michaelmas Cay by Sail', and 'Steam Trains to the Rainforest'. She picks up a handful of brochures and sits on a shady bench to read them while she finishes the last delicious drops of her ice cream. The amount of information feels overwhelming when she's barely worked out what time zone she's in. It'll be easier to go into the shop and ask for help.

As she goes inside the delicious coolness of the air conditioning strikes her. Nobody else is waiting, so she walks over to the counter. "Hi. I'm only here to two days. I'd like to see the best of the reef along with the mountains and rainforest. What would you suggest?"

"Okay, well I'd suggest an outer reef boat tour for day one, and train trip to Kuranda to see the mountains and rainforest on day two. There's a market up there where you can see aboriginal dancing and art and buy lunch," the helpful guide answers.

It seems like a good plan, so she nods.

"Do you have a preference for the boat company; there are several?" he says.

"Wherever the coral is best. Which do you recommend?"

I'd personally go with Quicksilver. The boats are new and fast, and they go right to the far edge of the outer reef where the water's clearest."

"That sounds good. And if I wanted to head off to Magnetic Island after my train trip what would be the best way?"

"I'll fix you up with a bus ticket and a motel room in Townsville if you like. You can fit it in after you leave Kuranda and then go out to Magnetic Island on the ferry early the next day. How about that?"

She agrees and pulls out her credit card. While she waits for the payment to process she thinks of how she first heard about Magnetic Island when reading about Captain Cook's discovery voyage. Then, earlier this year, a girlfriend mentioned this same quiet island where she'd enjoyed a steamy romance with a German man staying at the same backpacker hostel, situated right on the beach. Perhaps a place to start her own love life again, or at least relieve that ache of desire to be touched, an intimacy she's missed over the last few months thanks to that cheating bastard Edward.

As she leaves the tourist shop she's vaguely aware of a tall man, wearing an eagle motif cap and sunglasses, brushing past her. Abstracted by imagining her planned trips she looks away as he passes.

A chicken salad and glass of wine are lunch at a local café. They leave her feeling warm and sleepy. She makes her way back to her hotel and falls onto the bed in her cool shaded room.

Susan wakes as dusk is falling; she blames jetlag for her three hours of afternoon sleep. She feels mussy and her mouth is dry. She finds a mineral water in the bar fridge and goes onto the balcony to sip it in the dusk. Her plans to go out that night seem suddenly less attractive. She needs to be early away to the reef. Plus, the bed feels so good.

The bathroom has a Jacuzzi style bath in front of a large mirror; she assesses it then runs the tap. As it fills with steaming water, she takes a bottle of sparkling wine from the fridge and fills up a champagne glass. She tosses off her light dress and knickers and stands, half looking at herself in the mirror.

She remembers sharing champagne in a bath with Edward last year, him telling her, "I love your oval face and small nose. And I love your perfect pointed little chin."

She pushes her thoughts of him away and tries to see her body through the eyes of someone else, wondering how a new lover would see her.

She's of average height and, as a teenager, she'd wished to be taller, but she likes her body now. She sees smallish well-shaped breasts, round hips and slender legs. Most striking are her pale blue eyes, a Nordic feature that match her fair skin but don't quite gel with her abundant Mediterranean looking hair. Her eyes are the colour of a milky blue tropical sea—this morning's sea. Some poetic friends say the colour is an English summer sky bathed in bright sunshine. Men love her eyes. Perhaps a Spanish sailor, wrecked with the Armada, found his way into the family Anglo-Saxon gene pool. She never thinks herself riveting, but she is sometimes aware of other's admiring glances. Today she feels good about what she sees in the mirror.

Susan is never short of men trying it on—men interested only in a physical encounter. If she's honest, her relationship with Edward had a shallow edge. She craves something deeper. Still, for now, a man to give her pleasure will suffice. Deeper things can come in their own time.

Waiting for the bath she's suddenly hungry. She rings room service and orders salt and pepper squid—the house specialty. On being told of a half hour wait, she collects a glossy magazine from the countertop to flick through and plunges into the bath. Water up to her neck, Susan lies dreaming as she glances at pictures of rainforest, fish, exotic animals and Sydney Harbour Bridge. Bubbles of wine slowly fizz on the tip of her tongue.

When the bell rings for room service, she quickly dries and dons a bathrobe, then opens the door and the food is brought in. By the end of dinner, she's struggling to stay awake. Cursed jetlag. Leaving the plates, she casts her robe aside and falls, naked, onto the bed and into a deep and dreamless sleep.

She wakes, cold, at 3.00 am and snuggles under the covers with a novel until faint light on the horizon tells her a new day has come. She stands on her balcony watching the sky go through its colours, deep purple with pink edges, then reds and oranges, and finally brilliant gold as the sun bursts over the horizon, somewhere far out over the Pacific Ocean. It offers the promise of excitement in the coming brand new day.

She has a quick shower then finds her bikini, the pale blue skimpy one Edward bought her on a trip to Greece. He loved it because he said she looked "So-o sexy" and it matched the colour of her eyes—it too is the almost cornflower blue of a tropical sea. The bikini is the one thing from him she still has. At least something worthwhile came from that relationship.

Susan admires herself in the mirror. She has to admit, even if she feels vain for thinking it, she does look really good in this bikini; it works for her. She likes the idea of being eye-catching for handsome blokes on the reef tour. It's a delicious thought, and she feels a thrill of anticipation at the direction her imagination is taking her.

But time is passing, and she's keen to start her day. She puts on a T-shirt and shorts and heads to the breakfast café in the hotel lobby. Boat departure is half past eight, so she eats well, but with purpose, resisting the temptation to dawdle over the newspapers. Just before eight she heads out, carrying her underwater camera and a backpack of tourist accessories.

On the wharf she joins a hundred other passengers milling around. Someone checks her ticket and asks whether she wants to participate in snorkelling or scuba diving. She got her diving qualifications in the Mediterranean with Edward, and diving has been a great love since, that separate underwater world, completely removed from all else.

She says yes to both diving and snorkelling and her name goes on the list for the second dive.

She takes her bag below, finds a place to leave it, and returns to the deck. The crew make final preparations, then the line is cast off. They reverse away from the wharf and turn to face the sea. There are several other boats dotting the harbour; some look like fishing boats, and others have the sleek and shiny hulls of the pleasure cruisers. An orange harbour master's boat sits off to one side. In front of the boat on both sides rise the low rock walls of the harbour sides.

A few hundred yards ahead is another large catamaran, cousin to their boat. As she watches it powers up, white wash surging behind as it reaches the harbour entrance. It rises from the water, its silver body pushing out like a leviathan of the deep that bursts free. Soon it is skipping across the waves and curving steadily right towards a new destination.

Now they motor slowly across the glassy water of the sheltered inlet. Susan stands at the rail on the top deck looking out to sea, one of a dozen people standing side by side. The view out to sea is of endless rolling ocean with a few islands dotted here and there. Looking back to the town she sees mountains rise steeply behind covered in dark green foliage, with odd patches of bare rock and glimpses of glistening waterfalls.

The sun is warm on her skin but not yet hot. She turns to look back at the same time as the woman beside her. Their eyes meet in a smile, "Your first time on the reef?"

"Yes, first time in Australia, just arrived. You?"

"I come up here every year from Melbourne. It's freezing down there now in the middle of winter. The weather here is perfect. It's my yearly escape to paradise. I think getting out on the reef is the best part."

They're about to talk more when the captain comes over the intercom. "Ladies and gentlemen, welcome aboard. Soon we'll leave the harbour and head to the outer reef, where we'll tie up at a pontoon. It has an underwater viewing area, which gives a great view the fish and coral. You'll also have the opportunity to snorkel and dive nearby.

"It's a trip of an hour and a half and may get a bit rough with the swell, so please hold the rail or sit down. Once there you'll have over five hours of free time to swim, dive and enjoy the reef. A buffet lunch will be served. We depart at 3.30 pm, and we'll be back to port by five this evening."

A second announcement follows. "Those diving please come to the back deck to be fitted."

Everyone is fitted with masks and flippers. Diver's qualifications are checked, and the dive master gives an outline of the coming dive. They're instructed to assemble on the back deck at 11.00 am for an 11.30 am dive. She returns to the top deck, wanting to enjoy the view and the sea air.

Once outside port, the engines power up to a throaty roar. The Jet Cat cuts at a sharp angle across the wave tops of the half-metre swell as they maintain their line heading straight out of the harbour. From the angle of the rising sun she infers they're heading north east. Wind and salt spray whip her face. It's exhilarating, good to be alive.

The crew announce that tea, coffee and biscuits are available below, along with reef videos to show what they may see in the water. After five more minutes in the fresh air Susan heads below deck to educate herself on the new fish of this place, half a world away from where she's dived before. She's so absorbed by the images of fish and coral she barely notices the trip or the other guests. All too soon the motors slow as they arrive on the outer reef and nose into their pontoon.

Susan has an hour free before her dive, so she grabs snorkel equipment and is almost first in the water. The tide is low, and she feels protected in the shallow water around the fringing reefs. Keeping the boat in sight, she works her way around, trying to identify and keep a count of the myriad different fish she sees. She's blown away by colour, loves the different corals and the homes they form for fish. The highlight is a large stingray, more than a metre across; it slowly flaps on its way above the sandy sea floor, stirring up sand eddies in its wake. She looks up and sees the divers from the first dive returning. Her hour must be almost gone. She swims back and boards.

There are two instructors and ten divers in her group, which is broken into pairs, buddies for the dive, who will stay together and watch out for each other. Her buddy is a lanky man, probably in his early thirties, lean and fit without the body builder look.

"Hoho," he mumbles, as he fiddles with his snorkel fitting. "I'm Mark." He holds out his hand and she grasps it. His hand is strong and callused from manual work.

"Susan," she replies. She likes his smile, friendly and composed, not trying for over-the-top charm excess, a person who keeps his own counsel. She thinks his accent is Aussie—not quite definite; perhaps he's lived or worked elsewhere.

"Have you done this before?" he asks.

"Yes, got my ticket in the Med a couple years ago. Love it. And you?"

"Long time ago. I'm rusty. Looks like you'll be bringing me up to date."

They go off the boat deck into the water, a second apart, and swim side by side, following the lead instructor a few metres ahead. They swim slowly, slowing their breathing to an even pace as they relax. Mark waves to her.

She signals back: all good.

The instructor points to his left, down into a big hole in the reef where a huge cod guards his patch. Small brightly coloured fish swim around its massive head, staying just out of reach. Susan smiles at the cheekiness of the little fish. Mark seems to be grinning too. They swim on. She notices a disguised power in his long body; he diverts slightly then rockets back towards her with powerful kicks.

The hour passes too quickly. It seems only minutes before they're back at the boat. But wow, so much to see in this place: turtles, huge reef fish lazily working around the deeper holes, a group of white tipped reef sharks scouting the reef's edge, and so, so many brilliantly coloured fish and corals. She loses count of all their types but loves them all.

She can't help watching Mark as he pulls his wetsuit top down, revealing lean hard muscles. A scar, several inches long, runs high down his back, over his shoulder. Other smaller scars pepper his skin in various places. She turns away before he looks around, puts her own gear in the tub.

When she looks up, he's standing alongside her. "Don't know about you, but I'm starved. Are you travelling with others, or do you want to join me for lunch?"

"No, just me. Yes, let's have lunch."

They go to the buffet bench and pile their plates high with prawns, ham, salad and bread rolls. They find a table with two seats facing. For the first few minutes they're both too hungry to talk, as they cram their mouths.

Mark stops eating just as she takes a huge bite. He smiles, and the smile crinkles around the edges of his eyes. Captured in that moment he is striking.

"Looks like you needed that; you must have been even hungrier than me."

Her mouth is too full to reply. She points to her mouth. They both laugh.

Soon they're talking together, the way complete strangers do, exchanging details about lives, trips, plans, work. Mark has just returned from abroad and is planning to head across the top of Australia, maybe to get work in the Kimberley on a mine.

It appears he's a jack of all trades: stockman, miner, bush mechanic, mostly in the outback, but he knows big cities like Sydney and Melbourne too. He's also spent time in the Middle East, Africa and America, with a couple trips to Europe and England. Now his accent makes sense.

He seems warm and personable, but there's a hard edge to him, something she can't fathom—not quite dangerous, but at the far edge of unpredictable wildness. She tells him briefly about her breakup with Edward, saying, "I caught him cheating on me. I decided I didn't want to be with someone I didn't trust, plus we had little in common. So, I moved out of the flat we shared and decided it was time to get on with my own life. This trip is part of me getting on with my own life, learning to do things on my own. What about you?"

"Well, there have been a few girlfriends along the way, but most didn't last long. I am a bit footloose. I like the freedom to travel when the moment seizes me. A couple times it got serious, but things went wrong and it never worked out. I've got used to looking after myself. Perhaps one day the right one will come along and I'll find myself settling down. Meanwhile there's so much to see and do."

"And what did the serious relationships get right?" She laughs. "I can't believe I asked you that. Sorry. You don't have to answer."

"It's not really looks. Well, a little bit. But I think it's sparkle, taking joy in life, living in the moment, being willing to try new things. I'm like that. If there's something I haven't done before and it looks exciting, I'll have go. Sometimes it works out well, sometimes badly, but it's good to try. Life is for the living; it's sweeter at the edge."

"Not looking for the safe and predictable, finding someone you can trust?"

"Yes of course, but I don't want my brain to turn into mush. Safe's an illusion. It can vanish in a puff. Best not to assume it will last, but to learn to get back up when you fall flat. There's always another day, another horizon.

"And what about you? Is safe what you want?"

She thinks for a moment, feeling there's more to the question than the words. "I need to be able to trust. Nothing like seeing your boyfriend in bed with another to teach the value of trust. But I want more, shared adventures, doing new things. Safe on its own isn't enough."

Something about Mark draws her in like a magnet. Perhaps it's his understated way, his willingness to go anywhere and do anything, not tied to rules. He isn't classically handsome, but he radiates a raw vitality that's appealing. She senses a resilient tough independence, as if Mark's a man who takes hard knocks and bounces up with an undiminished life force. And she likes the way he tells stories with an edge of sardonic humour, hidden behind a slightly weather-beaten face and self-deprecating grin.

When they finish eating, Susan gets into a conversation with another woman sitting by herself at the table next to them. Her name's Maggie, and she's English too. They're soon swapping stories of London and enjoying their shared English humour.

Mark takes his empty plate away. She expects he'll return and join her conversation with Maggie. Instead he drifts off, heading outside; he seems to have lost interest in being part of this conversation. There is something solitary and a bit asocial in the way he leaves without words and moves away.

When it's time to go back into the water, she and Maggie agree to go snorkelling together. As they come outside, Mark is on the back boat deck. They smile to each other, and she says, "Maggie and I are off to snorkel and explore. Will you come with us, help us navigate?"

"Reckon you two can find your own way just fine." He shrugs and goes in a different direction, seeming content to do his own thing.

She feels a sharp stab of hurt at his curt indifference but pushes it away as she heads off to explore with Maggie.

She doesn't talk to Mark again that afternoon, but he nods briefly as they depart their own separate ways. She's sure that, if she hadn't started chatting with Maggie, she and Mark would have continued doing things together today. There was a definite spark of mutual interest. Now she'll never know for sure.

But she and Maggie have really hit it off, and they arrange to meet in a bar an hour later. After a quick shower at her hotel Susan puts on a fresh dress, light but classy and suitable for day or night, and heads out.

Maggie's at the bar with a couple from her hostel, Ryan and Trish. Drinks become dinner. Phone numbers are swopped. Susan and Maggie discover they're both going to Kuranda tomorrow. They happily arrange to meet on the train platform in the morning.

Susan's lightheaded with booze by the time she arrives back at her hotel. As she passes through reception the concierge waves and calls her over. He hands her a pastel envelope. Inside is a slip of notepaper with a brief scrawl:

Sorry I missed you.
I called to invite you for a drink.
I enjoyed our dive together and lunch.
Hope your trip goes well.
    Mark Bennet

Chapter 4 – Magnetic Island – Days 5-9

Susan enjoys a lovely day at Kuranda with Maggie. She's sad to say goodbye, but she has a bus to catch. They exchange details and promise to keep in touch.

The thought of she and Maggie going in opposite directions is a downer that leaves her feeling emotionally flat as she climbs onto the bus. Or perhaps she's coming down after all the excitement of the last two days.

She can't stop thinking about missing Mark last night either. The feeling stings her with a small twinge of regret. She mentioned his note to Maggie, who responded with a knowing look. 'Looks like you missed a nice little fling there.'

Perhaps Maggie was right. Who knows where an evening alone with Mark may have led. There was a definite spark.

She settles into a seat and watches green countryside, with mountains to the west, slip by. It's four hours to Townsville, with a half hour stopover midway. Tomorrow she'll visit Magnetic Island for three days before flying south to Sydney.

As the bus rolls along Susan's mood lifts again; there are new places to see, new things to do. The mountains fade into deep shadow, their tips washed by the final flares of the day's departing sun—it's an eerie image that's distinctly Australian in its beauty. Travel is such a mood aphrodisiac.

As the bus pulls into Townsville, Susan stifles a yawn. At least the jetlag is gone. She tumbles into bed at her motel and doesn't stir until bright daylight wakes her.

After a leisurely breakfast she walks to the jetty to catch the 9.30 am ferry to Magnetic Island and, once there, she catches a bus to Horseshoe Bay which, on her map, faces out east towards the vast Pacific Ocean.

Somebody in Cairns recommended this backpacker's hostel, apparently the best on the island, so she checks in. Nobody's in sight, so she drops her pack on a vacant bed, changes into her blue bikini and walks to the beach with a book and a towel. She sits gazing out over an aquamarine expanse, soaking in the pleasure of this warm, endless ocean space. Only a couple of others are on the beach and they're far away: it's her own private piece of paradise.

Susan moves into the shade and stretches out on her towel to read. Each time she looks up from the pages, she feels like her life also sits inside a holiday storybook.

Finally hunger brings her back to the hostel. In Townsville she bought a loaf of unsliced bread and a pack of ham and tomatoes. Now she makes an oversized sandwich using two thick bread slabs.

There are odd bedroom noises, but otherwise it seems she has the place to herself. She should really dress, but her hunger won't let her ignore it, so she carries her plate to a bench table by the window and sits facing out, looking away from the kitchen. Her view is along the beach towards a green headland. She eats with ravenous hunger.

Like a charged tingling up her spine, she becomes aware of footsteps behind her. Something else, familiar but not, catches her subconscious attention.

She turns around. As her eyes adjust from bright light, she realises it is him, Mark. He's standing a few feet behind her, tall and broad in the gloom. He looks at her with what seems like hopeful recognition.

Their eyes connect. It feels like an electric shock, tightness in the pit of her stomach, a raw flood of physical connection.

While this feeling flares within, she can't help a smile of delight, attraction and pleasure at re meeting one familiar in this country of strangers.

Mark smiles back, but the smile seems guarded and hesitant. "I thought it was you," he says, "but then I thought it was just my imagination. You look great, even better than the picture in my memory. I guess the absence of a diving mask improves us all, even me."

Susan bursts out laughing, a giggle fit that leaves her breathless and feeling flushed. Self-consciousness at being clothed only in her skimpiest bikini makes her notice Mark's awareness of her body.

She pulls herself back from her embarrassment by pointing at her sandwich. "Have you eaten?"

Mark shakes his head.

"I've plenty of bread, ham, tomatoes. Can I make you one?"

He nods. "Yes, that would be great."

They sit down to eat, side by side, facing out to the bay.

Susan cannot help chatting away and telling Mark what she's done in the last two days. Then she looks at him and says, "I was really disappointed I missed you that night at the hotel. It would have been great to go out and have a drink together."

"I felt a bit silly asking, like I'd barely met you with diving and lunch. But you were fascinating and we seemed to like the same things. I thought, what the hell, there's no harm in asking."

"I'm glad you did, even if it didn't work out. Now here you are. We have a second chance tonight."

A few minutes go by as they eat, both gazing at the view. Mark's body is so close it's almost touching. A couple times they brush each other and a little thrill runs through her.

"What are your plans for the afternoon?" Mark asks.

"I haven't thought about it yet. What about you? Do you know your way around this place?"

"I've been here a couple times. There's lots to do, horse riding, jet skis, sea kayaks, that kind of thing. Afternoons are great for walking in the national park. If you go out to the head of the bay, you'll often see dolphins and turtles in the sea;

sometimes you see a koala in the bush. There's a lovely little sheltered beach at the end where it's safe to swim."

"That sounds amazing. Do you want to walk out there this afternoon? And, if you're free tomorrow, perhaps we could do something more adventurous together?"

"Why not," Mark says, in his slightly droll way.

"Let me go put on something more suitable to walk in."

In the bedroom, she pulls on a light dress and sandals to protect her feet.

As she comes back to the kitchen Mark's filling a water bottle. He puts it in a small pack and drops this over a shoulder.

They head off, him leading the way, following the top of the beach. After a few minutes they come to a path that leads into a forest. This is a mixture of gum trees and other scraggly ones with funny pointed cones that poke out at odd angles.

"What are they?" she asks.

"That's a banksia tree, and those are the banksia men that live on it," he says, pointing to the cone-like things. "They attach themselves and wait until someone like you comes along. Then they jump out and grab onto you."

Susan widens her eyes. "Oh really! I may be only a dumb Pommie visitor, but even I know when I'm being had."

"Just testing you."

They walk on, climbing a rocky ridge. The view on the descent is breathtaking: a little indented rocky bay with crystal clear water opening out to a sweeping horizon of sea and sky, blending together far into the distance.

"Wow, you weren't wrong. This is really something."

As she speaks, barely out past the rocks, two dolphins, side by side, leap from the water and are frozen in a split second of perfect symmetry. Susan shakes her head in wonder.

"I knew you'd like it, but that was particularly amazing. I think they turned it on just for us."

She links her arm through his as they start to walk on, giving a squeeze of delight.

He turns to face her. "It was your smile that did it. I think they wanted to impress you. He brushes a stray lock of her hair back from her face and touches her cheek. Then he pulls away. "Let's keep going; it's a bit of a way yet."

They go on, mostly him leading and her following. Sometimes, when the path widens, she walks alongside. A couple times he lightly rests his hand on her shoulder as she walks next to him. It feels good, and she responds by smiling up at him and moving closer.

They come down off the ridge into a green depression. In its centre is a small swamp that the path tracks around. Odd trees with white papery bark grow in the centre. Huge gum trees ring the edge. Mark motions for quiet, finger to his lips. He pauses, standing stationary for perhaps thirty seconds. Then he points up high in the canopy, a place of deep shadow.

She looks, puzzled, shakes her head, unable to make out anything distinct.

He takes her hand and raises it to point at a high branch in a big gum tree. "Look on the big branch up there, the fork half way along."

She searches the canopy and, as her eyes slowly adjust to the gloom, a small movement brings the detail into focus. Sitting on the branch fork is a mother koala. She is pulling a higher branch down towards her, eating the leaves off it one by one.

Susan gasps. She knows it's a mother koala because on her back is a large baby, perhaps half her size. She watches as the mother directs the leaves towards her baby. It follows its mother's lead and begins to eat the leaves, one by one. It mimics her exact movements as it eats with apparent relish.

They stand transfixed for five minutes, watching until all the leaves are gone. The mother koala looks about briefly as her baby climbs on her lap. Then she curls around it and they both close their eyes. It seems, for all the world, as if they both just fall fast asleep.

Mark smiles. "Seriously something, huh!"

"I feel so lucky I got to see that."

They walk on again, now holding hands, not talking but moving along together, enjoying the peaceful forest. Gradually they climb the hillside again, tracking beside small rocky headlands fringed by sea. Finally, they reach a place where the path falls away to a little sandy beach. They stop at the edge of the sand and stand for a minute, fingers entwined.

Mark pulls away. "Come on, time for a swim."

He pulls off his T-shirt and plunges into the ocean in his shorts, hard muscles rippling as he powers away. Susan lifts her dress over her head. She follows him in, wearing her bikini. They splash and swim separately for a minute before she swims up to him and stands, the water up to her waist. She looks up at him. "Thank you so much for showing me all this. It's been the most wonderful afternoon."

He rests his hands on her shoulders and looks directly into her eyes. "It keeps on getting better from here."

She moves in close against him, feeling his hard body, and wraps her arms around him. His arms pull her in tight. She feels his maleness against her. She pushes her pelvis against his leg. A deep ache runs through her. Since Edward her body has longed for this sexual touch. Waiting is past. Here it is, in the middle of nowhere, in an idyllic paradise. Normal restraints fall from her mind; there is only here and now.

His hand runs down her back and over her bottom, stroking her, holding her buttocks. She feels his hand slip inside her bikini bottoms, touching her naked flesh with a sensitivity that makes her shiver all over. He pulls back slightly, runs his fingers through her hair.

He tips back her face. "You have the most wonderful blue eyes, just the same colour as this tiny bikini that barely covers you. Each time they look at me they make weak inside. Then I want to do this to you," he says, sliding his other hand down under her top and cupping her breast.

She feels a little moan escape.

They both know what they want now.

Susan feels his hands on her bottom again, sliding down her bikini pants. There is incredible pleasure as he strokes her belly and says, "Your skin is so soft."

She feels his hands slide down over her skin, all the while moving down and into that aching place.

Holding together, touching these places on each other, they return to the beach. He spreads a towel on the sand and pushes her down onto it. She arches her pelvis and he pulls off her bikini bottom. Now he is on top and astride her. His body above her looks huge; his face is a silhouette against the light.

"I don't have condoms with me." He says it like a question.

She parts her legs. "Don't worry. I'm on the pill." Mark's pelvis arches as he pushes inside her. It feels exquisite, this long-missed pleasure of a man's joined body going deep within her.

The surges of pleasure come faster as they ride this rising wave together. She wants to make it go on forever, so she pushes him to the side, says, "My turn on top."

She climbs above him and takes him back in, working herself up and down like a gymnast. He grasps her buttocks and stokes her as she moves; his mouth is on her nipples. More, more, deeper, deeper, harder and harder. It feels like she will pass out with building pleasure.

In a sudden move he grasps her and flips her below him. He drives in with incredibly hard thrusts, almost hurting. His sheer male dominance brings her towards a massive climax, as he comes himself.

At last she can hold back no longer. As Susan falls over the edge of the orgasmic wave she grasps him, wrapping her arms tightly around his hard back. "Oh God," she gasps. It's like a signal, and she feels Mark's body convulse above and inside her, as her orgasm rolls on, such a cascading, overwhelming release, and relief.

They lie together, panting and slowly subsiding. She feels their combined wetness flowing out over her thighs. She had needed that so badly. And it's been worth the wait.

They lie still together for a while before they feel the need to wash in the surf. Then they splash and swim in the waves, before she swims across to Mark, who is standing in waist deep water.

She dives into him, pushing her face into his belly and working down. She takes him in her mouth and he hardens again. She feels him lift her effortlessly and place her hips against his waist. He pulls her down onto him while his face is in her hair. They stay in the water and make slow love in the little wavelets, first standing and then, when it feels like it will overwhelm them, lying together in the shallows.

Desire satiated, they sit on a rock, their bodies soaking in the afternoon warmth. She makes occasional affectionate touches to Mark who responds in kind. She moves to sit on the sand in front of him and pushes herself back against him.

He wraps both arms around her as they sit in silence. At last he says, "I guess it's time to head back."

The walk back has a pastel feel, like a dreamy painting.

She says to Mark, "I'm still floating on a cloud. What we did was beyond words. I wanted that so much. Now I just want to let this afternoon last forever and slowly ebb away with you."

It's almost dark by the time they reach the hostel, which is now crowded with other backpackers. Perhaps because it's so busy inside, Marks says, "How about we sit on the verandah and have a drink?"

Perhaps he dislikes socialising with groups. She doesn't recall seeing him talk with anyone other than herself on the boat trip out to the reef. But she's enjoying his company and having it all to herself, so she smiles and says, "Thank you. I'd love that."

He returns with a six-pack, and they sit together, almost silent, sipping their beers, as light fades from the horizon.

At last she asks, "Do you make a regular practice of picking up female backpackers, taking them for a walk, wowing them with beauty and ravishing them on the beach, the way you did with me this afternoon?"

Mark half smiles. "I have done something similar a couple times, but none of those days were as good as this day I've had with you. There's something different about you; it's like you're a free spirit, one never quite captured by ordinary life."

She snuggles into him. "Well, I knew I wasn't the first, but this was really something for me too. I think it's your wild edge that gets me."

Mellow with beer they decide on a steak at the local hotel for dinner. They shower and put on their best clothes for the night out. Over dinner Mark tells her stories and offers her snapshots of his life working in the outback, working in mines, working on an oil pipeline in the Middle East. He's also had other jobs in Africa, Asia and America. It's clear he's done many things.

"Your family must have missed you," she says.

He studies her face for a moment, then shrugs, looking away, as if wanting to move on.

"Where do they live? Do you see them much?"

"A conversation for another time. It's getting late. Let's head back now."

When they return to the hostel it's quiet; it seems most others are already in bed.

Mark carries a mattress out onto the verandah. "Will you join me?"

She nods, wordless. They both undress and he stretches out and indicates a space for her. Susan snuggles beside him, laying her cheek on his bare chest. They cuddle then, as desire grows, they made languorous love, looking at each other in a faint glow of starlight. After they murmur dreamy half conversations and soon fall asleep.

In the early dawn Mark rises and directs her to her own bunk. He packs up his bedding and heads off into the growing light. She doesn't ask him where to and instead falls into a deep dreamless sleep. The sun is well up when she wakes again.

Mark is sitting alone with a cup of coffee at the kitchen table when she comes out. He fixes her another one to have with him.

They spend the next three days together, jet skiing, sea kayaking, snorkelling, sailing. Best of all is horse riding. They ride along the beach together after breakfast that day, on sturdy ponies. Although Susan has done the equestrian thing in England, it's the first time she's ridden bareback.

Mark is self-taught and is a superb rider, so well-balanced. She loves riding along with him, sometimes walking and trotting, knees brushing, other times a lolloping canter, and occasionally an all-out gallop as they race frenetically to get to the front, laughing and whooping with joy and exhilaration.

From the very first day, Mark seeks an agreement from the riding school for them to ride alone rather than go with the organised group, telling of his life working with horses on large stations. Once they've demonstrated their riding ability, they're given the same two ponies each day for two hours, to ride on their own. Their pattern is to ride along the beach to the furthest end, walking, trotting and an occasional gentle canter, moving slowly to draw out anticipation of the pleasure to follow. As they near the beach end their pace quickens as their desire grows.

Out of sight they fall into the water and swim, but soon, clothes cast aside, they ravish each other. The return ride—a wild gallop—their perfect way to end each morning.

Afternoons are spent on the water, sailing one day, jet-skiing the next, sea kayaking another, paddling around the point to their first day beach and repeating the pleasure they shared there.

On the second night, in the small hours, when she wakes up beside him in their bed, outside under the stars, her hand is resting across his shoulder. She becomes aware of her fingers touching a hard scar, something that goes down deep into muscle. He awakes to her touch and she says, unthinking, "That must have been a deep cut. It feels like you were stabbed or shot. How did it happen?"

She knows, even before he speaks, that he won't tell her anything real. Instead he mumbles, "Horse threw me into a barb wire fence."

She's sleepy and doesn't want to dig deeper. She lets it pass, kissing the place, saying, "A real serious scar for barbed wire."

He grins at her in the half light. They both know it's an untruth and yet each leaves the lie to lie there.

The next day another thing happens. They're sitting on the outside verandah, side by side, while she fiddles with her camera, thinking that tomorrow she'll bring it and try take pictures of some fish. Another backpacker walks past, a young Australian girl. Seeing the camera, she says, "Shall I take a pic of you two together?"

It sounds okay to Susan, and she'll have a photo of Mark remember him by. But, before she can answer, Mark firmly shakes his head. "Don't do pictures, thanks."

Susan says nothing, but gives the girl a small smile of thanks, not wanting to offend her for what seems like Mark's impolite response. She shrugs at him, as if to say that's fine, but something about his hesitance strikes her as unusual.

Then there is the time when a big loudmouthed American man tries to get Mark to join a card game—they need an extra player. Mark politely declines the request, but the man won't take no for an answer. He keeps pestering Mark in a badgering manner. He's three inches taller than Mark, probably three stone heavier, and it looks like muscle not flab. He's obviously used to getting his way, and it seems he assumes others will fall into line whenever he wants something.

Susan is sitting part way along the verandah, book on lap, watching from the mid distance. She watches Mark's face harden and his muscles tense. She wonders what will happen.

After a minute of this pestering Mark turns to walk towards her, but the American follows, talking loudly about how he must be a wimp if he won't play cards.

In a split second, Mark turns back to him and stares. "Mate, you seem to be missing something. I said no. I'll spell it out if you're a bit thick. It's capital N, capital O. It spells no and it means no. Now get out of my effing face. It won't end well if I have to ask you again."

That is all Mark says. Then he stands looking up at this big strong man, eyes full of cold intent and devoid of emotion. Susan has a strong premonition that it could end badly and not for Mark; he gives out such a sense of danger, like a snake in the millisecond before it strikes.

The other man drops his gaze, lost for words. He mumbles something and steps away, pretending he hasn't backed down.

Mark never moves a muscle until the man leaves. Then he says to her, "I hate bullies." An instant later it's like it never happened; he smiles at her saying self-deprecatingly. "Sorry, don't let it spoil our day."

Despite these odd things Susan's happy to have him fully to herself; he has such charm and captivates her so fully she doesn't desire more.

Susan abandons her plans to leave on the third day and stays for two more nights, unwilling to see their shared idyll end. But Mark has a week's work planned in central Queensland, after which he must head on to Alice Springs, and Susan is Sydney-bound and can't delay her flight any longer. At last, by the fifth day it's inevitable they must go separate ways.

Their ferry ride back to Townsville is sombre. Mark barely talks. An ache of impending loss settles over Susan. She's grown huge affection for this sun-toughened man from out the back of somewhere, in the middle of nowhere, wherever it is. She knows there are many more layers of what makes him up that she has yet to reach. She's sad her days discovering him are at an end.

As the ferry approaches the dock Mark asks, "What are your plans from here? Where to after Sydney?"

"Well, I've five days planned in Sydney, then three days in Melbourne. After that I've ten clear days until I'm due in Darwin for my flight home. It leaves on the Sunday and gets into Heathrow early Monday. I want to see the outback. Perhaps I could go via Uluru or Alice Springs or maybe to Perth and head up the west coast. Places like the Kimberly and Shark Bay sound amazing. You know your way around. What do you think?"

"There's a chance I could be in Alice around the time you come. Shall we try to meet? At least make space for another day and night or two, if you're keen."

She tries to read his body language; there is something inscrutable in his face. She doesn't know if his offer is just politeness or if he wants to be with her again, the way she wants to be with him, so she says, "If only, but don't make me promises you can't keep. How long will you be there?"

"I have to do a trip from Alice to Darwin around that time. It'll take about a week, going overland to some remote places, a detour into the desert and a night on a big crocodile river. Does that sound like something you want to do?"

"That sounds wonderful!"

Something in the way he says it makes it feel indefinite. She doesn't quite see it happening, believe they'll get together again.

A bus is waiting near the ferry terminal to take passengers to the airport and several others climb aboard. She buys a ticket on it, her plane leaves in another hour.

At final parting they hug tightly. As he starts to pull away he hands her a card with 'Mark' and a mobile number written on it. "Think about it. If you decide to come by Alice the week after next and you want to see the real bush, send me a text to let me know. Maybe you can join me on my trip from Alice to the Top End, that's if you don't mind my doing some bits of business along the way. It's your chance to see all the nature and emptiness. If it's what you want I think we can make the timing work. If you let me know I'll try to line it up. Until I get to Alice I'll mostly be out of phone contact, so a text is best."

Despite her uncertainty about his words and emotions Susan's spirits lift with a surge of hope. She tucks the card into her purse and gives him a brittle smile and a wave as she walks towards the waiting bus. Mark's expression remains inscrutable, but she's sure it holds more than indifference.

Suddenly she doesn't want it to end like this, with an almost casual goodbye. She runs back to him and he puts his arms out. She presses her body against him one last time, nuzzling her face into his rough cheek. "Mark, I really want to see you again. I hate saying goodbye. Meeting you has been so special for me. I want more."

"Me too." He holds her close. For brief seconds it's only the two of them, and the world beyond fades to nothing. Then an urgent toot of the bus pulls her back and they finally separate.

Chapter 5 – Sydney and Melbourne – Days 10-16

Susan is perplexed by her own deep sadness as the plane climbs away from Townsville. The view of the reef and mountains is as spectacular as it was on arrival, but she barely looks up, lost deep in memory.

Her time with Mark was wonderful but intense; their intimate connection barely stopped for a minute. Now she needs to catch her breath. Their physical and emotional contact was so powerful, and the sex, after a long deprivation, was beyond words. When she was with Mark she barely thought about anything else; it was an all-consuming pleasure addiction.

It had never been like that with Edward, despite sex being a great part of the lives, and one of the things that had kept them together, despite other differences. But Mark's wild physicality, coupled with a lack of restraint, was something else again. She feels that sexual part of her being is worn out and needs a good rest. But as she thinks of his sometimes sad and distant eyes and his warm hard body, she knows she'd do it all again without hesitation. The feelings he's awakened in her are something way beyond her control, like trying to stop a bolting horse or hold back a fast running river.

Can she trust these feelings? There's still so much she doesn't know about Mark. Sure, he's told her lots of stories of his work and places he's been, but they never did get the chance to talk about his family, friends, past relationships, or others in his life. Of these people she knows nothing. Not even where he came from or where he grew up. Uncertainty twinges in her gut. If she thinks about it, he hasn't told her a single personal thing about himself.

Her instinct tells her that he hides a dangerous edge, something ruthless and uncompromising that will not accommodate to anyone who tries to push him against his will.

She's seen occasional glimpses, like that first day diving, when she and Maggie had struck up an instant friendship. Suddenly, he didn't want to keep doing things with her; a shutter came down, and she was instantly blocked from his mind and plans. Then of course there was the time with her camera and the episode when he stared down the loudmouthed American. That time there was no mistaking the danger.

But that incident was an exception. Normally Mark was great fun to be with, absolutely fearless and willing to try anything. And he was kind and gentle with her, giving her his full, undivided attention whenever he was with her.

But she was certain, except for that first night when they went to the pub together, that he had a strange reluctance to go to public places with her, little desire to hit the town or socialise with others at the hostel.

He was also reluctant to engage in group activities—organised tours he did under sufferance. At the time she was happy to have him all to herself; his presence consumed her so fully she'd desired nothing more.

It was that his private life and emotions that were a hidden book. Every time she tried to find a way inside she drew a blank. She knew he really liked her, not just the physical pleasure of their sex. From the outset he'd said this was more and he had an intimate tenderness towards her which was quite breathtaking.

All in all, it was five wonderful days. She already misses his serious but smiling face, with those far away eyes, seeing places she did not know and could not begin to imagine.

She pushes thoughts of him away. Now she's off to Sydney, where she'll get her fix of city life and society. She's always wanted to see the famed city, with the sparkling harbour shown in boat races, the magnificent bridge and opera house, lit up each year with New Year's fireworks.

Susan has cousins living here who have visited her family a couple times in England where they had spent some weeks together and became close. They're great fun and have offered to show her the sights and nights and let her stay with them at their place in Newtown, close to the city, in what they've said is a done-up workers' cottage.

She plans for five days here, then on to Melbourne for a couple days. She still has a couple days yet before needing to lock in flights and travel arrangements for where to go after Melbourne. It will be good to let the decision sit for a couple of days until she's regained some perspective. With that settled she sits back in her seat, looking forward to her hours of solitude before her Sydney arrival.

Ruth, one of her cousins, meets her at the airport with girlish screams of delight. They drive through the first real traffic she's seen since London. Ruth gives her a running commentary on Sydney and all there is to see and do. Soon they're crawling down a main road, choked with cars and people, which brings them towards the city.

Ruth's older sister, Jessica, and Jess's boyfriend, Robert, own the Newtown house. It's in a narrow street, about a hundred yards behind the main drag, King Street. Ruth rents one of the three bedrooms.

Jess is two years older than Susan. Ruth is around Susan's age and they're good friends. Ruth's taken the week off her work to show her around and have 'girl fun together', as she calls it.

It's mid-afternoon when Susan unpacks her things. After a ritual cup of tea, with English chocolate and biscuits which she brought from England, especially for them, they walk along King Street inspecting a myriad of restaurants, junk shops, and upmarket places.

The place has great buzz, people everywhere of all colours, shapes and sizes, shop wares and café tables spilling onto sidewalks, bookshops and bars both doing a roaring trade, restaurants of every nationality, a bit seedy, but familiar in feeling to the area she lived in London with Edward. A strange sense of loss settles over her. She and Edward once had something similar to this. Even though she had not realised it when they split, she misses street society in big cities.

She and Ruth walk along, chatting and swapping stories, only half-looking at the sights. They pick a restaurant for dinner and make a reservation. "It's mainly vegetarian food, but there are a couple of good seafood options," Ruth tells her."

After dinner it is off to the Rocks, next to Circular Quay, a place of grand early 1800s Georgian style pubs with live music, facing out onto Sydney Harbour. They've arranged to meet Ruth's boyfriend at an old pub called The Orient Hotel.

They squeeze into a corner table. The music is loud but not deafening. Familiar songs by Queen and Meatloaf come on and they get up to dance. A few men try pick-up lines, but although they look good, and Ruth gives them thumbs up, Susan feels no attraction and declines. When the songs end they sit down again.

"When you rang me before you flew out you said you were keen to meet new men now that Edward's gone," Ruth says. "Why turn the dance offers down? You seem a bit distracted. What gives?"

"I had a backpacker fling at Magnetic Island. I think I need a night or two off, nights on my own, if you know what I mean."

Ruth gives her a knowing look and they giggle together before Ruth goes to the bar for another drink and then they dance some more.

Ruth's boyfriend, Stephen, comes along an hour later with another friend. Ruth introduces them. "This is our good friend, David. David, I'd like you to meet Susan."

David smiles and holds out his hand.

They find chairs and expand the table. Dave squashes into the corner next to Susan. He's tall, well-built and good looking, with sun bleached blond hair—close to gorgeous actually. Susan is engaged by his smile and charm. He seems to like her too, looking at her with interest.

"How do you know Ruth and Stephen?" Susan asks.

"Ruth was a friend of my ex. Stephen and I used to work together, so he met Ruth through us. The ex is gone but the friendship remains."

"What's your work?"

I used to work for an IT start-up, which developed software for doctor's surgeries tracking their medical tests. Then I decided to do it on my own. So, I launched my own start-up, similar concept, different but related field, secure data analysis and record systems for biotechnology firms." He explains some more, and she listens with interest.

"I'm pleased your eyes didn't glaze over when I talked about work stuff. Saying what I do has that effect on many people. How about you? What's your line of work?"

"I did medical science subjects at uni. Now I work in a laboratory that does medical tests. Once it was mainly pathology and blood chemistry, now more and more tests are DNA based. We amplify and test DNA markers, both for medicine and forensic purposes."

They chat for while about this common interest.

Dave absently puts his hand on her knee while they talk.

She involuntarily recoils.

He pulls his hand back. "Sorry."

She feels relieved. She knows she's not bound in any way to Mark, and Dave is handsome, charming and appeals to her taste, but she still doesn't want this presumptuous casual touch.

His gesture seems too intimate, yet she responded so positively to Mark, throwing herself at him, welcoming physical intimacy. The touch of this attractive man isn't something she's wants now though. She's sure she could enjoy Dave's company and a physical relationship with him, but her mind's not in that space—not now anyway.

Susan excuses herself from the table and goes to the toilets to give herself time to think. She'll plead tiredness and an early night, without pushing him away directly. His attentive behaviour suggests he's definitely interested in her. Who knows, she might like him more if she sees him again in a day or two.

They stay for another drink and another hour passes. Dave has picked up on Susan's body language and makes no further moves. His respect of her is attractive. Part of her wishes she hadn't pulled back.

The days in Sydney fly by filled with shopping in the city, visits to Oxford Street and various flea markets, days around the harbour, walking the two fluffy dogs of the house in local parks, nights of restaurants, music and meeting the innumerable friends of Jess, Robert, Ruth and Stephen in a wide range of bars and locations.

By the third day, she knows she must decide on the rest of her trip. While little misgivings prickle in the back of her mind, Mark's face and presence come back to her very strongly, and she feels an aching desire to see him again. She pulls out the card with his number, finds her phone, and sends off a text.

Hi Mark,
Susan here!
Fond memories of great times on Magnetic Island.
Let me know if you can meet me if I come to Alice.
Expect to arrive Mon next week.
Love Suz

That's it, the die is cast. Maybe he's forgotten her and hooked up with another woman by now. If she doesn't hear back from him by the end of the day she'll go to Perth instead.

Susan surreptitiously checks her phone every half hour during the day. No messages come back as the morning and afternoon roll on. She tries to ignore the anxiety, but is starting to feel flat and let down. Even if he's busy he could surely reply. She must stick firm to the airline's requirement and confirm her flights tonight—that's the rule.

At 5.30 pm, as they are getting ready to go out for an evening drink, her phone pings, a new message. Trying to look and feel nonchalant she picks it up.

> *Hi Mark here,*
> *Just got message, out of town*
> *Love to see you in Alice, Monday*
> *Can you ring day after tomorrow?*
> *Then we can work out details to meet*
> *Can't wait*
> *Mark*

Susan puts down the phone. Her hands are shaking. She feels excitement bubble through her, but also a strange dread; she really wants to see him again—her body craves him—but why this anxiety? It pricks at her and makes her feel uncomfortable despite her burning anticipation.

Susan tells Ruth to go on without her, that she'll meet them in the pub in half an hour, she just has to go out and do a couple things first.

Ruth looks at her inquiringly, "Sure, fine. See you then."

Susan finds an internet café and confirms her flight— Melbourne to Alice Springs, arriving at 11.30 am, Monday.

She's relieved it's booked, the decision point passed. She'll tell the others of her Alice Springs arrangements, let them know she'll go on from there to fly home out of Darwin, but she won't tell them about Mark. It feels like a private thing for her. She doesn't need to share him with anyone else.

She phones him on the specified day. It's a thrill to hear his voice, and she expects he'll want to chat with her, tell her the news of his recent trip, but he seems constrained and their conversation is brief, just a confirmation of time of arrival and flight details and an agreement he'll pick her up at the furthest end of the terminal pick up zone.

Her own chatter dries up when nothing comes back from him, after their initial hello and the pick up instructions. Perhaps he's with another and not free to talk, or perhaps there's a long term girlfriend or wife he's hiding. He was really secretive about his personal life.

She pictures another woman, blond and beautiful, sitting next to him, and resentment washes over her. She rationalises. He's probably just busy, right in the middle of doing something. Another woman is a figment of her imagination. But, if he was busy then, why didn't he just say so or offer to ring her back later to talk?

Her remaining time in Sydney flies by. She decides to catch the day train to Melbourne as she's been told it gives a leisurely view of the southern Australian countryside and arrives in the city in time for an evening of sightseeing. She's booked a small hotel in the heart of Melbourne, only three star but convenient and a good price. She's only there for three nights and wants to enjoy the city.

She sees David several more times, with Ruth and Stephen, and he's still clearly keen on her. Part of her is being pulled towards him too but, particularly now she's made her arrangements with Mark, she feels sure nothing will come if it.

She has no intention of sleeping with him. In fact, if someone had asked her about them becoming an item two days before she left Sydney and after she'd talked to Mark again, she'd have given an emphatic no!

Somehow Mark, the man from somewhere out of the back of nowhere, has changed something inside her, at least for the time being. She doesn't want any more entanglements while she's with him, or even while that possibility remains.

It is a strange sort of faithfulness to an idea of possibility, even though she can't conceive what real possibility there is; she and Mark, two people with totally different lives, different backgrounds and careers, who live on opposite sides of the world. Yet her mind is clear. Nothing can or will happen with David. And yet it does.

On the second to last night they go out as group until late, drinking in a small pub. She lets David take her hand and lead her to the small dancefloor. His body brushes up against hers, and she lets him. It feels good. She could easily spend the night with him. She knows he wants this, and he is patient in encouraging her.

At the point where the only normal decision is whether she'll go home with him or let him come back with her and share her bed, she freezes. She likes him as a person and physically, but there's an almost tangible block in her mind and body, like a closed door, that stops her short of intimacy.

Susan rationalises that it's because she'd gotten her period on her second day in Sydney. But her period is as good as finished by tonight, and she knows it's not the real reason. The real reason is Mark. What they'd had. What they may share again. Why is she feeling this way? She owes Mark nothing. He would expect nothing of her.

Eventually Ruth and Stephen head home saying they need to sleep, but Susan and David have watched them become increasingly intimate as the night progresses, and they share a knowing look and a smile when Ruth waves them goodbye. Knowing why Ruth and Stephen are really leaving arouses their sexual awareness of each other, like a spike of anticipation.

Susan looks at David. "I guess I should head home too once I finish this drink. It's getting late." She really intends to go home alone.

But, as the two of them sit there together in the late night, Susan can feel her own sexual appetite returning, and she doesn't want to have listen to Ruth and Stephen doing it through the adjoining wall—it will just make her horny.

It brings memories of her nights with Mark back. The thought that she'll be with him again soon arouses her more. She wonders where he is now. Perhaps he's with another woman, someone in an outback pub. She remembers a woman from the hostel, one who cast admiring glances his way. Could they be lovers? Or was there someone with him on the day she rang? The idea excites and enrages her. She knows there have been many women in his life, but she could not bear for him to be with another since her; she wants him for herself.

But Mark isn't here and David is. She feels like staying here for a bit yet with him. She tells herself it isn't sexual, her reason for wanting to stay with him; she's just enjoying being out and he's good company.

So, when he suggests they have another drink, she acquiesces. She suspects it must be a double because it tastes pretty strong, but she doesn't care because the lightheaded, carefree feeling that envelopes her is nice. When he suggests he walks her home, she says yes to that too.

Outside is cold with a winter chill.

"My place is a short walk from here. You want to come over and listen to some music?"

Susan nods and they walk into the night, arm in arm together at first, but eventually with his arm around her shoulder and she leaning into him. She's a bit drunk, but the feeling his body gives her as he walks alongside her, strong, solid and stable, is enjoyable.

Once at his place, he fixes them both a drink and puts on some music. They sit together on the couch just letting the beats thrum over them. As the alcohol flows through her brain, she becomes less conscious of where she is and what she's doing.

The music slows, transforming into a soft ballad—almost a waltz—moving and evocative. David pulls her to her feet and they dance together, bodies pressed against each other as they move with the music. She can feel his arousal against her belly.

She should stop this now, not go where this is leading, but she is unable to draw back. It is more comfort than sexual; she just likes the feeling of a male body against hers, holding her with strong arms in the late night. Her physical being has reawakened to male body contact pleasure and she now has an unmet need for it.

Before she fully comprehends what is happening, David puts his hands over her buttocks and strokes her bottom in an intense and intimate way. Susan feels his hands lift her dress upwards and slide it over the bare skin of her hips, feels his fingers slip inside her knickers from behind. Her mind is at the edge of a protest, but it does really feel good; she can feel herself becoming wet with desire.

David moves his hand around to the front and strokes her from outside, first on her belly and then on down over her knickers. She can't resist moaning and pushing herself hard against his hand. As she does it is as if what's happening is happening with Mark, that the intimate touch is really his. She knows it's not him, but the idea still arouses her further. Before she fully realises where this is all going, David leads her to the bedroom and undresses her. She feels his hands inside her.

Mark has taken over from David in her mind, and her body is responding to him. Her memories of Mark are so strong they transport her to that earlier place and time. As Mark takes over the role of her lover she finds herself responding enthusiastically, giving herself unreservedly to her returned lover.

She feels her body being opened up. He pushes her legs apart and pushes himself inside her. She finds herself moving, thrusting her pelvis back against him as his urgency mounts.

David is but a shadow at the edges, a jealous observer.

It is all a faraway mind-blur with Mark at its centre. And now there's another spirit within Mark that she see's too and it terrifies her. It's a crocodile like creature in the centre of his being, dark and hungry. She is both repelled and attracted as these two faces of Mark join together making love to her. At the same time another woman is there with them too, taking a part, one of Mark's many lovers

Her sense of jealousy spreads. This other woman takes her place. A bubble of rage rises. Mark is not doing this with her but with the other. She's not really with him. He's found another.

The stab of jealousy morphs the man above her back into David. And why should she not do this with him if Mark is with another. She will make love to David to spite Mark, or so her aching heart says.

David is whispering words of tenderness to her, and feelings of affection flow to him in return. She is being pulled along by the power of his need; it is a river and she is in the current.

David pulls a condom from somewhere and puts it on. She's vaguely aware of being glad of that, not because of a worry that she'll fall pregnant, but because she prefers not to have him naked inside her. The condom is a layer of separation that takes away her offering him total intimacy.

As his urgency mounts, she gains a peculiar sense of detachment, like an out-of-body experience. His body is convulsing in orgasmic delight, then it's over. It felt pleasant, but in a distant way. Still she likes the body comfort of him next to her. She distractedly strokes his head as she falls asleep.

It's daylight when she wakes. She has a dry, fuzzy mouth and the edge of a headache pulsing at her temples. David slumbers beside her, his tousled hair beautiful in the morning light. She finds him almost too attractive, something of the male model. At her core she's strangely unmoved by his physical perfection. She'd like to just dress quietly and go home.

But now her movement has aroused him. She feels him grasp her and pull her towards him. He has a throbbing early morning erection, huge and hard. While not desirous of more sex, it's easier to let it happen one more time than explain what's changed between last night and now.

Susan lies back and lets him thrust into her. She begins to enjoy it, the physical pleasure of a man's hard body moving against and inside her, her pelvis arching against him, his mouth on her breasts, strong hands grasping her buttocks. But it's over too soon, just when her own pleasure is building.

David drifts off to a semi-sleep state and Susan rolls to her side, facing away from him. She feels unsatisfied, as if something has been missed, part pleasure part emotional connection. She falls back to sleep.

The next time she wakes it's mid-morning. David has set up orange juice and croissants for breakfast on a verandah looking out over the water and the city. The view is sensational.

Most people would love to wake to this, but her emotions are mixed; she would almost prefer to wind back the night and wake in her own bed, alone, even though last night she'd been happy to go along with David pushing her to drink more knowing she'd likely then spend the night with him.

She's not angry at how the night turned out; it feels good being with him. But her liking of him is nothing more rapturous than that he's good company.

When he asks her about her plans for the day, she thinks immediately of Ruth. She didn't contact her to let her know why she didn't come home last night.

David must see the anxiety on her face. "I hope you don't mind, but I texted Ruth earlier this morning to let her know you'd stopped over. I should have asked you first, but you were asleep. I wanted her to know you were okay."

She would have preferred this remain a private affair, but she knows that chance has passed. And she could have sworn this night with David was something Ruth and Stephen had sought to aid and abet. Now it's out there beyond hiding.

"Thanks for letting her know. And in answer to your other question, I need to go home and change. I promised Ruth I'd meet her for lunch. I've planned a quiet afternoon and evening as I'm catching the train to Melbourne early tomorrow."

"Why don't I ring her and see if she can meet us? Perhaps Stephen can meet us too, flex off at two. We could have a late lunch at Watsons Bay, at the mouth of the harbour."

Susan nods, going with the flow. David is trying to be the perfect host. He is a nice bloke. She doesn't need to hurt his feelings. And so, her final lunch in Sydney is arranged.

It's a glorious mid-winter day. The sky is cloudless, and it's warm in the sun, with only the lightest cool breeze.

David drives her in his open topped BMW sports car, to collect Ruth. When David's back is turned Ruth looks at her and winks. The private joke is no more than she's expected. Soon they're in the car and flowing with the moderate mid-day traffic, along New South Head Road, passing Double Bay and Rose Bay, getting glimpses of boats and sparkling water.

Taking a circuit around Bondi, they stop for a walk on the beach. Susan and Ruth walk along in the shallows of the ocean as David walks ahead.

"So, you and David last night, hey?"

Susan nods; no use denying it.

"I'm glad for you both. Edward never deserved you anyway. And David's ex didn't deserve him. I used to be friends with her, but not since then. Did he tell you about her? What a piece of work. He was devastated when they broke up. He seems to really like you. If I wasn't with Stephen I'd definitely go there."

Susan winces. "Cut the match making. He's nice, but it was a just a one-night thing. I'm glad you're pleased, but why do I have the feeling you've been pushing us together?"

Ruth grins. "Maybe you're a bit right. Stephen and I wondered, when we went home together last night, if it'd be your lucky night. We wanted you and Dave to have a night of good fortune together. It seems our wish came true. I just wish you were staying for a few more days. Can't you stay a little longer? A week in the outback would be more than enough."

Susan rolls her eyes. "You're such an incurable romantic."

The lunch served at Watsons Bay is luscious seafood, washed down by bottles of bubbly and fine wines. Stephen joins them around three, and Jess and Robert arrive a bit before five, just as they're finishing. David insists on paying the whole bill.

"Not such a cheap night after all," Ruth ribs him.

They sit on a beach, facing west, watching the last sunlight leaving the Sydney sky, toes dipping in tingling cold harbour water. They take two cars back to the city, Stephen driving David's car, as David's a little drunk. "Intoxicated with Susan's lovely presence," he says.

As they sweep down the road from Vaucluse to Rose Bay, the lights of the city and the Harbour Bridge rise to meet them, creating a magic place like a winter fairy castle, as the towering buildings sparkle and the surrounding harbour glitters. Susan takes a deep breath as she absorbs the beauty. She could live in such a city, and perhaps with this man, next to whom she sits, bodies pressed together. David is a good person; the word honourable seems to fit.

The six of them, now arranged as three couples, stop at quiet little café in Oxford Street for an intimate dinner. By 10.00 pm they are home to the Newtown house. Susan needs to pack so she can be up and off early to catch the train.

It isn't quite planned or agreed, but David ends up in the bed with her. The sex is better than the before. It lasts longer, and their bodies are starting to synchronise. His ability to pleasure her is increasing, not quite orgasmic but nice. If they do it a few more times she knows she'll enjoy him more and more. This time the condom is forgotten, but she likes the feeling of his naked male body adding to the wetness inside her. She sleeps a deep and dreamless sleep, enjoying again that physical comfort of another body lying close alongside.

Then the alarm is ringing: time to rise.

She showers and dresses quickly, then Robert drives them all to Central Station.

As they stand waiting for her train, David says, "I wish you could stay another week or two. You don't fly out for a fortnight. Why not stay a few more days? You'll still have more than a week in the outback? I'd love to show you our family farm in the country, the beautiful mountain rivers, our horses, the kangaroos and other wildlife."

"It sounds lovely, but my plans are made. Too late to change them now."

"Maybe I could call you some time before you fly out? Or even fly and meet you somewhere for a while?"

"I'm not sure that'd work. I just don't know where I'll be."

David looks dejected, so she gives him her mobile number and address in England. "Why don't you write once I'm home? I love letters. Send me a letter with your news. I promise I'll write back and tell you about the rest of my trip."

"Thank you. I will. Perhaps I'll see you again some time."

"Come back again soon," Jess says. "There'll always be a spare bed for you here."

"And, of course, next time a country trip to David's farm," Ruth suggests.

She hugs them all goodbye and boards her train. She waves as the train rolls out of the station, then settles back into her seat. Sydney and David are done. Only in her history now.

As the green countryside flashes by, thoughts of Mark return. Part of her wishes there'd been no one else since him. They'd made no promises of faithfulness and, until the trip to Alice Springs was arranged, there were no definite plans about them seeing each other again. Still the feeling's there inside her.

Why should she have this strange feeling of almost shame? She hasn't betrayed Mark by being with someone else. She's a single woman who's free to enjoy the feeling of someone else's body enveloping hers.

It's strange how enjoyment and guilt can share the same space. Perhaps it's only the primal sex drive in all humans, where faithfulness is a lovely, imaginary concept, but where, in real life, when opportunities come one takes them. Even more so because, as a visitor to these shores, it's done without any consequences; pleasure's briefly shared and life moves on again.

It's like sliding doors. She stepped through one sliding door when she left England and came to Cairns, and she stepped through another when she travelled to Sydney. Now she's passing through yet another door as the train leaves Sydney behind. It's curiously enlivening and exciting, a life lived this way. So why is doubt still nagging her?

The train rolls along, and she enjoys the peace of looking out across green fields and hills, not unlike England except for different gum tree colours and horizons.

Thinking of England brings her family to mind. She must say hello. She pulls out her phone and thumbs off a quick text.

Hi Mum,
Just left Sydney and on train to Melbourne.
Barrier Reef was brilliant and loved Sydney
Stayed with Ruth and Jess – great time
Next week fly to Alice Springs then overland to Darwin.
Looking forward to seeing you in a fortnight or so
Please pass on to others.
Love to you, Dad, Tim and Gran
Suz xxx

The day drifts by in a leisurely haze. Morning turns to afternoon, and then to dusk. The last of the trip reaches into evening, and the lights of towns and cars twinkle as they pass by.

Finally, a big city is evident, continuous lights and buildings. The journey is over for now as they pull into Southern Cross Station, destination Melbourne reached.

Susan's heard lots about the cultural life of Melbourne, its museums, art galleries and inner city delights of trams and street-side shopping. She knows she can easily pass the two full days she has available here.

She's also heard great things about Melbourne Zoo. Zoos are a passion of hers, something she and her father have done together. They've both always been fascinated by the large animals of Africa, especially the superbly adapted predators like lions, leopards, hyenas and crocodiles. Together they've visited Regents Park Zoo, Jersey Zoo and Whipsnade, as well as some of the other great zoos of Europe.

She's looking forward to visiting Melbourne Zoo so she can sit and observe these incredible animals for an hour or two.

Melbourne is easy and comfortable as she settles in. She's made lists of places to visit and things to do. It's great to have full days where she can immerse herself in all there is to see and enjoy. With just herself to please she's amazed at how much she manages to fit in. Melbourne consumes her so fully that, until she's getting ready to leave, she's thought of almost nothing else; her visit here has been her own time in her own space.

As she's packing, on her final night, she pulls her phone from her shoulder bag. She hasn't looked at it since this morning. There's a text from Mark, sent three hours earlier at 7.00 pm. He's going to be delayed getting into town and asks if she can catch the shuttle bus to the Alice Springs Mall. He'll let her know when he arrives so he can arrange to collect her. She has no idea where they'll go or what they'll do from there.

He offers no explanation of the delay, and there's no missed call indicating he rang earlier to explain. She feels a twinge of unease. Is she being too trusting? She could ring him now to ask what happened, but it's getting late. Plus, she'd hate to disturb him with another, says a little jealous voice.

She thumbs a quick text, "That's fine. See you there."

As her plane departs from Tullamarine Airport, next morning, she thinks she must visit Melbourne again, maybe stay a while. There's still so much more she wants to see and do in this city. It has a welcoming and homely feel, much more like the European cities she knows, despite not sharing Sydney's natural beauty. Perhaps it will be here for another trip, in another life, perhaps with another somebody, a person yet unknown, who will one day become a part of her life.

Chapter 6 – Alice Springs – Days 17-18

Susan feels she does her best thinking on aeroplanes, those crowded places in an empty sky. While you're jammed in with other people, you're almost entirely disconnected from all else in the world, giving you free hours to sit and contemplate.

Despite gorging on movies, magazines, drinks and junk food on her other flights, today she just sits, thinks and wonders what might be.

She doesn't regret her decision to come to Alice Springs to meet Mark. There's no part of her that fears travelling with him as she knows he's so thoroughly competent and in his element.

Thoughts of Sydney and of David have already been pushed into a remote corner, somewhere in the back of her mind. Whether or not she'll hear from or see him again already seems far away and unimportant. As does her worry about whether she should feel ashamed at taking two lovers in less than a week, with neither knowing the other exists.

She lets Mark fully recapture her mind. There's something in what makes him up that she can't fathom. It adds an edge, makes her uneasy and nervous in a way she can't define, but it also draws her inexorably towards him. Perhaps this will be a journey of discovery of the real Mark, that he'll be more able to show himself in a place where he feels at home, with no need to conform to the expectations of others. All she knows is that he exerts some powerful force over her, and the thought of seeing him soon gives her butterflies of anticipation. The time she's spent with him is far and away the most exhilarating thing to ever happen to her thus far in her life.

So now she follows his instructions and brings herself and her backpack on the shuttle bus from the airport to the mall in the centre of Alice Springs. In anticipation of seeing him she's bought him a beautiful little calendar notebook from Melbourne

Zoo, each month separated by its own animal picture. In the flyleaf she's written:

Dear Mark,
Really looking forward being Out Back with you
From Suz, with love!!

She finds a small café in the mall and enjoys lunch there while she waits for her phone to ring, still a little bit in her own contemplative world.

She becomes aware someone has stopped directly in front of her table.

She looks up.

It's him.

Today he's wearing a bright blue check shirt and denim pants with a broad brimmed hat pulled down over his eyes to shade them from the glare. He looks just great, so seriously together. Breathless with delight she springs to her feet, spilling coffee, and hugs him tight. She doesn't care. She feels his hard arms encircle her; it feels good. All her doubts are gone.

He looks at her with a quizzical expression. "I wondered whether you'd show. When people get a taste for bright lights and the big cities they often don't want to come out here."

"I wouldn't have missed it for anything. And anyway, it was you, not the Outback, I most came to see."

She fumbles and finds her present, passes it to him, feeling shy. He takes it and flicks through it, his pleasure evident. Then he returns to the front page and rereads her writing with a half smile on his face.

"Well, I hope not to disappoint. Out here's lots of space, but with not much in between."

He looks at her half-eaten lunch. "Do you want to finish up? We have a way to go this afternoon."

Arching her eyebrows, she says, "Oh, so secret, where to, pray tell?"

"My surprise."

He leads her to a car park around the back of the mall, flanked by a dry riverbed. Parked amongst other vehicles is large white four-wheel-drive. "That's mine, a tray back Toyota Land Cruiser. I think of it as my little truck; it's my home of wheels. It takes me and my gear anyplace I want to go."

On the back is a cage and a built-in white structure, like a large cooler box or an oversized fridge, with a locking door and padlock. There's also a big swag, an overnight bag, some locked metal boxes, a water tank in a front corner and two spare tyres attached to metal brackets in each back corner.

"What's that?" she asks, pointing at the cooler box.

"Sometimes I catch a lot of fish, sometimes I shoot a camel or a buffalo and take the meat to the local aborigines. It goes in there, with a great pile of ice. That keeps it cool for a few days. Today there's only a carton of beer and a couple of juicy steaks."

"What about the cage?"

"Sometimes, when I go hunting, I bring a dog. They're great for pigs. The cage stops the dog from running away or biting someone when I don't want it to. And a dog eying you off has a great calming effect on anyone who wants to help himself to what's on the back of my truck."

He puts her pack inside the cage and unlocks the doors. "Time to go."

Susan climbs in. With a clattering roar the diesel engine fires and they're away. They drive through a gap in the red broken hills, heading out of town along the edge of a wide sandy riverbed. They pass more low hills along the road, red rocky hillsides with olive-green trees and bleached grass, vibrant against the clear blue sky.

Susan recognises this as the way she came in to town from the airport. She sees various landmarks she passed then: the train line, the Ghan Museum, a Road Transport Hall of Fame—lots of big trucks there. Just when the airport comes into view and seems like their destination, they turn right. A big sign says 'Stuart Highway' and points to Adelaide.

"Thought we were going to Darwin. I know I'm not real strong on Australian geography, but I'm sure Adelaide is the opposite way."

Mark cracks a grin, "Really, can't pull one over you, eh? Well spotted. We're doing a slight detour. I thought you might like to see that big red rock, the one bloody tourists rave over, before we head north."

Susan smiles. "That is a big surprise. I thought we were going out into the 'Never Never', yet here we are heading for Tourist Central. You know I could have flown straight there?"

"You could, but there's something I really want you to see along the way."

They rumble along at a steady pace, passing around the edges of more low red rocky ranges and sand hills, featureless but pretty country, mixed low trees and bushes, occasional roadside patches of desert flowers. It is vast and empty, different from anything Susan knows. She sits there, letting the country roll by, feeling content and enjoying Mark's profile as he gives attention to driving, throwing her odd descriptors of the country and places they pass for commentary.

After an hour, as they are coming to some larger hills, Mark slows and turns left off the bitumen, following a small sign that says Rainbow Valley. "That's our destination, not far from here."

The road is just sandy wheel tracks, which cross orange-red low sand dune hills. Occasional patches of heavy sand cause Mark to drop a gear. They pass a tourist four-wheel drive going the opposite way. About fifteen minutes further on they pull off the road, at the side of a low sandy ridge. Mark indicates to get out and they walk towards the ridge top. It's three or four times higher than the car, and doesn't look like anything special, just loose orange coloured sand covered by wiry grasses and stunted trees and bushes.

As they crest the ridge, there, opening before Susan, is the most spectacular sight she's ever seen. Below the sand dune is a claypan, part covered in water. At its far side is the most incredible low range of hills, their eroded, broken and jagged peaks pointed skywards. The colours are what hits her; some parts are brick red, others fade into a rainbow range of soft pastels of orange, salmon, yellow and white. The hills are reflected as a perfect silhouette in the lake, so it seems a second mountain range sits there, just below the first. It is not on large scale, but the perfection of weather-sculpted nature is here on display. The beauty takes her breath away.

"I wanted you to see it from here," Mark says. "It's the best view of the whole."

Susan stands alongside him, resting a hand lightly on his arm and her head against his shoulder. "Worth coming just for this."

They drive on down to the car park next to the claypan, and spend an hour walking and viewing it from all angles in the afternoon sun. As the sun falls towards the horizon, its light reflects back from the hills, lighting them in ever more iridescent hues of glowing colour.

"I love sunsets here," Mark says. "For five minutes, right on dusk, it's like the ghosts of people past, those who've lived in this place for over 50,000 years, come out and walk in the twilight, living in the magic of the colours. Then, as the light fades, they sadly leave behind this beauty and return to other lands which we, mere mortals, can't see.

"In that soft shining light, I feel as if I leave my body and walk with them, hearing their whispers and songs telling me of times long gone. Perhaps one day, when I die, someone will scatter my ashes here, to mix with the spirits of these wise and ancient beings. I'd like that."

Goosebumps rise on Susan's skin. She'd never have imagined a spiritual dimension to this bush-hardened cynic. This is a window into his soul she is privileged to see.

Mark abruptly pulls back from the moment. "We can't stay for this evening's dusk. It's still a long way to the rock. Let's push on."

They walk back to the car and drive on, sharing silence for a couple hours, back onto the bitumen and turning south, winding through more hills, crossing two large and spectacular rivers, the Finke and the Palmer, which are more and more surreal in their colours as the sun sinks westwards. Then they pass over vast short grass plains, the grass glowing golden in the fading sunlight.

Another road sign points to Adelaide straight on, and Uluru to the right. They go right, driving towards a red sun disk on the horizon. Half an hour later she sees a roadhouse sign for Mt Ebenezer Roadhouse. Daylight is gone by now, diminished to a dull red glow in the sky.

"Still 200 kilometres to go; I thought we'd stop for a cold beer and a burger."

They perch at the bar where the beer is icy and the burgers good. They eat with simple enjoyment. Then on they go, into the dark, as the stars come out. After another hour a silvery light seems to glow. Susan looks behind them. A near full moon is rising, bathing glimpses of grass plains and sand hills in silvered light. Far to the south is a large flat-topped mountain, seen as a moonlit reflection. It's how she imagines that Table Mountain, over Cape Town, would look.

"Mount Connor, similar in scale and spectacle, but not in fame, to its Uluru cousin," Mark says.

Another roadhouse appears, its sign proclaiming Curtin Springs. White-faced cattle stand near the road as they pass. Then desert returns. Spinifex sand hills roll on past for an hour or more. Finally, distant lights twinkle on the horizon. As they crest a sand-ridge Susan sees a massive bulk ahead.

It's another incredible sight: a dark mound with shadow stripes running up and down its massive half-circle form. It glows in the moonlight, an almost deep purple with silver hues, growing ever larger, dominating earth and sky, a huge elephant shaped lump, fast asleep in the middle of the sand under a near full moon. This is Uluru.

They swing away and it fades from view behind more dunes.

After a few minutes they roll into a well-lit town. Hotels, caravan parks and wandering tourists are reflected in their headlights. They enter the car park of a modern hotel complex called Desert Sails.

"I thought we'd treat ourselves to a night of the good life before we seriously leave civilisation behind," Mark says.

"Here I was expecting a bush camp, not a five-star resort," she answers.

The desert night air is icy, and Susan shivers as she emerges from the warm cocoon of the car. They walk into the hotel, side by side, holding hands. Susan squints in the bright light and stands back as Mark goes up to reception, looking at the pictures of aboriginal art and local scenery on the wall behind as he signs the check in forms. He already has a booking slip, so it's a minor formality. The receptionist gives him access keys, a map and a brief introduction to their hotel and location.

Now it's just the two of them. They follow the directions and walk along a passage to their room, which is in a back corner looking out over sand dunes towards distant dome shaped hills.

Trepidation at being alone with Mark settles over her. Their lovemaking has always been out amongst nature or in hidden moments in public. She's never been alone with him in a totally private space or spent an uninterrupted night with him in a full-sized bed. She hopes he won't find this intimate experience with her a disappointment, after the frisson of their almost public past lovemaking.

But Mark is totally calm and reassuring. They walk out onto the verandah and savour a blast of cold night air for a moment. It's as if he's slowing the reconnection process down, giving her time to get comfortable and occupy her own space. She moves in next to him, puts her arm around him, enjoying his solidity and warmth.

He points to the bathroom. "You probably want to freshen up after a long day, or maybe, you'd prefer a drink from the bar fridge. I'll get the bags from the car."

She smiles. "A hot bath sounds just fantastic."

Mark leaves and she turns on the tap.

Susan removes her clothes while the bath runs and the bubbles froth. She notices her reflection in the mirror. She runs her hands over her breasts and has an overwhelming desire to have Mark touch her like this. The prospect of a full night together is thrilling.

She climbs into the bath, leaving the door open six inches, so he can't help but see her when he returns. She lies stretched out for a minute, letting the warmth penetrate all her pores. Then she pushes herself deep into the water, submerging herself completely. She lies there for a few seconds, an upside-down underwater dive.

When she lifts herself and opens her eyes Mark is standing there, silent as a cat, looking down at her. He holds a large bottle of bubbles. "Compliments of Management. Thought you might like one," he says.

She yawns sleepily, like a contented kitten, and says, "Lovely. But really, all I want is you. God, I've missed you over the last week."

He looks at her intently, his eyes glinting into the start of a wicked smile. "It's taken all my effort to keep my hands off you until we got here. Now I intend to spend the whole night catching up on lost time. I want to make you beg for rest. But, to begin with, let's pop the bottle and drink a glass of these bubbles to celebrate."

With a flourish Mark removes the cork and pours two glasses. He sits on the edge of the bath while they sip together. Then, with his free hand, he scoops up some soap bubbles and places them on her nose. Susan takes his fingers and kisses them, one by one, then moves them to her aching nipple. She arches herself towards him, bubbles sliding off her naked form. She reaches up and undoes the top button of his shirt. "I want you in here with me. I want to see you naked too."

She watches him peel his clothes off and slide into the bath beside her. His mouth is on her breast, his hand stroking her thighs. His body moves above hers, as he pulls her towards him, trying to join himself to her in the bath.

Susan giggles, playfully pushes him back. "This is crazy. We have a king bed waiting for us."

Mark stands and reaches for towels to dry them. Then he picks her up and carries her to the bed, where he gently lays her down, his eyes full of intent.

It is a night burned in her mind for all her life: she like a sex starved kitten, her ravisher as a rampaging lion.

They begin on top of the covers but are soon under them as they explore each other's bodies with their mouths, reaching a joint orgasmic climax. They watch a raunchy movie. Then another slow languorous bath after which gentle lovemaking sees them drift to sleep, until early light reflects back off the hills behind them, to bring them awake. They find each other again in the early morning, him telling her he loves seeing her naked body, she thinking the same about his.

"That's it. You win; I can't take any more. I'm worn out," Susan says. She jumps up and pulls on a top. "And I'm absolutely starving! Let's have breakfast then go see this famous lump of rock."

They eat a leisurely breakfast: great piles of bacon, eggs, tomatoes, sausages, and mushrooms, then pastries and multiple cups of coffee.

"I'm so full," Susan says, looking at him with a slow smile, "A breakfast to remember after the best night of sex in my life. What can you do to top that?"

Mark, smug faced, says, "I can't think of anything, except to do it again tonight, and again the night after, and the night after that, under star filled desert skies."

They climb Uluru and marvel at the view across to the Olgas and Mount Connor, amidst end-to-end sky sitting over endless spinifex sand-plains. They walk around the rock base. Mark shows her where Azaria Chamberlain's dress was found; she knows the story of the dingo and of Lindy who had carried the blame for her daughter's death. They drive on to the Olgas and walk up the Valley of the Winds.

Finally, touristed out, they head back in the direction of Curtin Springs, stopping in the mid-afternoon for a beer and a local steak sandwich—juicy, tender, well-flavoured beef, which the owner tells them is station grown.

They drive on into the late afternoon's fading light, following a different route, which brings them towards Kings Canyon. It is a bitumen road so the driving is easy. They see camels and brumbies walking through scrubby bush, their silhouettes outlined in the late afternoon shadows.

An hour before dusk, they turn east onto a dirt road and drive a few kilometres before taking a side track north. They come to the edge of a broad sandy river that Mark calls The Palmer. He turns along a set of wheel tracks, following the river edge, and drives for few more minutes. They reach a waterhole nestled in the riverbed, viewed from a high rocky bank on their side, where he stops. In the stillness of the evening the landscape glows in reflected light, rocky bank, clear water, sand and dry grass behind.

"I think this might be our campsite for tonight. Happy?"

"Love it," Susan says.

He pulls his swag off the car and places it on the top of the ridge, so they have a view looking down and out across the river. "Why don't you sit and enjoy the view while I get a fire going."

She sits, alone and quiet, while Mark forages for branches. She contemplates her return to Mark, something beyond words, the intensity of their night of loving, the togetherness of their day of walking, talking, at times holding hands, at times sharing a laugh and a smile, other times sharing silence.

In the gathering dusk, an endless succession of brightly coloured birds come to the water to drink, small finches with a zebra tail stripes, others with red and diamond patterns on their plumage, beautiful blue wrens, and turquoise coloured parrots.

Susan hears a twittering noise and looks up. Perhaps a thousand iridescent green-yellow birds, silhouetted in the last sunlight, come swooping in to drink. She realises these are the real wild budgerigars, the original form of those she has seen in cages. Thump, thump, a blue-furred mother kangaroo and her joey hop cautiously across the sand below her and come to the water to drink. Her heart pounds; it's the first wild kangaroo she's seen. It's like she's on the set of a wildlife movie.

Mark returns with an arm full of timber. He says it's mulga wood. Soon a roaring fire is burning. He leaves again but soon returns dragging a medium sized twisted log. She helps him; it's incredibly heavy. He puts one end into the fire. "Best wood for cooking coals, gidgee. It'll keep our fire going all night."

He opens a metal tucker box. Inside is a cast-iron pan and pot, a selection of food tins and jars and, tucked in a corner and wrapped in a tea towel, a square glass bottle. Mark pulls out two tin cups, pannikins he calls them, dusts off the bottle and hands it to Susan. "Would you like to try some Bundaberg Overproof Rum, OP for short? There's ice and Coke in the Esky if you prefer it that way." He pours an inch into a pannikin and hands it to her. The fire of the drink almost takes her breath away.

She coughs. "Think I'll try it with ice and Coke."

Mark nods and fetches a Coke and a handful of ice from the car, which he adds to her drink. He adds a liberal splash of the rum into his own cup and takes a deep sip.

"Just the thing for a cold night! When I started in this outback country, I had a week out northwest of Alice, out towards the Georgina River, with an old-timer. I asked him what to bring, and he said a carton. So I went to the pub and bought a carton of beer. Next morning, when he picked me up, he pointed to my carton and said, 'What's that rubbish? That won't last us a night. I meant a carton of OP Rum.' So we stopped at a pub on the way out of town and I bought a carton of OP Bundy Rum. We almost finished it in that one week." He laughs. "My liver never recovered, but I got a taste for it."

Susan laughs too. "Sounds like I'll need lots of practice to catch up."

Dinner is steak and jacket potatoes, cooked in the coals and washed down with some more rum.

As they sit staring into the fire an eerie howl reverberates through the stillness. A few seconds later another howl comes from a different location, then another.

"Dingoes hunting. Soon they'll make a kill," Mark explains.

"I wonder what it was like for Lindy Chamberlain. Did she hear that noise before the dingo took her baby. It gives me a chill to think of her searching that night with her baby gone."

"Probably not. The word was that it was a pet dingo that the park rangers were feeding, tame enough not to be frightened of people, wild enough to hunt and kill. They're the most dangerous kind."

"What happened to that animal, the pet dingo?"

"A local aborigine said the ranger killed it later that night, took it far out into the desert and dumped it where it would never be found. He didn't want anyone slitting it open to see what was inside."

They retell more of Azaria Chamberlain's story, each contributing parts and emotions, she from reading and seeing the film, he from talking to locals. Neither doubts it was a dingo. Their conversation has an eerie poignancy, spoken to the sounds of hunting dingos calling into the night.

And then the talking is over. For a moment they look at the fire in silence. But quickly they roll out the swag and lay in it together, not moving for a long time. Susan feels incredibly dreamy and content, and drifts to sleep. She wakes as the fire is dying down.

Mark is looking down at her with an electric smile. "You didn't think I was going to let you sleep the whole night through without something more, did you?"

"Sleepy," Susan says through her drowsy state.

But Mark is insistent. "All the more fun to wake you." He turns her face towards him and kisses it with a ferocity that Susan is almost unprepared for. Then he's on top of her, forcing her legs apart and her body open, as he seeks to push himself inside her. Susan's first inclination is to clamp her legs shut and push him away, but he is too strong. She is pinioned and powerless, with just a pimple of fear at how unrelenting he is.

But, as she looks at his face, half seen in the moon light, something melts inside her. She has lost her power to say no to him; she really wants this as much as he does. Her body opens and responds to him. Soon she is as insatiable as he, a tigress, uninhibited, crying out with pleasure and pain as she climaxes. They take each other three times more before dawn lights the sky. There is not a single inch of her body or soul not touched, entered and pleasured. She loves this newly discovered wild sexual being within her.

She lies there thinking about what has changed inside her with this man. She's never thought of herself as sexually repressed, but there has been a conservatism in her upbringing, a family of Scottish Presbyterians which shaped her, with Sunday school and weekly church, and while never a strict adherent, it has shaped her morality. But Mark has no rules, at least not of that kind, and now she wonders who is right.

In the early dawn Susan falls into a deep sleep. She wakes a couple of hours later with the sun well up. There's no trace of Mark, but the fire has been stoked, a billy sits at its edge with hot water, and a basin of cold water, soap, and a towel have been placed nearby.

She realises this is for her and adds hot water to the cold, until it's pleasantly warm. She washes her face and sponges her body. She dresses in a tracksuit to push back the morning chill. She sees a pan with rashers and eggs sitting in it. She places the pan with rashers on the fire. When it's sizzling, she cracks the eggs and drops them in.

As the eggs are finishing, Mark emerges from the trees fifty yards away, carrying a rifle on a webbing strap, over his shoulder. He waves to her and she waves back. "Breakfast's ready. What did you get?"

"Nothing today, just scouting. You were sleeping so peacefully that I didn't want to wake you. I often go for an early morning walk. Sometimes I bag breakfast, like a rabbit or wood duck, but not today. That smells really good," Mark adds, looking at the bacon and eggs.

He drops two pieces of bread on the dull coals and, after a few seconds, flips them over. After another ten seconds there are two perfectly cooked pieces of toast. He passes her one and puts a handful of tea in the simmering, half-full billy. He finds two camp chairs tucked away on the truck, sets them up and pours two cups of tea. They eat side by side.

"How would you like to see the real desert?" Mark asks. "We could cut across to the east, around the edge of the Simpson Desert today and tomorrow, before heading up to the Gulf. You said you need to be in Darwin on Sunday week to catch your plane, didn't you?"

Susan nods. More than a week seems an eternity away.

Chapter 7 – Simpson Desert and On – Days 19-21

Susan and Mark pack quickly after breakfast. Before they get on the road, he checks the two spare tyres, the water and fuel tanks, then the engine oil. "I fuelled up in Yulara, so we have enough fuel to go about 1000 kilometres yet. But it's still important to check. You wouldn't want to run dry in the middle of nowhere."

Once they're on their way, they turn back onto a main dirt road going east. A short way along Susan sees a sign to the left for Henbury Craters. "What's down there?"

"It's still early. Why don't we take a look?"

They detour and gaze at a large hole seemingly punched out of the dry stony hillside. A sign says it was due to a meteorite impact that happened about 5,000 years ago.

Considering the age of this land this seems very recent to Susan. She asks, "Would aborigines have been living here then? It must have caused a big bang and a shockwave."

"They have local story that says it was made by a fire devil, which came out of the sun and burns and eats bad people. So they clearly saw something, probably felt and heard a massive explosion. I'm sure it would have scared them half to death. It would scare me too."

"I had an impression you're scared of nothing. Is there really something that can frighten you?"

Mark raises an eyebrow. "It's foolish not to fear obvious danger. What you do when it happens is what counts. For me, courage is to look danger in the eye, stay calm, maybe even smile back. We had a famous horse breaker the British executed in the Boer War. The story was he murdered people. As they pointed the guns he said, 'Shoot straight, you bastards.' I'd rather be him than cower in fear when my time comes."

Susan feels a chill. "Surely you don't plan to follow him?"

Mark gives a distant smile, as if his eyes glimpse dark shadows. "Bad stuff is part of life. You learn there's nowhere to hide from it."

She shivers wanting to push away this sense of doom.

Mark puts an arm around her. With his touch sun returns.

"Come on let's keep going," she says.

They walk on briskly in the still chilly morning air, circling the craters. No one else is in sight as they return to the car.

"If we came here two hours later the place would be crawling with tourists," Mark says. "Better early when this is here just for us."

They reach the bitumen of the Stuart Highway and follow it as it sweeps down into a valley where Mark points out the green line of the Finke River ahead. Soon they turn off again, following a sandy dirt road heading towards the morning sun. Another hour and a half of driving along a series of back roads, crossing a succession of sand dunes interspersed with flat areas of grass, scrub and small claypans brings them to a solitary rock outcrop called Chambers Pillar. It pokes its nobbled sandstone head fifty metres above the barren sand plain. They have a late morning tea at the base of this ancient monolith. It stands alone, a silent pale ochre sentinel. Perched up high, surveying their empty desert kingdom, are two lonely crows.

Several tourists arrive as they're drinking their tea. These people wave and call out distant hellos, before climbing up the base of the pillar to look out upon the sweeping views, but otherwise they remain alone.

They continue their drive alongside ever-bigger dunes that mark the edge of the Simpson Desert. Mark pulls out a map which he sits on the seat beside them to help Susan understand where they're going.

He seems to have an encyclopaedic knowledge of all these back roads, turning this way and that, cutting his way across the country while maintaining a broad direction. He tells her how many creeks and rivers flow out from the Alice Springs ranges and run south east towards the western edge of this desert. Here they end in a series of swamps, which he calls flood-outs. These become massive pools of water after rain.

Now, with the heavy rain of last summer a fading memory, these flood-outs are drying, but still lush. Roads, that six months earlier were underwater, are now becoming trafficable. They pass through remnant swamps where lush vegetation grows to the height of their car roof. Susan glimpses mobs of cattle, mostly enormous bullocks. With little to do but eat, many have grown so fat they waddle. A profusion of waterbirds such as ducks, pelicans, swans and waders seem to live here too. As they pass by these fly off in dense white clouds.

Soon the swamps are left behind and they drive alongside vast sand dunes, bank behind bank. Here she sees occasional cattle, camels, fences and windmills in the distance. She points towards a distant building. "What's that?"

"It's a cattle station homestead, the last one before the real desert begins."

Now they drive between massive sand hills along a set of faint wheel tracks. All signs of human habitation drop away.

Susan follows their progress along a squiggly dotted line on the map. She looks up the map legend and sees a symbol that refers to a local road of unknown condition only suitable for four-wheel drive vehicles. She follows this road with her finger for a long way until it seems to vanish into nothingness at a green patch in the middle of the desert.

She points to the place. "Is that place our destination? What's there?"

Mark nods. "We're heading for the very end of the Finke River in the desert at the border of South Australia and the Northern Territory. That's what that green place is. It's where its final floodwaters vanish into sand. Beyond that is a flowing bore where we'll camp for the night. It forms an oasis in the desert."

"That sounds amazing. I can't wait to see the oasis."

In the mid-afternoon they stop at a claypan where water has pooled between two mighty sand dunes. They light a fire, drink tea and eat bread and cheese. This is followed by a mug of cool water that Mark pours from a waterbag hanging behind the vehicle cabin. It had a slight canvas taste but is deliciously cold and refreshing.

They haven't seen another person for hours. Susan's never experienced such a sense of total solitude. Should she feel scared, being isolated in this remote place with a man she barely knows? She doesn't though. Instead, she feels content and elated. With just the two of them this is a place of perfection: the desert's endless red hues of sand, splashed with purple, yellow and white desert flowers and an intense blue sky stretching out to infinity. It gives rest to her soul. It's pure joy to be in the company of someone who draws sustenance from this peace and beauty as she does.

After eating, Susan and Mark sit silent and peaceful, absorbing their own quiet solitude and the land around them. This moment is something beyond words. People have come to deserts for millennia to find this, man lost in vastness, on a scale that exceeds the imagination.

She must doze off, sitting on the sand with her back against the swag. The movement of Mark packing to go snaps her from her daze. With reluctance she rises and they drive on.

Susan loses all sense of time, distance, and direction—other than an awareness of the sun and where it sits in the sky. The glowing disc, now behind them, casts long shadows, and the colours of the sand grow ever brighter in reflected light.

An unknown time later, having passed yet more sand dunes and flood-outs, they come to their destination, the flowing bore.

Susan looks out as they stop and sees an area of green grass and dense bushes which runs alongside a series of pools of water. It runs off into the distance, vanishing behind a low sand ridge as it curves around.

"Decades ago, a drilling rig sunk a bore here," Mark says. "As they reached the water a huge blast of pressure blew out the wellhead, and for fifty years it has flowed, huge amounts of water, rising from far below the earth in a thing called the Great Artesian Basin. It's an aquifer that covers half of inland Australia. It lies under this entire desert and extends a thousand miles beyond."

"Everything is so big out here; it's hard to comprehend."

They get out of the car and walk along the edge of the water heading towards its source. A couple hundred yards along they come to a place where water is bubbling out of the ground, rising to the height of Susan's chest. She looks at this vast flow. "So much water in the desert. Does this flow ever stop?"

"It's been like this as long as I've been coming here, at least ten years. They say it's been flowing non-stop for fifty years, and when it began it shot thirty feet into the air, like a massive geyser, before it slowly died back to this. A professor guy I knew once wrote down a number for how much water he reckoned had come out. The number was too big to make sense, but he said it would fill Sydney Harbour. Now they're talking about capping bores to stop the waste of water. There are others like this scattered around. I suppose it makes sense, but it's a pity about all the birds and animals that have made it their home."

Susan contemplates then says, "Australia is supposed to be mainly dry, so where could so much water come from?"

"Some say the water starts its journey in the New Guinea highlands, where hundreds of inches of rain fall each year. I've been told that slowly, over hundreds or thousands of years, it oozes through rocks far underground until it fills the ground below this place. I picture a vast ocean flowing beneath our feet which brings life but remains unseen."

"I like that image, like a second Pacific Ocean under the sand. I wonder what creatures live down there?"

She walks alongside Mark as they follow the water. Trapped between low hills it runs through shallow pools. At first it trickles steadily along, then it slows until it barely oozes. At its edges she sees drinking places of desert animals, muddy footprints marking their comings and goings, patches of green grass, trees and bushes with many birds dotted through them. After a few hundred yards the pools shrink and vanish until only green grass remains. Soon all sign of water is gone, returned to the sky or its underground source, and there is only desert again.

They make their camp on a dry claypan within sight of the bore flow. Mark finds a pair of binoculars that he passes to Susan, along with a 'What Bird Is That' book. He encourages her to try to identify some of the innumerable birds that come here to drink and suggests she keeps a lookout for other animals that may come to seek out water, perhaps a camel or an old bullock.

In the late afternoon they sip a rum sitting on Mark's swag. "Apart from showing me, what brings you here?" Susan asks.

He takes her hand and leads her to a muddy place at the edge of the water and scours the ground with his eyes. Where the mud has dried he points something out. It is a big footprint made by what looks like a cow, two distinct half moon hoof indents joined together, nearly the size of a dinner plate. "Do you know what made that?"

"A cow, a very big cow. I know what their footprints look like from our farm in Scotland, but this one must have been huge," she replies.

"Actually, a huge fat bullock. It's a footprint made months ago, but you get the idea. Sometimes at night they come here to drink, and I want to find one. They're very wary and rarely come before the evening dusk or full dark. Tonight we wait and see.

"Most are escapees from stations way up north, many hundreds of miles away. Floods or storms break down fences, opening paths into the empty desert. They live there for years and years, out in its farthest reaches, walking ever onward between the huge sand dunes running southeast until they emerge here."

"It sounds huge and a bit scary, but I'd still love to see one in the middle of the night. How do they survive out here?"

Mark walks to a low succulent bush with bright pink flowers that grows in clumps around their camp. He breaks off a piece and crushes it between his fingers, so the juice runs out and drips to the ground. "This is parakeelya. After rain it grows between the dunes. Where it is cattle don't need to drink. This plant gives both food and water. They can walk hundreds of miles, living only on it. But, when a long dry comes, it dies away and then they must come here to drink in the summer heat.

"Right now, it's growing across the desert, so they don't need to come here. But cattle are creatures of habit, so perhaps there'll be one tonight. If there is I'll take its meat, either as it drinks, or by following its tracks in the early morning. They don't usually walk far before they stop to rest after they've had a big drink. Their meat is good for trading with the mines and aboriginal communities where we'll be going."

"And you're allowed to shoot them without a licence?"

"What lives out here no one else can lay claim to, so they're free for the taking, that's if you're smart enough to find them. But it's easier said than done. They're clever animals. They only survive if they can avoid people. I like to try; I enjoy the challenge. Sometimes I succeed."

It's an hour until dark, so Mark suggests they climb up a nearby sand dune for a wide view of the surrounding countryside. The dune is surprisingly high and hard to climb. But they work their way up, puffing as they go. At the summit they gain a panorama of the desert as evening settles. They sit in the lee of the dune, just below the top, where they can look back towards their camp. It's silent in the evening stillness, and they sit in this silence. After a long minute Mark points out a huge eagle, circling above them.

"A wedge-tailed eagle. It must have a nest somewhere around. It's looking for something, perhaps a rabbit, for its dinner." As he speaks the eagle folds its wings and plummets down to where the grass grows green on the edge of the soak. As it soars again, Susan sees it's carrying a brown furry object in its talons, an unfortunate rabbit, now dinner.

A little later they see movement perhaps a kilometre away. Susan's eyes try to pinpoint where it comes from, but it's indistinct in the evening haze. She picks up the binoculars and zooms to where she sensed motion. Now it comes sharp in her focus, a group of camels walking through the mixed trees, browsing as they go. There are six large ones and three smaller ones, females with some calves. About a hundred yards behind is an even larger animal, a bull camel tracking along behind the female group. Despite feeding, they move along rapidly. Before long they reach the edge of the soak. There one raises its nose in the air, tasting the breeze. Without an obvious signal they form into a file and drift away, fading into desert and vanishing from sight at a steady trot.

"Like ships of the desert, the way they silently come and go," Susan says. "But why head away before they drank?"

"Out on the stations, back towards Alice, people shoot them because they break fences. Others round them up and catch them. To survive, most camels try to keep away from people. They probably caught our smell, wafting in the evening breeze, and decided they'd rather leave drinking to another day."

There's a scurrying noise in a clump of spinifex near where they sit. Mark puts his finger to his lips. Seconds later a small, furry, mouse-like creature runs out. With a springy step it sniffs here and there, making little darting movements as it scurries this way and that. Suddenly it springs high in the air and catches a large beetle, almost half its size, in its paws. They watch as it proceeds to eat it with apparent relish, crunching every last morsel then licking its lips. A few seconds later it's joined by a second, identical creature. The sniff each other warily, then, as if frightened, spring back into the spinifex together. The shadow of a hawk passes a few feet above.

Susan hears a faint chirp and looks to her other side. In a bush, so close she might touch it, is a mother blue wren with a nest of chicks. The mother makes little cheeps as she dips her beak towards each open mouth, transferring food to each in turn. She moves so fast it's like little flashes of light as she darts amongst the low branches alongside the nest. The female's mate appears, his plumage even more brilliant than hers, and he repeats the feeding of the chicks. For a brief second, the birds sit side by side on a small twig, making a ritual of reacquaintance before flitting away.

Susan shivers as a chill falls in the still evening.

Mark notices. "Time for dinner. It gets really cold out here at night, so you'll want to wear warm clothes."

"I expect you to keep me warm tonight. That's what you're here for," she says in a cheeky tone.

As they reach the bottom of the dune, coming alongside the soak, there's a whirring sound in the sky above. They look up. Framed in the last rays of the sun is a vast cloud of iridescent budgerigars, tens on tens of thousands, a number far beyond counting. They circle in a tight spiral whorl then settle in a huge mass to drink. With another whir they're away, vanishing into the sky. Susan's never imagined the wealth of wildlife that lives here in this remote desert place.

She and Mark settle in next to a fire, with sizzling sausages and another pannikin of rum. There are no signs of old bullocks. They'll probably arrive like phantoms, coming only when they're not expected or when she's looking another way.

Susan sleeps soundly, cuddled together with Mark for warmth. Lovemaking is forgotten until the call of a bird brings them awake in the early dawn light. Then, well refreshed, they pleasure each other and sleep again.

When Mark gets up to stoke the fire, Susan thinks about joining him, but it's too cold out of the swag, so she burrows deep under the covers.

Later, hidden in her cocoon of comfort, she hears a noise above her. She pokes her nose out. Mark holds out a steaming mug of tea and a plate of toast, bacon and eggs. "Something for her ladyship, made while she slumbered. It's so cold out here there's ice at the edge of the soak, and the car cabin thermometer reads minus six, so I thought you'd enjoy breakfast in bed before you emerge to face the day."

Susan puts down the plate and cup and takes his hand. "While this looks and smells fantastic, what I most want is for you to come in here and warm me against your body."

Mark begins to climb in, food forgotten, body aroused. Susan puts up her hand. "First we must eat. We're going to need the energy." She makes space beside her, and Mark lays his body there as she climbs astride him. She places pillows under his head and feeds them each alternating mouthfuls of food.

Mark hardens against her belly. Still feeding him, Susan aligns her body and pushes him within her. Sex merges with breakfast. They devour food; they devour each other, alternating steps, increasing gusto, until all control is gone.

Afterwards, she lies in his arms. "You're the sexiest, most precious man I've met. I don't want this to end. Do you think we could stay here in the desert forever?"

Mark tightens his arms around her and pushes his face into her hair. No words are said, but his actions feel like an emotion that mirrors hers. His body shakes slightly; it's like he's crying inside but hiding his face.

She runs fingers through his hair. She loves this man.

Later, Susan will remember this moment as their most perfect place of existence, simply being together in this place before any shadow darkened their sky.

After breakfast Mark scouts the water's edges. "Nothing came last night, no tracks. Still, I'm glad you came here. Very few do."

Susan nods. "Amen to that."

They walk for an hour along the soak and amongst the dunes. Sometimes she skips, her joy outpouring into physical exuberance. Sometimes they hold hands, or she hugs herself to him as he walks along. Once she climbs a dune high above his head and, rushing down, flings herself into his arms. He catches her and swings her through the air with effortless strength. It's an aimless rambling walk, more about each other and their delight of togetherness than about a place in the desert. But the desert is their playground, and the warming sun gives a sense of immortal delight. For a short time, she allows herself an image of their life going on together, forever, just like this.

It's mid-morning when they pack and head off in the car. They return the way they came from, following yesterday's tracks for the first couple hours. Then they take a different road, which travels further along the desert edge. The trip rolls along, not unlike yesterday, but with a sense of kinship between them that Susan has never experienced with anyone else. She's sure Mark feels something similar. A couple times they stop the car on a high desert ridge and gaze away into the endless space. They make occasional aimless conversation, but these are like punctuation marks between empty spaces, spaces without need of filling, which is befitting in this land of emptiness.

As they drive between two large sand dunes, in the mid-afternoon, Mark sights a big bullock trotting east towards a ridge of sand a couple of hundred metres away. He pulls the car to a halt. "I've been looking for a big fat one just like this." They get out and he opens a long steel box on the vehicle tray behind, sealed with a lock. He slides out a heavy hunting rifle with a gleaming polished scope. He cracks the bolt open and feeds a round into the breach from the magazine, then clicks on the safety catch. From his confident handling, it's clear he's often used guns before.

Mark walks to where a bent tree forms a natural rest at shoulder height. The bullock has stopped with its head poking into a bush at the foot of a big dune.

Susan estimates it's now a good 300 metres away. It's barely visible, its head little more than a black dot as it eats some succulent foliage. She watches Mark ease off the safety catch and steady himself. There's a pause for maybe two seconds, then crack. A bare second later the bullock falls down as if poleaxed.

Mark drives them to near where the animal lies, then they both pick a path over the broken ground with care.

Susan looks at the body of this massive animal, at least a ton, with rolls of fat flesh bulging around its hips and tail. She can't see where the bullet has hit; it must have been a head or spine shot to fall the way it did. She finally finds a small red dot in the skin, just below and behind the ear. Under this mark she can feel smashed bone. She's is a fair shot herself, and her father is good, but Mark has real skill to pull off a shot like that, accurate to an inch over 300 yards.

In half an hour Mark has boned out the carcass, and loaded the meat into clear plastic bags, which he puts into the cooler on large blocks of ice. Susan helps carry the smaller cuts and clean up. The large pieces are very heavy, completely beyond her to lift. Mark carries them with apparent ease. They pack up and head on again.

It feels like a movie set from *Out of Africa* or *The English Patient*, with panorama after panorama opening before their eyes. Over each ridge new rows of dunes emerge. Gradually, to the north, blue in the distance, mountains ranges grow out of the horizon, the East MacDonnell Ranges, with Arltunga, their evening destination.

Finally, in late evening light, the hillsides glowing an intense blue, they arrive at the Arltunga Bush Hotel. A booked cabin with a hot shower awaits them.

Mark carries a large slab of meat to the hotel manager, a good friend. He's back in a minute. "We're expected for dinner and drinks on them, in return for the meat."

They shower, dress and go into the bar. Dinner is homemade bush tomato flavoured sausages along with a slab of roast meat, said to be camel, and vegetables. Their glasses are endlessly full, and the cheer flows.

This is the first time she's seen Mark among friends; these people greet him as someone they know. He greets them back, and they all laugh and joke together, always making Susan feel welcomed and included too.

After dinner a guitar is found and country songs are sung: mining songs, stockman songs, songs about the country and its people. Songs by people called Slim Whitman and Slim Dusty. 'A pub with no beer', 'Leave him in the long yard'. Susan tries her best to sing along. This is the Australian bush of legend. She loves seeing Mark fully in his element, amongst his friends.

Sometime after midnight, last drinks then stumps are called. She and Mark walk, arm in arm, to their cabin. Their lovemaking is perfunctory, both full of drink, and they're soon asleep. She lies cuddled into him and feels even closer than before.

In the morning they eat a cooked breakfast served in the pub. After many backslapping farewells, they're on their way, heading across some of the biggest mountains she's seen so far.

They stop for a cup of tea at a little mine that ekes out a living from the rocky hills and their minerals. As they pull up two burly blokes come out of a tin shed that seems to serve as a house. One calls out to Mark. "Hey, stranger, long time, no see, where you been?"

"Off travelling, a trip to another desert on the other side of the ocean. It's good to be back. Let me introduce you to my friend, Susan. She's out from England to see this God forsaken place. God only knows why.

"Susan, I'd like you to meet Vladimir and Goran, Serbian brothers, my long-standing friends. They hope to get rich here someday."

Susan puts her own hand into each man's battle scarred one. She smiles and says, "Hello," to each in turn.

"I've got something for you," Mark continues. "I hope you've got something for me." He passes a slab of beef to the grateful miners.

They hang the meat in a nearby scrawny mulga tree.

Mark points at the slab. "It will hang and dry over several days, up to a week. With a dry outside crust, it will keep and not spoil. The flavour and tenderness will improve, day after day, until it melts in your mouth."

They all sit around a battered table under the shade of the tin roof, which extends out from the side of the house, sipping tea. Slices of a honeyed cake, not unlike baklava, are passed around.

It seems that Vlad is the business man, as after a while he says to Mark, "I have something to show you. I think you will really like it."

Mark looks to Goran. "How about you take Susan for a tour into the workings while Vlad and I do business."

Goran leads Susan to a shaft cut into the side of the hill. He's a grizzled bull of a man, with little English, but a friendly manner. He shows her how they prop the walls and chip into the shiny seams. He brings her to a seam that holds possible gemstones. Pointing his torch, to capture glints and reflections, he shows her how to look for the colour.

Susan looks back to the outside and sees Mark deep in conversation with Vladimir. She sees him open a case to show Mark something. It seems to interest him greatly. He's totally absorbed. Goran notices her looking back. "Maybe they trade. Mark only buys the best."

Susan finds the tour interesting, but now appreciates what backbreaking work it must be. They have some mechanical equipment, but a lot seems to depend on a pick and a shovel in a dark dusty hole, working in strange shadows cast from the electric bulbs. Still, she can sense Goran's excitement as he tells her how, on rare occasions, they find fantastic stones hidden amongst all the muck.

When they return Mark and Vladamir are drinking another cup of tea, having concluded whatever their business transactions were.

Mark and Susan wish them goodbye and drive on. The roads are rough and stony, and the mountains are steep. In places the road is little more than wheel tracks over the rocks creeping around the sides of huge hills. The side slope makes Susan nervous, knowing where they'll end up if they lose control, but Mark is concentrating hard and seems in his element, fully confident. His great confidence allows her to relax and trust herself to his care.

Sometimes he drives in low gear creeping over broken ground as the engine chugs, other times they come across flat valley floors, where he accelerates and goes up through the gears. They traverse broken-up sections of washed-out creek crossings, picking their way around rocks, holes and obstacles. It seems very few people ever come this way.

Mark is knowledgeable about the country and its geology, giving her a running commentary as they go. Thanks to him she's gaining a unique view of this country of childhood stories and imagination; it's becoming ever more real and fascinating as they drive on.

They see plenty of huge bullocks, along with scrub bulls. Mark explains that these are owned by the station they're driving through. The cattle are like a piggy bank full of thousand-dollar notes. It can be opened when money is needed. Now, when times and seasons are good, these backcountry cattle are left alone to grow big and fat. When dry times come again this four-footed gold will be turned into cash.

There are also lots of brumbies, proud stallions. With their necks arched and ears laid back, they herd and harass their broods of mares. They spy two brumby groups meeting near a waterhole. The stallions' rear and bare their teeth in threat. One backs away, herding his mares. The victor gallops behind him for a few seconds biting at his rump. But he quickly returns to his own harem, perhaps fearful that another will steal them away.

Around lunchtime they come to a place where a soak runs out of the side of a hill. Hoof marks indicate recent cattle and horse use, but just now they share the place with multitudes of little zebra finches and an occasional iridescent parrot.

Mark lights another fire of dried mulga, which burns fiercely. As it burns down he takes a heavy, black metal plate, about a foot long, from beside a spare wheel. "It's my mobile barbeque," he explains. He slices two, inch thick slabs from yesterday's bullock meat, and puts them on the grill, along with half a kidney and a liberal sprinkling of salt.

The scent of the meat is delicious. Marks serves it on a slice of bread with pickles. The meat is rich flavoured, tender, best restaurant quality.

"Not bad, but it would improve more if hung it for at least three more days."

Susan laughs. "You're getting way too fussy."

In the mid-afternoon they emerge from the mountains onto a wide, open grass plain.

"Yambah Station. It's one of the best blocks in the Alice," Mark says.

They're heading for Barrow Creek pub where, that night, a bush band is supposed to be playing. It's over 200 kilometres away, so they have a quick drink from the waterbag then go on.

Two and a half hours later, with late afternoon drifting towards dusk, they come around a bend and, alongside low rocky hills, see a sign pointing to Barrow Creek Hotel.

The rooms are booked out, but many people are camped out on the flat ground nearby, come from the stations and aboriginal camps to enjoy the night. Mark drives to one side and rolls out their swag. Half the population is aboriginal. This is Susan's first introduction to these people who all seem to know Mark well.

Mark explains he has done a lot of work around here over the last decade, mining work, station work, building work in these aboriginal communities: sinking bores, putting up windmills, fixing houses and anything else needed. These people have become his friends.

He calls to an older man named Johnnie, who he tells Susan is a tribal elder. "Hey, Johnnie, I've got something for you."

Johnnie walks over and shakes Mark's hand. Mark turns to Susan and says, "Allow me to introduce you to an elder from the Kaytetye people; they are the people who belong to this place. And Johnnie is their best hunter, better than anyone I know at tracking a kangaroo."

Susan shakes his hand and smiles. "Hello, Johnnie. Pleased to meet you. I'm Susan."

"Very nice to meet you, Missus Susan."

Mark goes to the back of the truck. Lifting out a piece of meat he offers it to Johnnie. "This one good bullock, Johnnie. Him eating parakeelya, out on edge of desert country. You know, that other side Arltunga. You take this one for your dinner. Pay back for that kangaroo you gave me last year."

With a broad smile and gesticulating thanks Johnnie carries it off. He shows it to others in his camp who wave their thanks.

Over near the pub the band is warming up, playing reels and jigs. A few bare-footed aboriginal girls dance in the dust. Alongside are several cut down metal drums, like the ones used on the farm for fuel, with roaring fires burning inside them to ward off the evening chill. Most people are drinking beer, though a few old-timers can be seen with their rum bottles and pannikins. A barbeque, with steak, sausages and onions, along with piles of buttered bread, coleslaw and tomato sauce is being cooked up. Someone says the price is a donation to The Flying Doctor Service.

Groups are mingling, coming and going, warming up for the evening dancing. All at once the band strikes up a jig, and the caller tells everyone to put down their drinks and join in for the first dance. He leads them slowly through their moves at first, and then they're on their own. The music gets faster and faster and most people join in and keep up. When the song is over there are cheers and calls of, "More! More!"

Susan dances with Mark, but sometimes other men seek her out. Eventually a supper break is called, and weary legs rested, before the band resumes for their final bracket. It's a great night, carried along by the music and the dancing in the dust.

In the late-late night only a few remain, hunched around the fires. Mark, deep in tales with a couple old-timers over a bottle of rum, sits amongst them around a fire.

Susan stays on a while, but finally signals to Mark that she's off to bed. She yawns as she walks to their campsite and crawls into their swag. This is the first time she's gone to bed alone. While part of her misses Mark's strong, warm body, she's also content lying out in the incredible star filled night, as the fires slowly gutter and die away. The only noise is a distant hum of a diesel generator and a mutter of soft conversation. A bright shooting star flashes across her vision. She's happy in this remote but amazing place.

She wakes in the early dawn. Mark is lying beside her, fully dressed and snoring quietly. As the dawn lights the sky she goes to the temporary shower block and washes herself, shivering in the cold. She walks back, gazing at the eastern sky. It is just another desert sunrise, but the light captivates her, golden lance shafts spearing up from the horizon. Far above, at the outer edges of the world, they light fine filaments of clouds in endless hues of shifting pastel pinks. Extraordinary light, extraordinary colour, everyday desert ordinariness.

Mark sleeps on; she can smell rum on him now she's washed. She cuddles into him in the bed, content to be with him, enjoying their small window of time together. The sun is a hand width above the horizon when Mark stirs. As he opens bleary eyes he becomes aware of her.

"You look so fresh and pretty," he says sleepily, as he admires her freshly washed face. "Must be time now to give a man his pleasure."

"But, Mark, I'm dressed; it's daylight. All these people will see us."

He reaches out and pulls the canvas swag flap over their heads. "Not now, they won't." He directs her hand to his hardness.

This lovemaking has an illicit thrill, with the noises of people waking up and moving around them. This is their cave of delight, under the shelter of the canvass. She knows this strange man is taking over and consuming her life. It is beyond any power she has to stop it.

Chapter 8 – The Big Waterhole – Day 22

An hour later Mark goes off to shower and shave. They eat breakfast together, this time steak and eggs at the hotel bar. Mark leaves her there, saying he's off to top up the fuel tanks and give the vehicle another careful check over. They'll be cutting though some rough country to the east, where they'll camp overnight at a big waterhole, before heading up into the Gulf, leaving the desert behind for tropical scenery, weather and fishing. It is now mid-August, the end of Australia's winter, but it's still cold here. Mark says the weather will warm up fast as they travel north.

Susan sits at the bar and looks around. There is a collection of curios spread over the walls. Lots of photos of people, some recent, some decades old—mostly station people and truckies, but some who look like tourists and also many aboriginal people.

Susan's attention is drawn to an old newspaper story that someone has pinned up titled: 'Revisiting the site of the Coniston Massacre'.

Fifty miles from here is a place called Brooks Soak, which it says is the site of the last big aboriginal massacre in Australia. It was led by the policeman who lived here at Barrow Creek. She's heard of aboriginal massacres in the 1800s, but this wasn't back then; it was after the First World War. By that time, she thought countries like Australia had moved past a frontier mentality to become places with laws and consequences. But this happened within the lifetime of her own extended family; her grandparents and many other people she has known were alive then.

As she reads the journalist's story of two decades prior, she realises this journalist actually talked to people who had lived through this time, both children from the stations around who had known the perpetrators, and relatives of the aboriginal victims—old people now. These were survivors from Coniston's community who had been there, felt the terror and seen what happened as dozens of their brothers, sisters, mothers, fathers, uncles and aunts were rounded up and butchered like cattle.

It was payback for the death of one white dingo trapper, who'd stolen from his killer. Estimates were that at least sixty, and probably over a hundred, men, women and children were butchered. What followed was a travesty of justice. At first no action was taken but, following heated demands from other parts of Australia and around the world, the ringleaders were taken to Darwin for trial, only to be acquitted. The local jury considered that the actions taken by these 'upstanding citizens' were justified.

It's shocking to discover this callous event so close to here, a dark underbelly of the country, beautiful outside in its rugged remoteness; this brutality lies just below the sunlit surface. Susan shivers, glad this happened in another time and is now passing from human experience, or at least from the places and experiences she knows.

Susan walks to the other side of the room to read more clippings. Here she see's something more recent, a story of a girl who went missing almost a year ago, last seen in Adelaide, but believed to be heading for Alice Springs and perhaps further north. It's a copy of a standard missing person's photo with contact details for the Northern Territory Police. The quality is poor, like a faded photocopy on which somebody has spilled a beer, making the ink run, and gathering dirt and other muck. The woman's name is almost illegible. It ends in a smudged 'o' or 'e' then an 'na' –that's all she can read, perhaps Lena or Shona or something like that. But the image of the woman's face is still quite clear.

As she looks she gets a shock. The woman has dark hair and an expression which could be herself from a few years ago, an enigmatic half smile. For an instant she feels like she's looking at her vanished self, but it can't be real. It scares her. She walks over to the bar to get a drink, something to calm her nerves.

As she stands, musing, in this black mind space, Mark appears alongside her. She points to the first newspaper article, just to her side, the one of Coniston Massacre. "Did you know about this?"

"Of course. I've worked there. Some of those who lived it told me."

"Isn't it awful that it could still happen within the lifetime of these people?"

He shrugs, looking a bit perplexed, "Why do you find it surprising? Out here life is cheap, death is easy, and the pretence of civilisation is thin. It's how it is in most places around the world and always will be. For the dead it's no big deal: one minute alive, the next gone. But the living must protect themselves, take their own retribution. I would have put my own bullet into that policeman and each of his mates, then dumped their bodies in the far out desert where no one would find them. I wouldn't have sent them away hoping for justice. Better to kill bad bastards than pretend justice can be done by others."

There is something ruthless in his voice. His words don't sound like idle talk; she senses Mark really would have done the killing himself if he thought it was needed. It would have been done with no compunction and no questions asked. Still, Susan can't disagree that his way would have served justice better for these people.

She thinks of pointing out the picture of the missing person, asking him if he thinks it looks like her. But there is something dark and ugly in his manner which scares her. She pushes it out of her mind.

Now she doesn't want to talk about it anymore. She doesn't want her image of Mark, so kind and gentle to her, being mixed with such brutality. All those days Susan has spent with him out here have been filled with a bright sunlight. She doesn't want darkness intruding and spoiling it.

"You're probably right, better not to think of it anymore," she says, flashing him a smile and walking away.

It's mid-morning before they're away, and the sun is well up. Leaving with them are many other late risers from the previous night of revelry, now much subdued.

They travel a few miles before turning off the highway, taking a medium sized gravel road. They pass battered old signs for places that Susan assumes are stations or aboriginal communities: Murray Downs, Elkedra, Epenarra, Erelola Rockhole and Frew River, their distances ranging from one hundred to three hundred kilometres away. Alongside these old signs is a much shinier, new looking sign that bears the names of Davenport Range National Park and Old Police Station Waterhole, with symbols for camping and rough roads.

The first hour is a smooth dirt road, but this ends with a turnoff sign to Murray Downs. After this the road deteriorates rapidly, with many areas of sand and corrugations along with patches of broken stony ground. They often follow along dried up creeks, their rock littered beds running between stony ridges, flanked by coarse spinifex sand plains. They drive through lots of small broken hills, the orange-red stony sides beautiful as sun flashes off them. The wealth of wildlife is astonishing in and around these hills, innumerable bright coloured birds of many shapes and sizes, large goannas sunning themselves on rocks, snakes that slither across the road. On the hillsides they watch large solid-bodied wallabies hop away on their approach.

They pass a sign for the Erelola Rockhole. Two rusted-out car bodies are visible in the bush nearby. "Who'd leave rubbish like old cars in such an untouched wilderness?" Susan asks.

"There's an aboriginal camp near here. They buy old cars, but they don't last long on the rough roads. They're abandoned where they stop. Then the occupants return to time-honoured foot travel, like they did before for tens of thousands of years."

Once they leave this turnoff behind the road improves, with less traffic wear and tear the corrugations are minor, but the country gets steadily rougher. Susan's bottom aches from endless bouncing over the rocky road.

Finally, they come to a sign to the left that reads: 'Frew River 4WD Loop Track', and below it 'Old Police Waterhole 8'. Another sign reads: 'Rough Road – Only for experienced 4WD.'

Mark stops at the corner, gets out and stretches.

Susan climbs out too. "Is something the matter?"

"No, just a real bad road from here; it's only eight kilometres, but it'll take an hour. There are lots of parts where walking is faster."

After five minutes of walking and stretching they climb back in. Mark puts the car into low range four-wheel drive and they head off.

He hasn't exaggerated. It's slow and rough. Yesterday's drive through the mountains was rough, but this is at another level, not big hills, but continuous ups and downs as they cross small broken ridges and endlessly follow, cross and recross the same rocky creeks. There are times where they barely crawl up hills covered with loose stones, with all four wheels spinning in the rock scree, gradually inching forward, as one wheel and then another finds temporary grip.

Finally, they crest one more ridge, and there before them is a vast waterhole, broad and clear in the midday sun, sitting alongside a broken red range. It's isolated yet beautiful, a sparkling jewel in a desolate landscape of rocky spinifex hills. They haven't passed another car since the Rockhole turnoff.

This is their own private paradise, laid out before them. They are its sole inhabitants.

They park just back from the water, on a flat green grassy foreshore, interspersed with large shady trees. They're both starving, so lunch is quickly made, slabs of cold beef, sliced off a piece of cooked meat, laid over bread slices and topped with tomato relish and a liberal sprinkling of salt. They wash it down with two cold beers each.

The water beckons. The afternoon is warm and the sky cloud free. A sandy beach in front of their campsite leads to water so clear it sparkles like a shiny glass, freshly washed. The air is still. Opposite, red hills make almost perfect reflections on the smooth water. Occasional light wind puffs and small fish splashes cause tiny ripples, fractures through this mirror. As they settle, the glassy perfection reforms.

Susan walks down onto the sandy shoreline and stands, toes sinking into the wet sand of the edge, absorbing the atmosphere.

Mark suddenly rushes at her, pushing her into the deep. She ducks under his arm and, as she does, scoops a handful of water and splashes the length of his back, still covered by his shirt. The water is freezing. Mark yelps and spins, two hands flinging water to drench her. She responds in kind. They both laugh and splash until they're completely saturated.

It brings to mind their first day on the little beach. Susan's desire for Mark wells up with the memory. She's facing away from him as she grasps the hem of her shirt and lifts it over her head. Her bra had disappeared in their morning passion. She spins around so Mark can see that her nipples are erect, then laughing she pushes her breasts into his face. "Well, what will you splash now?"

Mark picks her up and carries her out into deep water, his mouth on her breast. He trips and falls over, pulling them both below. They surface together, both spluttering. They look at each other and laugh, both knowing what they want now.

After their lust is satiated, they lie together, side by side in the warm shallows, sharing stories and memories of other bush and camping trips, he telling her of safaris in Africa, and she telling him of hunting with her dad in Scotland. The stories ebb into silence. "I had a wonderful childhood, what about you?" she asks him.

He looks at her with a thoughtful look, not quite open but not closed off either, as if considering, but no words come.

She finally plucks up the courage to ask him directly about his early life and where he learned his bush and shooting skills. "I wish you could meet my father; I'm sure he'd like you. You both like the outdoors, hunting and going to out of the way places. Did your father take you bush or teach you to shoot like mine did?"

Mark remains silent, as though weighing something up. A brief flash of openness shows in his face, then the shutters come down. "What does it matter? I don't want to talk about my father. He was a dick. A lazy, useless drunk and a bully."

Susan should leave it, but a voice inside her head won't let her. "Surely someone in your family was good to you? What about your mother?"

Mark winces and turns away. "I really don't want to talk about it, but seeing as you seem determined to know, my mother died when I was little. I can barely remember her. I suppose she was okay, but she was totally scared of my father. One day she just wasn't there anymore. A long time later my father said she'd died in an accident. There was no funeral. It was like she was written out of our lives. Later I found out it was suicide, but I don't think he cared or missed her."

Susan put's her hand on his. "That's awful. I'm so sorry."

"She never did anything for me. As soon as I was old enough I went bush. Since then I've worked all over, doing anything that paid and getting on with my life. I haven't seen my father since then; perhaps he died one time when he was drunk, or he's a bum who sleeps on the street. Perhaps he's locked up in jail, but whatever, I don't think he even noticed I was gone."

Mark stands, brushes himself off and says, "If it's okay with you, I'll go off on my own for a while and do some hunting?"

While it sounds like a question, Susan knows it's a statement of fact. This is what he will do and she's not invited. His rejection stabs her, but she smiles and says, "Sure, I'm happy to rest quietly for a couple hours and read a book."

Hearing her words, Mark seems to relent a little. "If you feel like trying you might catch a fish on a line. You get yellow bellies in here, and you can sometimes catch one on a piece of meat."

He returns with a hand line, fitted with a hook and sinker, and an off-cut of beef, which he places on a rock beside her.

Turning from her, Mark takes a medium sized rifle and box of ammunition from his truck. He drops them in a backpack, along with a water bottle. With a nod of his head he's gone. Susan watches his retreating form until he's out of sight.

He doesn't turn back or wave.

It's like he's instantly severed her from his life, and the tenderness of their lovemaking together, bare minutes before, has vanished.

Susan feels deflated and alone. She pulls out her phone and looks at it. She wishes it had a signal so she could ring her mum or Maggie from Cairns, just to have someone else to chat with.

She hasn't spoken to family of friends to let them know her movements since she arrived in Melbourne over a week ago. Mark has totally consumed her life from the minute she touched down in Alice Springs, five days ago. No one even knows his name, let alone that she's travelling with him in the far away Northern Territory.

She's barely been anywhere in mobile phone range since she met up with him again. She charged her phone at Arltunga, two days back. There was no reception there and she's not looked again since. To be truthful, she's hasn't thought of contacting others until now. Deciding she doesn't want to waste the 30% charge left in the battery, she turns it off completely for now.

The afternoon sun is hot on her skin. She's starting to turn pink. To avoid being red raw tonight, she'll have to put on sunscreen or go into the shade. She's seen Mark with sun cream at some point.

Susan climbs into the car and opens the glove box.

No sun screen there. She tries the door compartments. Still nothing. Perhaps it's behind the seats? She slides the driver's seat forward to look behind it, then does the same on the passenger side. Nothing anywhere.

There's a big plastic box with a first aid sign strapped to the wall behind her seat. Perhaps there's something in the first aid box. She unclips it and sits it on her seat. The kit has three slide-out drawers and a flip top. She starts systematically at the top, sees lots of little things, band-aids, tablet blister packs, small tubes, sewing needles and some syringes. On the next level are bandages and dressings, plasters and tapes, but still no sign of any sun cream. The third level looks more promising: bottles and larger tubes of various liniments, alcohol, disinfectant, cough medicine; but *still* no sun cream.

There's one more drawer at the bottom. It's tightly packed full of things in cloth packages. The drawer is hard to open, but she wiggles it and it comes out. It doesn't look promising, but she's come this far, so she may as well look inside.

The first package is full of surgical instruments, obviously for more major accidents requiring stitching. Susan's surprised when, instead of finding something similar in the second cloth wrapped package, she finds three car number plate sets, each held together with a rubber band and all wrapped together in an old calico bag.

She lifts one out, separates the two plates, and finds a tiny sticky label on the back of one plate which reads 'Butler'. Curious, she separates the next set, which has a similar sticker with the word 'Brown'. The final label reads 'Brooks'.

This seems strange. But after Mark's negative reaction to her recent questions, it's not something to ask about on his return. No doubt there's a good explanation.

Susan carefully wraps up all the bits, just the way she found them, and puts them back in place. Then she returns the first aid box to its exact place. The discovery is a thing to muse over for a day or two. Why would he need extra sets of number plates?

She sits on the passenger seat for a second, thinking about her afternoon. Will she fish or read? Glancing up, looking over to the driver's corner of the dash, Susan smacks her hand to her forehead. There it is; a battered bottle of sun cream sits on the dashboard, clearly visible. She wonders how she missed it in the first place.

That decides her; with sun cream on she'll fish and read, sitting at the edge of the water in the afternoon sun. Susan covers her face, hands and legs with cream, finds a long-sleeved shirt and floppy hat, and takes a novel from her pack.

She threads the meat on the hook and casts it out a few yards into the deep. Sitting on a rock with her toes in the water, line loosely wrapped around a finger, Susan opens her book and enjoys the warmth of the afternoon sun as she reads.

She's read one chapter and is just starting the next, fishing forgotten, when the line twitches—a definite bite. Butterflies of excitement stir in her stomach. Imagine that, catching her very own fish, all by herself, out here in the middle of Australia! That really will be a story to tell.

Book cast aside, she turns her attention to the fish. She's fished in England with her father and has a sense of how to do it. Show patience, allow the fish to explore and nibble the bait, no hasty pullbacks. She settles her nerves and waits, suppressing a desire to rush.

The gentle tugging resumes. Let the fish investigate and pick up the bait. Imagine it feeling and tasting it in its mouth. With luck it will pick it up properly, taking it fully into its mouth.

Suddenly it all changes; the fish has clearly taken the bait and begins to swim off, giving the line a powerful pull. Her heart skips a beat, but she calms herself. Applying steady pressure back through the line with soft hands, Susan works the fish towards her. There's a sudden violent surge of tugging as it realises it's trapped, but she holds steady and tries to smooth out the more severe jerks with her hands. The jerking stops, and she pulls in the line, hoping it hasn't got off, but no, it has just swum towards her. There it is again, making a last desperate attempt to get free. But the hook holds, the fish stays attached. Soon Susan has it in the shallows, and then it's over and the fish is on the sand next to her. It seems huge, perhaps one or two kilos, with glistening golden scales on its sides and belly.

It looks something like the perch she knows from England, but without the stripes on its sides. Part of her feels sorry to bring death to this creature, now helpless at the water's edge. Another part feels proud of her own success, without help, catching this fish for dinner. She can't wait to show Mark. He'll be impressed, she's sure.

Susan finds a knife in a box on the back of the car. She dispatches the fish, the way her father has shown her, then, feeling slightly squeamish, she opens its belly and removes its innards. She casts them out into the water. First there is splashing as small fish feed, then a sudden swoop. A large bird, like a hawk or falcon, swoops down from the sky and plucks the remnants up with a talon. With a screech of success, it flies across the water to a dead tree where it sits and eats.

Susan's excitement surges. It's as if she's mastered a part of this remote place. Reading is forgotten. She covers the fish to protect it from other hungry animals and decides to do her own exploring, walking along the water's edge to where it ends in a dry riverbed.

At its edge she finds a path of sorts, a track where animals use a gully to come down to the water. She works her way up this for perhaps a hundred yards until she comes to a place from where she can climb up to the top of the red rock hillside.

Here Susan sits at the cliff edge, gazing out across the hill to the tree lined riverbed and water below, her view extending to the far horizon where endless yellow spinifex covered hills meet blue sky. Something in this harsh stone country is eating its way into her soul, a different but kindred desolation to that of the sand desert of days just past.

She watches the comings and goings of the desert animals that rely on this oasis. Three kangaroos: mother, large offspring and a small joey, its head out of her pouch, approach cautiously. They drink in quick sips, alert to any other visitors, then hop a short distance away where mother and her large offspring nibble on some green riverbed grass. The baby comes out to explore before a noise causes it to startle. A quick, headfirst tumble later, the baby is back inside the mother's pouch of safety. They move out of sight.

Minutes later a tan coloured dog emerges from the river's edge scrub and comes down to the water. It laps quickly, then it too vanishes. This is the first time Susan's seen a wild dingo. Now only birds, lizards scurrying over rocks, and herself are left as sole occupants of this place.

Perhaps half an hour passes in solitude. Her eyes spot distant movement. It's Mark, walking down the riverbed, carrying something over his shoulder. She clambers down and runs to meet him.

"What have you got?" she asks.

"Just a couple ducks. Thought we might have them for dinner," he replies, indicating two birds tied together on a stick over his shoulder.

Susan shuffles her feet awkwardly and says, "Sorry about before. I know it's not my business."

Mark's hard expression softens; Susan moves in close and hugs herself to him. "Thank you for bringing me here; this is something really special, every bit as special as the sandy desert in its own way."

Mark's expression seems to struggle. She thinks he might say something—anything—that will tell her more about who he really is or what's going on inside him. But instead he just pulls her close and holds her against him. After a minute, he moves an arm's length away, gripping Susan's shoulders tightly in his hands. "We should enjoy our trip together then get you to your Darwin plane. After that, who knows? Like you I want more, but I hate to make promises I can't keep."

Her heart leaps. It's not quite a statement of commitment, but it's something more than nothing.

She's almost forgotten about her fishing success, but as they walk back, Susan glimpses the fish's tail from beneath its covering. Almost bursting with pride, she points to it. "Mark, I caught a fish! A big one, a golden yellow colour."

"A big one, eh?" He reaches for her hands and holds them a couple of feet apart, "This big?" he asks, gesturing to the distance between her hands.

She laughs with bubbling excitement, "Well, not quite, perhaps half that, but really big for me."

Susan races ahead, uncovers her fish and presents it to Mark.

"You're right," he says, with a smile, "it is pretty big, actually. It's just the right size for our dinner."

They light a huge fire and, while the coals form, Mark digs a pit with a shovel off to the side. He half fills it with hot coals from the fire, lays leaves over it and places the ducks and fish, with salt and bush herbs in their bellies, over this. He covers them with more leaves and then another layer of coals. His final step is to cover it all with larger branches and some earth.

Mark dusts off his hands and reaches for a large cast iron pot—a camp oven he calls it—and shows Susan how to make a damper and brownie for dinner and breakfast. These roast side by side as the fish and ducks cook.

After an hour and a half Mark pronounces their dinner ready and uncovers the pit. Susan's mouth waters as he peels back the burnt skins to reveal the succulent flesh of the ducks and fish. A final sprinkle of salt and it's ready to eat.

They feast with their fingers, eating morsels of meat on pieces of fresh-cooked damper. Dinner is accompanied by a cold bottle of champagne, a Moët no less, that Mark finds in the fridge. After they eat their fill of the meats they lean back against the swag and eat brownie and butter, washed down with large mugs of tea. They watch in quiet stillness, as the light fades from the western sky and the first stars appear in the clear night.

She thinks this is the best night of their time together so far; it is their magic place. They're even closer now than the night they shared in the desert.

In all her happiness, the mystery of the number plates now seems unimportant. It had felt unusual at the time, but now she looks at Mark and knows there will be a rational explanation. She would trust this man with her life.

Chapter 9 – To the Gulf and Hell's Gates – Day 23

SNAKES
LIGHTS ATTRACT INSECTS
INSECTS ATTRACT FROGS
FROGS ATTRACT SNAKES
SNAKES BITE!
TURN OFF LIGHTS
FLYING DOCTORS ARE 2 HRS AWAY

This is the sign at Hell's Gate Roadhouse, which greets their arrival after a long day of driving.

After their idyllic afternoon and evening at Policeman's Waterhole on the Frew River, they'd risen early, when there was barely light in the eastern sky. Mark insisted they not waste time, as they had a full day of driving ahead of them.

Breakfast was a mug of tea, warmed on the still glowing coals of last night's fire. Mark ate some leftover cold duck. Susan contented herself with leftover damper and brownie, which she coated liberally with butter and golden syrup.

Then it was an hour of slow and rough four-wheel driving until they came out on the road to Epenarra, a nearby cattle station. From there they followed a proper dirt road, not just a set of wheel tracks.

They stopped at a roadhouse mid-morning, on the Barkly Highway, where the road to Borroloola and the Gulf branched north. Mark showed her where they were going on a map. They had a half hour break to have a second late breakfast, before Mark did vehicle maintenance. While Mark was topping up the fuel, Susan freshened herself in the bathroom. She thought of using the roadhouse's payphone to ring home and say hello to her parents, but with the time difference it was late at night in

England, and her parents would be asleep. Besides, travel news could wait until she saw them in a few days' time.

Instead she bought a second cup of coffee for herself, and one for Mark, and sat on an old bench in the shade watching him work. He was so focused. His effortless strength and skill were incredibly attractive. Perhaps sensing her gaze, Mark glanced up and noticed her. Susan waved before gesturing to the coffee mug. As Mark walked over, Susan tapped her feet happily. Mark took the coffee, downed it in one gulp and punched her affectionately. She just smiled.

"Ready for a long day's boring driving? If you wanted to, you could do part of the driving today. It's a long straight road for the next couple hours, not much to see. I thought I could play at tourist while you take the wheel for that bit."

His offer thrilled Susan; it was a symbol of the trust growing between them. She climbed into the driver's seat and, after introductory instructions on how to operate the car, they headed off. She drove cautiously at first as she got the feel of the heavy vehicle, but soon drove with increasing confidence. The road was a narrow strip of bitumen with an uneven edge, just wide enough for one car. A couple of times, Susan had to pull over to share the road with cars passing or going the other way, steering carefully to keep control.

At first Mark watched closely to be sure she was okay, but quickly paid no mind to her driving and looked around. Susan was pleased with his display of confidence in her.

As they continued, they left the desert scrub behind and emerged into what Mark said was the start of the good cattle country. It began as open grass plains between low scrubby ridges, then it was just vast rolling miles of grass, golden tips swaying over green tinged stems, extending from horizon to horizon. Mark told her how, when a storm came rolling over this land, you could often see it a hundred miles away.

They passed occasional groups of big shiny-skinned cattle. "They're Santas," Mark said. "Short for Santa Gertrudis."

Susan drove on for another hour and a half, to what Mark said was the northern edge of the Barkly Tableland, then he took over again. The landscape outside slowly changed, more scrubby patches than rolling grass plains and less shiny and fat cattle.

They veered east, heading away from the afternoon sun. The cattle country was left behind. They were now driving through broken landscapes of fast drying creeks and little gullies. The ground was mostly covered in coarse gravel and wiry dead grass, with no cattle to be seen.

In the mid-afternoon, they took a small track that turned off the main road, with a sign for Nicholson Aboriginal Reserve. After few minutes they pulled over and stopped as Mark said he wanted to test and sight-in his rifles. "It's a total no man's land here, so we won't disturb anyone."

After long hours of driving, Susan was happy for the break. She helped Mark measure out fifty metres using a tape measure, and then put targets in place. Mark used the truck door to steady himself as he shot groups of five shots into each target. His shots were close together, all within a one-inch circle, though for one rifle, which he said was a 223, they were all about an inch low of the bullseye. Mark made a minute adjustment to its sights and then shot off a single round. It was almost dead centre.

Mark passed her the rifle. "Do you want a go?"

Susan nodded and took her place, lifting the rifle to the target. She flinched on the first shot and it went wide, but then steadied herself and controlled her breathing. Her shots hit within a ten-centimetre circle. She punched the air with delight.

"Not bad for a Pommie girl from the city," Mark said, sounding pleased too. He put that gun aside and pulled out another, much bigger, gun with a glowing polished telescopic sight. He handled her this new gun with loving care; it was clearly his pride and joy. "It's a 30-06. This is my safari gun from Africa; I shot an elephant with it once. Do you want to try? It kicks a fair bit."

She gave a tentative nod. It felt huge and very heavy.

Mark lifted out his swag and spread a groundsheet. "Why don't you try a lying shot. The swag will help keep it steady.

She took her place, deliberately cleared her mind of everything, and then concentrated on the target. She slowly squeezed the trigger. The blast felt huge and the jolt massive to her light frame. But she had done it, shot straight and steady without flinching.

They walked over to the target. Her shot was a perfect bull. She couldn't have placed it better if she'd used a tape measure to mark the spot and then shot it from an inch away.

Mark whistled. "No one can beat that, eh? Not bad for a first time."

"Beginners luck. I'm sure you'll easily equal it."

She felt inordinately pleased, glowing with pride as they walked away from the target. Mark took the rifle and shot three shots to follow hers. All were very close to the centre, but none matched hers.

"Your father must be some man, teaching you to shoot like that," Mark said, tipping his hat to her. "Not only beautiful and fantastic in bed, but you're the hottest hotshot I've ever met."

Susan blushed with this praise.

As they were both hungry, Mark opened a packet of oatmeal biscuits, some of which they ate, accompanied by water from the waterbag, before they left. He found a detailed map of the region to give Susan an understanding of its geography. He spread it out on the bonnet and indicated the main features before they started driving.

"This is the top of the Gulf Fall. From here the country drops away going down to the sea. Our last four hours have been spent travelling over the Barkly Tableland. It's a huge flat plateau. Out on it the creeks run nowhere, but pool in huge swamps that form in depressions on the plains.

"We're about to come into the headwaters of the big rivers that start at the top edge of the Tablelands and carve their way down into the Gulf of Carpentaria, that's this huge bite out of the top of Australia. Just north of us you have the Calvert and Robinson Rivers, which you'll see tomorrow. We're coming into the headwaters of the Nicholson River, a huge river running east into Queensland for two hundred miles, before it flows out into the sea at a place called Burketown."

They drove on and continued to chat about the river they were following. Mark described how the river and its tributaries passed through some fantastic gorge country further downstream, places like Lawn Hill National Park and the Riversleigh fossil deposit, where a huge array of bones of early Australian animals were being found.

"I studied some of the Riversleigh finds at university. It fascinated me. I'd love to go there."

"Unfortunately, time is against us. Long way to go and limited time to get you to your Darwin plane."

Soon they came to a big sign saying: 'Aboriginal Land. Permit Required'.

"Doesn't that apply to us?" Susan asked.

Mark nodded. "It should, but I've done work with most of these people. They know me and even gave me a skin name. They tell me I don't need permits or any of that 'white man rubbish'. I often give them a bit of beef or a kangaroo I've shot. We're more in danger of being invited for a dinner of goanna and snake and of being here all night than getting into trouble for not having a permit."

"But I'd love that. You know I studied aboriginal customs at university, but I've never met any traditional aboriginals."

125

Mark raised an eyebrow. "Well, they're traditional here: utes, guns, fishing lines, power boats, you name it, they have it. But they can still go out with a spear and digging stick and get dinner from the land. I like their attitude and their way of life, take the best of the new, when it suits, but also keep the best of the old."

Mark seemed to deliberate for a second. "Tell you what. There's a camp where they live an hour up the road, and I still have one slab of meat in the Esky that I was thinking of passing on to them. Maybe we can call in for a cuppa and early dinner. I'm sure they'll have a fire going and something on offer."

As they drove, their conversation went deeper into the past world of this place, as revealed by the fossils. "I wonder what it was like to live in this place when giant animals roamed, marsupial lions and the like." Susan said. "Do you know if the aboriginal people were here then?"

"The way I heard it was that they came first and a few thousand years later the giant animals disappeared. Some say they caused it, some say it was because the climate changed. The inland was wet and lush back then, and slowly it dried out and the animals could no longer survive. Ask two experts and they give two different answers."

"Imagine that," said Susan, "coming face to face with a lion creature as tall as you. What would you do?"

"Well, I'd run away at a million miles an hour, crawl into a tiny cave. Only the crazy brave would stand and fight with a flimsy spear. But I'd have loved to watch it; that would have been something."

"Me too, oh for a time machine. How do you know so much about all that stuff, the pre-history of Australia? Did you study somewhere?"

He grinned ruefully. "Nah. More to do with time spent as a labourer and dig assistant in the hot sun. That and many books read. I met all those professors who wrote the books at the digs.

Sometimes they'd sign their books for me. I think it was their way of getting rid of books no one would buy, and even fewer could understand. Still, it's amazing how, when they show you all their finds and explain what they mean, it all slowly begins to make sense."

The sun was falling away behind them. They drove on steadily, winding their way down into a valley. The road ran, mile after mile, below a high cliff, whose western faces were lit in late-afternoon sunshine, a dazzling fiery orange red, while the gullies and eastern facing edges glowed soft pink in the shadowed light.

"That's the China Wall. Pretty amazing, huh?"

Before she knew it, they turned into a local camp road. Aboriginal children ran screaming in excitement from all directions, and Mark greeted them like he knew them well. An elderly lady, walking with the aid of a stick, grinned broadly as she approached. She had grey hair, thin bandy legs, and wore a tattered blue dress. She carried herself with obvious authority, like the tribe's grandmother.

"Dat you, Mark? How ya going, young fella? Got any beef in your tucker box? We bit hungry here."

"Go way with yer der, Judy. I can see that kangaroo from here. What, not enough for an old friend?"

Soon they were sitting on tin drums round the fire, sharing a mug of sweet tea and slices of half pink kangaroo on damper. It tasted good, even if a little raw. Susan could understand little of the excited, voluble conversation, which flowed between the dozen people gathered, but she felt the welcoming spirit.

As they were making their goodbyes, Mark pulled out his last slab of meat and waved Judy over. "Probably don't want this eh, seeing as you got so much food here, but it's yours anyway."

Judy waved a stick at him, "You one cheeky fella. Someone should give you good hard belting with stick like dis."

Susan laughed at the thought.

From there it was a couple more hours of driving in fading light and then full dark. At last they came to Hell's Gates.

As their headlights pick up the sign, Mark says, "When the first settlers came, their aboriginal guides told them they would take them no further, as the black-fellows past here were too wild and dangerous. That's why it was called Hell's Gates. Enter at your peril."

They drive to the camping place behind the roadhouse and park in a corner. There are no other guests in sight.

"I have to go and meet a man, do some business. It will take about half an hour," Mark says. "We'll be gone before he gets out of bed in the morning, so I need to do it tonight. Do you mind if I leave you alone to set up the camp?"

Susan raises an eyebrow. "Sounds like secret men's business. No laws broken I hope. Anything I need to know?"

"Nothing so exciting, no drug running or the like. You've probably gathered I'm a bit of a wheeler dealer, trading things here and there, but it's small time stuff. Still most people I deal with would prefer the tax man didn't know. I reckon that's a matter for their own conscience."

Susan smiles. "Off you go then. See you when you're done."

Mark goes off with a jaunty walk, seeming happy with the world at large. Susan feels happiness well up inside her too; this man has that effect on her. Still she wonders what his business is, how he supports himself, something he's vague about. She has an impression he's trading precious stones, like what she glimpsed in the hills near Alice Springs.

Left alone, she takes out the things she knows they'll need tonight, the swag, chairs and a billycan for tea. She enjoys being entrusted with these jobs for them both.

When everything is arranged, she looks for matches to light the gas barbeque, which is next to their campsite. Not that she's really hungry, but she can use the gas to heat some water, and they may want to heat up food. She's sure the matches are in an obvious place, but they elude her first search, like the sun cream did yesterday. She starts to search systematically through potential storage places, glove box, tucker box, under seats, toolbox, all negative.

She remembers the barbeque plate used for lunch in the hills two days ago. It's stored beside a spare wheel in the back corner of the tray, in a space between the tray and wheel mount. Perhaps there are matches there. She slides out the barbeque place and slips her hand into the narrow space to feel around. As her fingers slip in, a fingernail catches on something. It slides away as her hand goes past. Her fingers feel a gap behind it with something in it. It feels like a box, a smooth metal box.

She gets a torch to look properly. She sees the metal plate. A top screw keeps it attached. But the bottom screw, which would stop it sliding aside, has fallen out, probably due to the vibrations of the rough roads they've driven over.

With one hand she pushes this metal plate aside while she holds the torch with the other. Sure enough, in a compartment behind the plate sits the metal box she'd felt before.

With a fingernail she catches a corner and eases it out. It's about six inches by four inches by two inches thick. It's like an old tobacco tin, with the lid jammed on tightly. She tries to lift the lid but it won't budge. She shakes the tin, nothing rattles, no matches sound emerges. The tin is heavy, packed tight with something. There's no point trying to get the lid off; there won't be any matches inside it.

The tin is grey, flat and looks well-used, but otherwise it seems unremarkable. Where it's hidden seems strange though. It's not a place where anyone would keep something they were using. Mark would either need to take the spare wheel off or use a small screwdriver to remove the screw to gain access to this space. That seems like a lot of trouble unless he wants to keep something well out of sight.

Susan is tempted to investigate further, but her English sense of privacy makes her put it back and finish setting up the camp. She catches herself occasionally looking towards the car, her curiosity niggling at her. This discovery makes her uneasy. She can't put her finger on exactly why. It's as if something is being deliberately hidden from prying eyes.

Mark returns five minutes later and shows her the true location of the matches. Susan lights the gas to boil the billy. She says nothing about her new discovery.

They share a supper of more biscuits and tea before they crawl into bed together. As she drifts towards sleep she recalls the box, and wonders again why it's been put there, hidden in a place far out of sight.

Chapter 10 – Fishing Calvert and Robinson – Day 24

They're up early again next morning. Susan is yawning and feels tired as she gets up and says, "Can't I sleep a bit longer?"

"Not today. We have a full day ahead. I've got a special surprise for you."

"Special surprise. What special surprise?"

"You'll have to wait and see, busybody."

They leave Hell's Gate and drive for half an hour until they come to a sign for a roadhouse named Wollogorang. "This place marks the boundary of the Northern Territory."

Susan has seen this name before, and now she remembers where. It's the name of a grand old house a couple hours south of Sydney. She read about it in a travel brochure for the Southern Highlands that somebody left behind on her train to Melbourne.

"Do you know why it's called that name?" she asks him.

"It's the name given to the cattle station that we're on by its first settlers. They came up from down south, somewhere near Goulburn. They must have been homesick because they named their new station after their house back there. It's one of the Northern Territory's most famous stations, the very first one settled. It's been here since the 1880s."

Mark is full of stories of the area. He's a goldmine of knowledge of early NT history.

"Where did you learn all this local history from?"

"Oh, from lots of places. A bit from reading books about it, but more from talking to old timers across the country. You'd be surprised at the stories they tell, sitting around a campfire over a mug of tea or sometimes over a pannikin of rum. While many tales get stretched in the telling they often start with the truth."

Susan watches the changing scenery outside. After driving up a valley for maybe twenty miles the road begins to climb. It winds through a series of gorges and cuttings as it works its way precariously up the side of a mountain, until, at last, they come out onto a flat and barren plateau at the top, a wasteland of dry sandy spinifex and scrub.

A few miles later they come alongside an airstrip that runs next to the road. At its end is a sign for Redbank Mine. Mark turns onto a track that brings him onto the airstrip. Near its end is an assembly of fuel drums, all marked with the label '*Avgas*'.

Alongside the drums is a helicopter with a large round clear bubble. Susan thinks it looks like a giant insect, perhaps a dragonfly—the round bubble at the front is its head, two holes on each side its eyes, a rotor blade wing above and a long metal tail with a smaller tail rotor. It rests on two skids, its insect like legs. It seems alive and exotic, not like sleek, streamlined modern helicopters she's seen before on the English evening news.

A slightly built man, with darkish skin and dark features, is pumping fuel from one of the drums into the helicopter tanks. He calls out with obvious familiarity. "Hey, Mark, about bloody time! Did you sleep in?"

Mark pulls to a halt and waves to him. "How ya doin, Vic?"

Susan walks, side by side with Mark, towards him.

"Yeah all right," Vic replies.

"How's the old Bell 47?"

"Still firing on all cylinders."

Mark turns to Susan. "Sorry, I'm being impolite. Let me introduce you to a good friend of mine and the best helicopter pilot I know. His proper name is Vikram Campbell, but we all call him Vic."

Vic waves at Susan. "Hiya."

Susan nods and smiles a greeting in return. "I know an Indian called Vickram in London. Do you have Indian or English relatives?"

Vic grins back. "Not in London to the best of my knowledge, though they tell me it's a big place full of Pakis and Indians, so who really knows. Bound to have some in India, but again nobody knows.

"My great grandfather was called an Afghan in Australia, though nobody knows where he really came from, some story about Kashmir. He worked the camel trains between the Alice and Adelaide a hundred years ago. He had a family with an aboriginal woman in Alice Springs. His name has sort of continued down through the generations, most typically shortened to Vic or Victor.

"As best I can tell I am descended from a big mixture, the Afghan, a bit of Arrente, that's the aboriginal tribe, and then other bits of Scots, English, Irish and God knows what else. The Campbell is from the Scottish branch.

"So I suppose the Afghan could really be Indian, but the name is common in that part of the world. There are probably a million other Vikrams, and the detail of that part of my ancestry has got lost. But the name keeps some bit of that man's memory alive. Now most people call me Vic, but Mark knows the story and does his bit to keep it known."

Mark points to the helicopter. "I guess you figured we might need a bit of fuel. Beats a hard landing in the middle of nowhere." Mark turns to Susan. "Fancy a ride in this old girl? She's a bit long in the tooth, but they're super reliable machines, provided you look after them properly. They're also cheaper to run than most of the new-fangled jet turbine jobs."

"Is this the surprise?" she asks.

Mark nods. "You got it. Only way to see this country properly. Vic used to chopper muster scrubbers for me, now he owns his own machine.

"I knew he was working nearby, so I rang him and asked him to take us for a spin this morning. Want to go for a ride?"

"Of course, I would love it!" Susan exclaims.

"Glad that's settled then."

"What you reckon Vic?" Mark continues. "Thought we might go along the gorges of the Calvert and Robinson Rivers, see if we can catch a few barra, perhaps get a pig or two. There's one huge boar in particular I've been looking for as a hunting trophy for more than two years now. If we get real lucky we may find him today. Can but hope."

Vic replies, "Sounds good. It'll give you a bird's eye of some spectacular NT scenery, Susan."

Susan is amazed all this is for her. Like her own private safari, with her own private safari guide. She's tongue tied for a minute. Finally, she manages to say to them both, "Wow, that would be brilliant."

While Vic continues pumping fuel into the helicopter, Mark loads two fishing rods, his 223 rifle, some ammunition, a water bottle and some other bits inside. He indicates the middle seat to Susan. "That's where you sit. Hop in when you're ready. I'll be a few more minutes."

Susan climbs in and looks around with wonder at all the gauges and controls. A long stick comes out of the floor with various buttons and knobs attached. Then there's a radio, headsets and lots of dials, other knobs and yet more buttons.

Vic finishes pumping fuel and walks around completing a careful check of all the parts of the helicopter. He offers her a big smile as he passes her window. "He sure pulls the beautiful ones. How did he find someone as drop dead gorgeous as you? And him just a busted-arsed ringer. If you find you want to trade up to a bit more class let me know."

Susan likes this man's warm open face and sardonic humour, particularly when he smiles. She also thinks his wiry body and dark features are seriously cute.

"I'm sure you have a lot of far more beautiful girls than me on a string, offering to take them for mile high rides in the sky."

Vic laughs. Then he pats the clear Perspex bubble of the helicopter. "How I wish! Ever been in one of these before?"

She shakes her head. "No, first time and I can't wait!"

He gives her a quick explanation of the main controls before saying, "I'll just be a couple minutes. Mark and I have a bit of business to do, and we need to finalise our route on the map so I can call flight control." He points to the seat belt. "Why don't you strap yourself in. We'll be with you in five."

She clicks her seat belt in, feeling a buzz of excited tension. Maybe she should be nervous, but all she can feel is a huge thrill of anticipation—primal and almost sexual. It flows through her. The more she sees of Mark, his generosity and sense of fun, the more she's captivated by him and this whole experience. It's far beyond anything she could have imagined. Huge warmth and affection flow out from her towards him.

Mark and Vic board and Vic starts the engine. The rotor whirls, going slowly at first, then faster and faster; the machine roars, wind blows up dust eddies.

Mark passes her a headset and shows her where to push the button to talk. He indicates they should postpone conversation until they're in the air, as Vic has called Air Traffic Control.

Vic is concentrating on all the controls, checking and zeroing various instruments. Then he slowly dials up the engine and rotor revolutions until a thing called Manifold Pressure is in the dial's green zone. He looks across at her and Mark. "Ready?"

Mark sticks his thumb up in the air. "Good to go."

The motor surges further then the engine note drops as Vic adjusts a control on the stick. The blades change noise and start to bite into the air. The whole helicopter shakes like a caged animal seeking to flee its bounds.

Vic lifts the stick up an inch. The helicopter rises straight up, imperceptible at first, and then it is several feet into the air. He pushes the stick forward and their motion changes from a hover to sliding forward, going straight ahead. They pick up speed and make a slow circuit over the airstrip while he logs his trip with Air Traffic Control.

Then, with another small move of the control stick, the helicopter flares up into the air and banks over to the side, making a steep turn right. The compass in front of her points to the northwest.

It is spellbinding. She splits her time between watching as Vic deftly manipulates dozens of controls and gazing in rapt awe as the country opens before her. At first, they fly across the barren flat plateau, a sand plain covered in spinifex with occasional broken boulders. Soon they pick up a watercourse that snakes out of the flat lands, first as a small scrub lined creek, then growing in size and cutting its way down into the increasingly rocky hillside. Pools of water start to appear along it.

"We're following the headwaters of Karns Creek, a creek through a piece of tiger country flowing into the Calvert River, cutting through a series of gorges," Mark says over the intercom. "Vic and I contract mustered here maybe ten years ago. We got out some of the maddest and wildest scrub bulls I've ever seen. They'd try to crawl under the bushes and into the creek to get away from us. Sometimes they got so mad they'd try and hook their horns up into the sky to catch our helicopter."

Soon Karns Creek widens to the size of a river, with cliffs beetling two hundred feet high along both sides. Magnificent paperbark trees and water lilies fringe the edges, and the water is the colour of clear weak tea, with a bright surface refection of trees and cliffs. They follow its winding length, staying just below the cliff line. Abruptly the helicopter flares up above its sides, and then there before them lies a huge river, the Calvert, cutting its way down through a gorge, running hundreds of feet below. She briefly sees where Karns Creek joins the river before they're back down flying between the monstrous river cliffs.

The beauty is striking. The cliffs are several hundred feet high and sheer. Their sides hold myriad colours and details: vibrant red, orange, yellow and black rocks. The dark openings of caves are dotted along the cliffs, and trees grow in incredible places, twisted roots probing their way into cracks in the rocks. Perched along the cliff, leaping from narrow ledge to narrow ledge, are numerous rock wallabies. In a mad panic they seek to evade the helicopter, making phenomenal leaps from rock to rock. Occasional waterbirds are disturbed by their passage. Susan glimpses occasional shadowed outlines of large fish in the water below. Several times she sees reptiles, perhaps one to two metres long, sunning on rocks. They fling themselves forward and dive in the water at the helicopter's approach. It's exciting to realise these are crocodiles. She looks at Mark and points down.

"Just freshies, but you do get big saltwater ones here too."

The river valley widens slightly. It's the confluence of another creek and, on one side, there's a small green area with paperbarks and swamp grasses. Mark gives a sign for the helicopter to come around. They circle tightly above the swamp, perhaps fifty feet high.

Vic spots something on the ground and points. They see a place where the swamp grasses have been rooted up. In its centre stands a huge black pig, with wicked tusks, several inches long, protruding from its mouth.

Mark smiles. "There you are. After all this time I've finally found you. Looks like today's your date with destiny."

He indicates to Vic to land a hundred yards from the swamp in a flat grassy opening. As the helicopter touches down Mark is out, gathering his rifle and running in a half crouch across the intervening ground.

Vic indicates with his hand that Susan should stay sitting. He lets the rotor slowly wind down. When the blades cease movement, they sit still for perhaps five minutes, Vic whispers to be quiet and stay put.

Finally, a sharp crack breaks the stillness followed, a minute later, by a second bang, then silence again until a whistle comes. Vic gives Susan a sign to undo her belt, and they walk across the ground towards where Mark has disappeared. Half way there Vic calls out, "Yoo hoo."

"Come on, he's dead now," Mark calls back." They continue and Mark meets them another twenty yards on. He leads them to a thick clump of paperbark saplings where, almost completely hidden, lies a huge boar. It's longer than either man and twice their girth. One tusk is dug into the mud, as if in a final act of outrage at its untimely death.

"So you finally got him," Vic says. "I spotted him once, about six months ago, but I didn't have a rifle that day. And I knew you wanted him more."

Mark grins widely. "This fellow will easily pay for our trip. I know a taxidermist who'll give me at least two grand for this one. He's easily the biggest I've ever shot and close to the biggest I've ever heard of. You must be the source of my good luck, Susan."

"You don't need any help from me in the hunting department. Apart from one other thing, which we'd better not talk about here, hunting is what you're best at."

Susan and Vic both laugh at Mark's uncomfortable expression.

"Was he easy to find?" Vic asks. "Last glance I saw him heading for that thick patch at the other side of the swamp. I thought you'd be hard pressed to track him in there."

"I thought he'd gone that way too, so I cut to that side of the swamp, but there were no fresh tracks. I realised he must have been trying to outsmart us and had cut back to the centre. I found a track coming back, so I scanned the swamp carefully, but nothing was in sight. This little patch of saplings was the only place he could hide without being seen.

"So I worked back, real slow and steady, watching for anything. When I was only thirty yards away, I saw a tiny movement in the shadow, the smallest flick of his ear in reflex to a fly. So I brought my gun up and there he was in my scope. He was so well camouflaged he was almost invisible, facing me with his head up sniffing the wind. He was so surprised when the first bullet hit he didn't know what to do. You can see how mad he was by the way his tusk ripped into the ground."

They agree they need to get the boar to the chopper, but there's a lot of weight. All straining together, they pull him a few feet out of the patch of paperbarks. Mark carefully slices him open and removes his innards. Then he uses a short piece of rope to tie his back feet together.

Vic heads back to the helicopter to bring it to them. After a few more minutes Susan and Mark hear the helicopter roar to life and fly towards them. Hovering the helicopter directly above, Vic lowers a chain with a large hook hanging on the end of it. Mark lifts the pig's feet towards her, and Susan guides the hook between them. When the pig's attached Susan steps back and gives the thumbs up sign to Vic.

With a burst of power, the helicopter pulls the pig up into the sky. It hovers, holding the pig well above the surrounding trees for a couple seconds, then it's off, flying in a straight line away from them.

"Vic will go back to the airstrip and arrange for the boar to be placed in a cool room at the Mine, until transport's organised to take it to the taxidermist in Mount Isa. That leaves us a couple hours for fishing and lunch before he gets back."

Vic has left the rest of their gear at the landing site. They collect it and walk towards the edge of the river. A sandy bar runs out from the bank, going a few metres into the water. It has the branches of a large dead tree to one side and clear water on the other.

Mark puts his hand on her arm to slow her motion, "There are some really big crocodiles in here. They can sneak up underwater and grab a person off the bank. So you need to be extra careful."

Susan thinks of the article she saw in the hotel a couple days ago about the missing backpacker, the one who looked like her. She wonders if a person could disappear without trace from a place like this. If a crocodile pulled her off the bank and consumed her in the water who would ever know. "I read, back at Barrow Creek, about a tourist who vanished somewhere in the NT. I wonder, could something like that have happened. If a crocodile grabbed her from a river bank who would ever know. There'd be nothing left to show."

"Don't let your imagination run away. They don't come from nowhere. But it pays to be super careful."

She puts her arms around him. "I trust you and know you'll keep me safe, no matter what."

As she says these words she feels a flinch run through him.

He hugs her tightly, saying, "That's what I'm trying to do."

As he says these words, an image leaps into her mind, unbidden. It's a huge ancient crocodile floating in the water behind her, staring intently at her with hungry eyes.

She suppresses a shudder as she glances back towards this place. But there is nothing to see, the surface remains unbroken. She decides it's only a figment of her overheated imagination

They come to the river's edge looking out towards the sandbar and sit high up on the bank. Mark watches closely for a couple minutes, scanning the banks and water, looking for any signs to indicate that a large saltwater crocodile might be lurking. While he sits he pulls an object, about hand's width long, carved from dark timber and brightly painted in ochre colours, from his pocket. A miniature crocodile is resting in his palm. He looks at it closely and then at the water, as though he's talking in his mind to both.

After a couple minutes he says, "It seems okay, but don't get too close to the water's edge. I'll fish on the side of the sandbar with the dead tree. There could be a big barramundi lurking under the snags. You should try the open side. There's a good chance for something there. Have you ever tried lure fishing?"

She shakes her head. "No, only bait fishing. My father tried to teach me fly fishing for trout a couple times, but I never quite mastered it."

He gives Susan a rod with a floating fish lure attached. It's about four inches long with two three barb hooks, a blue-grey colour with red and black side stripes. "It's a barra lure. You need to cast it into the middle of the clear water then wind it back in at a steady walking pace."

He puts a small lure, with green and yellow markings, on his rod and looks for some clear water, amongst the branches, to cast into.

Susan's first cast doesn't go according to plan. She doesn't time the line release right. The line flips to the side as the lure jerks back, landing a few yards from her feet.

Mark leaves his rod and helps her, putting his hands over hers, guiding her with slow, deliberate movements. "Don't try too hard until you get the hang of it."

It's hard not to get distracted by his closeness. Together they do a gentle cast and release with the lure hitting the water about ten yards out. "That's it. Work on improving from that."

She winds in and concentrates on getting her timing and direction right. Her next cast goes out straight about fifteen metres, and the third one goes a good twenty. She's only wound in a metre when the line jerks and snakes through the water in a crazy zigzag.

"Mark, I have something," she calls.

He comes across, but it's clear by now Susan has it well in hand, so he stands back to watch.

Her heart pounds when she hooks the fish, but she knows she has to remain calm and focused to reel it in. With a jerk the fish explodes out of the water, skipping across the surface in a tail dancing run.

Susan shouts, "Did you see that? It's huge!"

"It's probably half a metre long, a good five pounder," he calls back.

Five minutes later Susan has the gleaming barramundi lying on the sand.

"Well, as you've caught our lunch, I'll get a fire going."

She can't restrain her elation. She feels like jumping up and down as she chatters with excitement. "Wasn't the way it jumped out of the water and stood on its tail just amazing! I was sure it was going to get off."

Mark laughs. "First time is the most exciting, isn't it? Barramundi are great fighters and often manage to shake the lure out of their mouth and get away. But you kept it steady and did just great."

Using a similar technique to the night on the Frew River, but without a pit, they build up the fire to make coals to cook the fish. Mark shakes his head when Susan suggests gutting it. "No need when it's this fresh."

Once the fire dies down, he lays the fish in the middle of the coals and pushes coals from the sides up and over it.

Fifteen minutes later he says, "I think it's done."

He scrapes the coals from the fish's centre across to one side and gently pushes a hole in the charred surface with his knife.

There, below, is succulent white fish flesh, looking well cooked. He pushes the rest of the fire away and lifts the burnt skin carefully off the top side of the fish. From his pack he finds a metal plate and spoon for them each.

They sit on the sandy riverbank and eat plate after plate of white fish flesh, sprinkled with salt and washed down with cups of river water. Even when neither of them can eat any more, half a fish is still left.

Susan stretches out, feeling sleepy, laying back on the sloping sand, looking across the river to where the cliffs rise sheer on the other side.

"How incredible is this!" she says. "This is a life out of someone else's story book, my own Northern Territory safari."

Mark is silent but gives a half smile back, truth acknowledged.

It's hard to believe this will end in a few days and she'll be on a flight back to the other side of the world. Will she ever see Mark again after she leaves? It's almost too perfect the way it is now. Trying to reconcile their different worlds is something she can't conceive. Perhaps this time with Mark and her visit to Australia is only ever destined to be a wonderful memory once she's returned to her English life. Perhaps she'll meet and marry an English man and Mark will carry on with his outback life.

Could she and a man like Mark ever join their lives together? Or would it all tear apart, through difference and distance, when reality returns? Half of her thinks it's better she accepts this as a fleeting romance; the other half cries out against the profound loss and sadness she senses will be left in her soul after their separation happens.

Mark lies back silently staring at the sky. His face is a mask giving no clue as to what he feels, whether he cares if they continue their lives together or not. She wants to ask what he feels and thinks, but no words will come. She remembers the small carving he held on his palm earlier and asks, "What was the carved crocodile you took out earlier?"

He looks at her, as if deciding whether to reveal something significant, before he brings it back out. He hands it to her, placing it in her upturned palm.

She looks closely. The object is only little; it sits easily in her palm, but the creature it represents is not. It's crafted from a heavy timber, with char marks in places, as if it's been hardened and marked in a fire before painting. It's surprisingly solid to hold, and the ochre painting detail is intricate and lifelike. It is a crocodile, of great girth, broad head, body and tail. This little object represents a huge, ancient creature. As she holds it, she feels as if she's holding a live crocodile spirit in her hand.

She returns it to Mark. He's watching her curiously, as if waiting and seeking for her response.

"It feels so lifelike, like I hold the spirit of a real crocodile."

"It's my totem, Baru, Crocodile Spirit of the Dreamtime, the ancestor spirit of all crocodiles, formed when the ancestors of today's first peoples of this land created all the plants and animals living here."

Before she can reply, a distant throbbing in the air signals the return of the helicopter. They turn their heads skywards, and the moment between them passes.

Five minutes later the helicopter settles nearby. Vic joins them and helps polish off the remaining fish.

Vic has brought his own rod. He tells them he knows a great pool on the Robinson River, the next river over. "It's alive with barramundi at the moment. They've been trapped in a small pool since the river fell away to a trickle, after the big rains of the last wet season. I'm pretty sure the fish will still be there."

They walk back to the helicopter and fly west, until they come to the Robinson River. They follow it back inland, a wide river in its lower reaches, without the massive gorges of the

Calvert River. After fifteen minutes they cross a big dirt road, the main road on to Borroloola, and minutes later they pass to the side of an aboriginal community.

Soon they're in a gorge, every bit the equal of the Calvert, but with wider and higher sides. The river forms a series of large broken pools spread out far below them. At first there are roads, tracks and signs of human occupation but, as they climb towards the plateau, the gorge narrows and signs of people disappear.

Rounding a bend in the river they spot the waterhole Vic described. It's almost circular, with low rock shelves extending three quarters of the way round, and one side backing into a sheer cliff, which rises about a thousand feet above it. A great eagle is circling overhead, riding thermals high up near the cliff top, its white chest bright in the sun. Mark points it out. "See that sea eagle up there, watching and waiting for an opportunity. I'm sure it will join the action."

Susan looks below as they sweep over the top of the waterhole, sees glimpses and shadows of fish as they swim and dart in the shallows.

They land and take out their gear, moving quietly so as not to alarm the fish. From the flat rock alongside the helicopter they survey the pool, a stone's throw away and twenty feet below. In whispered voices they work out for each to take a sector and get set up, perched on the low rock shelf that runs around and a few feet above the pool, positioned so their lines will not cross.

Susan moves to her allotted space, a couple metres above the glassy pool surface. The water is so clear she can see down into its depths. She sees the shadows of fish as they cruise by.

Vic is the first to cast out. On his first cast they all see a big fish trailing his lure, but nothing happens. The same happens the second time, but the first fish is joined by a second, following just behind. When the lure is almost at Vic's feet, a third, huge fish comes surging out of the shadows and grabs hold of his line. Susan barely has time to watch his battle before her line explodes too.

Suddenly the whole pool goes crazy. It's as if a signal is sent to tell all the fish they'd better get in on the action or they'll miss out on dinner. Often, she sees that Mark and Vic both have fish on their lines at the same time as she does, their tails dancing across the surface, fighting to cast the lures from their mouths.

In half an hour it's all over. Twenty-one glistening fish lie on the rocks beside them. Susan has six, following Mark with seven, while Vic tops the tally with eight. The biggest is the first monster that Vic caught. He takes a spring scale from the helicopter and it weighs twenty-three kilograms. Susan holds up her own biggest to weigh and watches as it reads thirteen kilograms. Mark has one almost as big as hers. The rest of the fish range in size from eight down to two kilograms.

Vic eyes the big pile of a fish dubiously. "I'm not sure whether we can lift all this and ourselves in the same trip."

Thinking some more he adds, "Actually, I think it'll be okay. I'm down to half fuel and Susan's not heavy; plus, the air is cool in the shade of this rock. That'll help with the initial lift off.

"Let's give it a go. I'd hate to have to leave a fish behind or have to do a second trip. If I get airborne we'll be right. There's a run straight ahead down the valley. I'll be able to pick up speed before I need to get height on to climb out above the cliffs."

Mark finds a knife and quickly slices open each fish and removes the innards. He passes each down to Susan who rinses it clean in a shallow corner of the pool then passes it to Vic to take over next to the chopper.

As she works, head down, shadows flash above her. She looks up. A cloud of hawks and eagles are circling overhead. At the centre, commanding the field, the white breasted sea eagle maintains a tight spiral. The boldest of the hawks shriek as they jockey for position, bare feet above Mark's head.

When cleaning his last fish is done Mark steps back. Susan watches the screaming melee descend and fight for their pile. A whistle and a whoosh causes them all to scatter. The eagle lands in the centre of the pile. It walks around calmly, surveying the booty. It selects a suitably large pile of innards, which it picks it up with its beak. It walks clumsily to the edge of the rock ledge and launches itself into the air, its great spread wings beating slow time. It rises into the air ponderously and laboriously until it reaches its eyrie half way up the cliff face. Two screeching chicks raise their heads above the parapet at its approach.

Vic grins. "That's a good omen. The fish guts must have weighed as much as it does, and it still got airborne, so I'm sure we'll be right."

Susan and Mark help Vic load the fish aboard, stacking some in wire baskets on the skids and others in the cargo hold. When Vic is happy the balance is right, he signals them aboard. Susan sits in the middle with a panoramic view of all the controls.

She watches as the rotor begins to spin, slowly at first and then as a whirring blur. Vic talks her through what he's doing as he dials on the power, pushing the throttle steadily down. The engine revolutions rise up to the top of the green zone, tipping into yellow. Vic adjusts another control. Now the sound of the rotor changes, and the machine shakes beneath her as its blades cut deeper into the air, clawing for grip. The engines die back as it struggles with the load, but Vic keeps dialling on the throttle and the engine surges again.

Slowly the skids rise above the ground. Once it's clear by ten feet Vic eases his control stick forward and they're away, surging down the valley, piling on speed on his downhill run.

Gradually the ground falls away as they start to hold altitude. Soon the river falls far beneath. Vic starts the second phase of the flight and they slowly climb out of the valley, foot by foot, at first pulling barely a hundred feet per minute of climb as they creep up. As the altimeter passes five hundred feet, he directs their course towards the airstrip, flying more easily as they go on.

By the time they approach their destination they've topped out at over a thousand feet, enough to clear the highest hills with a hundred feet to spare. Vic lands at the airstrip and offloads Mark to collect his car. Susan stays aboard as they fly on to the mine a mile away. They circle over the mine and watch as a man walks out of a hut and waves them in. Once landed he comes over, and introduces the mine supervisor, Rod.

By now, Mark has arrived and he and Vic divide the fish. Mark packs his in fresh ice from the freezer at the mine. Mark pulls aside his biggest fish. "This one is for you, Rod, in thanks for your help. It weighed in at twelve kilos. It should give the camp a feed of fresh fish for a night. Next time I come past I'll bring half a side of a bullock."

"No worries mate, you're welcome. Why don't you all join us for beers and a feed at the mess. Dinner's on in half an hour."

"Sounds good to me," Vic replies.

"Thanks, just one beer. Dinner will have to wait for next time," Mark says. "We've a way to go tonight. I promised to be at Seven Emus tomorrow early."

They sit in the shade and drink a quick beer, then they're ready to head off. Vic walks out with them to say goodbye. He and Mark hug like brothers. Then Vic turns to Susan and winking at Mark says, "Well, if he does decide to let you go your own way, don't forget about me. Always happy to show you what a real good time is."

Susan laughs and gives Vic a spontaneous hug too. "I think one outback man is more than enough for me, not to mention my home is on the other side of the world. But thank you for the kind offer."

Mark laughs too. "As you know, my brother, I've my heart set on this one. She's is the best in every way, not for sharing."

Susan's feels a twinge of embarrassment to be the appreciative subject of their conversation. "Time to change the subject. Thank you both. I'll leave now before you really embarrass me."

It's late afternoon and they drive steadily, coming off the plateau and winding down a twisting road into a river valley below. They cross an unremarkable sandy river, with odd pools of water fringed by large trees and a sign saying 'Calvert River'.

Susan points. "That's nothing like the Calvert River we saw today. Is it really the same river?"

"Yes, you'd never know though. We're a mile above where the gorge starts and seeing this would give no clue of the wonders below. A helicopter is really the only way to visit."

They drive for another hour along a nondescript dirt road though featureless scrub, a mix of stunted trees with big palm like leaves, half grown gums and dense prickly scrub that Mark says would be lucky to feed two half-starved goannas.

As the sun is moving into their eyes, making it hard to see clearly, they come out onto an open plain, patches of bare ground and dried grass interspersed. Mark tells her this is the edge of the Robinson River, which they flew over today before they reached the gorge and their fishing spot. They turn right, following a maze of tracks. After driving a few kilometres downstream, they reach their intended camp site, a patch of open sandy ground just behind the river bank.

Even though it isn't as cold as it has been in the desert, or even at Hell's Gates, it's well and truly dark by arrival, and they want the comfort of a fire to sit by. Susan feels tired from her two full days of activity, but also in a relaxed, mellow mood. Her mind travels over all she's seen and done today, the helicopter, the scenery, the fishing. And sitting below these warm memories she has a sense that she and Mark are beginning to connect emotionally at a deeper level.

Mark sets up two chairs beside the fire and pours them both a drink. She sits at his side, exchanging half smiles and odd touches, experiencing a tingle each time his hand brushes hers, and at times when she sees a half flash in his eyes as firelight flares. They don't talk much, but their silence is a continued space of quiet contentment.

"How about I make us a stew with the leftover beef, carrots, onions and potatoes from the tucker box?" Mark suggests. "Something a bit different for a change."

"That sounds amazing. Shall I have a go at making us a brownie for dessert? I'm craving something sweet."

"Sounds good to me."

While Mark starts on the stew, Susan makes a mixture of flour, oil, golden syrup and dried fruit, and sets it aside while the stew bubbles. They sit companionably again, sipping pannikins of rum, making occasional aimless conversation.

It is then that Susan is struck by a guilty conscience. Mark has paid for every part of their trip so far: all the fuel and food, the accommodation on the nights they didn't camp and, particularly today, for the helicopter.

She doesn't know how he makes his money, apart from odd jobs for various stations and mines, maybe a bit of gemstone trading, but it's hard to see how he can be rich from jobs like that. She's allowed at least two thousand Australian dollars for this part of the trip and has barely spent a cent since arriving in Alice Springs. She'd had only a little over a hundred dollars cash on her when she arrived, as she'd planned to go to an ATM in Alice Springs, but everything happened so fast she never did. So, while she doesn't have cash with her right now for a major contribution, she feels she needs to make one. Mark has never looked for anything, but she must find a way to pay her share, even if broaching the subject feels awkward.

"Mark, I've had the most fabulous time with you. But you've paid for everything, and that's not right. I want to pay my share. Tell me what you think is fair and, next time we pass through a town with an ATM, I'll draw out the money to square up."

Mark looks at her, his eyes seeming to see all the way through her. "You know you don't have to. I've loved having you along. You're great company and no bother. Most of this trip I was going to do anyway. Despite appearances I'm not short of a quid. I'd much prefer if you just enjoy the ride and leave it all to me to sort out." With that he grins.

His offer is kind, but she knows she'd be much happier if she paid her share. "Please, it doesn't feel right for me not to pay a fair share."

He looks at her. "Your expression is so serious. It bothers you doesn't it? Tell you what; we'll be in Darwin the last night before you fly out. We can stay somewhere nice, go out to a flash restaurant, enjoy a good last night together. Rather than trying to square up for everything, how about I let you pay for that? Much easier than trying sort the money out here."

She feels reluctant about this plan but drops it so as not to spoil their bit of magic together. They share the stew and brownie and join their bodies together under the stars.

As she drifts off to sleep, Mark says, "I'll get up early in the morning. I want to go hunting down the river. There are often pigs along it. The Seven Emus mob, the station where we're going tomorrow, are always keen for fresh pork. They have a Chinese cook who does amazing things with it.

"So I'll let you sleep in for an extra hour or two. The people we're calling on never rise early. I figure we should leave here about nine to be there in time for morning tea around ten."

Susan drifts off into a dreamy sleep, liking the idea of an extra hour in bed in the morning. She is vaguely aware of Mark getting up when there is barely light in the sky, dressing quietly and heading away. Susan wakes perhaps an hour later. It's still early, the sun just touching the horizon, perhaps 7.00 am. She gathered, last night, that Mark wouldn't be back for an hour or two yet. She thinks another hour asleep will be nice.

But she can't get back to sleep because discomfort about paying her share is still nagging in the back of her mind. Mark has indicated nothing to her about the cost of the trip, and particularly the helicopter, but she saw Vic hand him a sheet just before they left last night. It looked like a bill. She remembers Mark put it in a black plastic folder in the compartment on the driver's side door.

Now a clear thought comes to her waking brain. She'll take a look at the bill. That way she'll know the real cost of the helicopter yesterday and have an idea of how much to pay.

Susan pulls on a track top and pants to ward off the morning chill. After she puts a couple of fresh logs on the smouldering coals, she goes to look for the bill. She finds the black folder easily.

The bill lists three hours of helicopter time at $600/hour, giving a total of $1800, with a 10% discount coming in at $1620. Not too bad. Her half share is about $800. She can easily pay that plus for a final night in Darwin.

She's about to put the bill back when she notices something odd. The name on the bill is different.

Chapter 11 – Discovery – Day 25

Susan looks at name on the bill, perplexed. She heard Vic calling him Mark, so Vic obviously knew his name, which she assumed meant his surname as well as his first name. And she saw Vic pass him the bill, which he'd happily accepted and countersigned without question. But the name on the invoice is Mark Butler, not Mark Bennet. Perhaps it was a mistake he'd missed, signing without looking.

She's ready to dismiss it as that but, as she opens the wallet to put it back, something falls out onto the floor, a plastic card. Susan bends to retrieve it, not wanting to leave anything to incriminate her for snooping.

It's an expired driving license, from the NT with a Katherine address. The man in the license photo is Mark. She reads the name—*Mark Butler*—the same as the invoice. But why use two names? The names are so similar, both creating the initials MB.

Something about the Butler name rings a bell. With a spark of fresh recollection, she realises she's seen it before. It's the name on one of the number plates, written in tiny writing on a stick-on label on the back of one plate. The other names come to mind as well, Brown and Brooks, MB and MB.

This is seriously odd: four men with the same initials but different surnames, four number plates for the same vehicle. Who is *her* Mark? Is his one of these names? Or are all fake? Is he really someone else again?

It's as if multiple odd, missing pieces about him are starting to connect.

She really likes Mark. If she's honest with herself, she's falling for him big time, getting in way too deep. Before she lets herself fall any further, she needs to know who he really is.

Susan knows he keeps business papers in an attaché case that he puts behind his seat in the cabin. Perhaps she'll find an answer there. She lifts it out and notices the little copper monogram, MB, just below the handle. The case has a combination lock on the latch, which she can't open. She tries obvious numbers like 0000, 1234 and 9999. No success, so she puts it back. It isn't going to help her.

The box she found the night before last jumps back into her mind. A sixth sense tells her it's significant, particularly with the clever way it's hidden. Her instinct says she should look in there.

Susan is conflicted; she wants to trust Mark and she wants to ask him directly who he is. But he reacts badly to any personal questions. Something in the way he's looked at her when she's tried to probe really scares her, like there's a demon lurking deep inside waiting to be unleashed. It reminds her of the horror film *The Omen*, where there is the beautiful child with the malevolent core. She shivers. No, such worries are nonsense. She's letting her imagination run away.

But still she must know the answer. Susan looks around in all directions; there's still no sign of Mark, and she doesn't think he'll be back for at least another hour.

Well, she won't die wondering. She finds a torch, goes to where she found the box that night and shines the light in. Sure enough, the bottom screw is still missing. She puts her hand in, wiggles the plate out of the way and, with her fingernails, catches on to its edge and eases the box out. She holds it in both hands and looks at it.

It's just a plain grey metal box; there's nothing remarkable about it, but it looks like it's seen a lot of use. The metal has that polished lustre that comes from regular handling.

She tries to lift the lid, but it's stuck tight. She's just about to fetch a screwdriver to lever it when, in the bright light, she notices another odd thing. Sellotape has been used all around the edge. It isn't obvious unless you look closely. It's like a wax seal. If you break it someone will know the box has been opened.

Susan makes a snap decision she isn't going to let something like this stop her. She knows she has steady hands and good manual skills; this goes with the territory for a lab technician. What she needs is a clean place where she can work slowly and carefully. She climbs into the passenger seat of the cabin, resting the box on her lap. She looks out to check she's still alone then at the tape closely until she finds the end.

Slowly and with great care she works this end up, lifting it with her nails, until a centimetre is sitting free. Gently, but firmly, she grasps the end and slowly eases it away—one side, two sides, three sides, four. Now she has half a metre of free tape. Carefully she attaches both ends to the dash, making sure it is clean and out of the way, so she won't catch it as she works.

Inside the box are two tightly packed brown envelopes, both about the same size as the box. Neither is sealed. Each is a couple of centimetres thick, and their outsides are unremarkable.

She lifts out the first envelope. Inside are three bundles of documents, each kept together by a rubber band. She separates out the first bundle, careful to keep the order. This is Mark Butler, his passport, license, credit cards and a range of other documents such as a rates notice, a bank statement and an electricity bill, the sorts of things needed for an identity check.

She pulls out the bank statement; it's from the Katherine ANZ. It lists a current balance of over $200,000, a serious amount of money to just be sitting there.

She puts these documents back together and examines the second bundle. It's largely the same, the Brown documents, different name and address, but otherwise near enough to the same, including a photo ID of her Mark. Brooks is yet another clone. And the three bank accounts have serious money, over half a million combined, a lot of cash to splash.

Now she knows this is real and not just imagined. It's creepy, but not really scary. Maybe he works for the Secret

155

Service, MI5, or whatever they call it in Australia. That could explain the money.

Opening the second packet she discovers four passports: one from the UK, one from Sweden, one from France and one from the USA. She flips one open, expecting to see another Mark grin back at her.

Now she is scared. A spasm of anxiety knots her insides. There is a face, but it isn't Mark. It is a woman, a beautiful Swedish woman called Elin. Her entry visitor visa is stamped over five years ago, but there's no exit stamp. What happened to her? Why is her passport still in Australia? She should have left years ago. Did she decide to stay and go underground, get new identity documents? Has someone stolen her passport, sold it on the black market?

There is also another explanation, but she doesn't want to think about it. She tries to lock it out. It sneaks instantly back into her thoughts. She recalls stories she's heard about missing backpackers, and other stories of rape, abduction, even murder. Those are the sort of words the newspapers have used.

She can't believe that of Mark, her tender, gentle Mark, the man who is her lover, but she also knows there is something unpredictable, even dangerous about him. She can't say it is definitely impossible.

She realises this box needs to be put back and quickly. But before she does she needs some details to check on. She finds a tiny notebook kept in her wallet and writes down this woman's full name, nationality, date of birth and passport number.

Her nerves are jangling; Mark could come back at any time! She gets out and looks around. The normalcy surrounding her is discordant, but nobody is in sight. She must finish this quickly.

Her hands fumble as she rushes. She goes on to the next passport and isn't surprised to find that the French woman is similarly young and beautiful, but dark haired and with a look that seems vaguely familiar. She studies the photo in the passport and looks at the name, Isabelle' It's not someone she knows; but a person with a look she's seen before in another, though who escapes her. She hasn't time to contemplate; she must keep moving. She writes down the details.

Next comes the American woman. She looks like a stereotypical all-American varsity girl: freckles, brown hair, big smile, radiant beauty.

Finally, she comes to the British passport. The woman is Scottish. There's something in this face that makes the blood drain from her own face, and her hands feel numb. Susan has seen this face before—she's certain—it was the face in the picture on the hotel wall in Barrow Creek, the one she thought looked like herself.

She remembers Mark standing by her side just after she saw it, but by then she had moved across the room to the bar. She recalls how she drew his attention to the other story about the Conniston Massacre but said nothing about this. What would he have done if she had? And, even more chilling, how does Mark have this woman's passport? It means he's met this woman, maybe done more. She can't let her mind go there just now.

It's now she realises she's seen this woman's picture even before the photo in the hotel at Barrow Creek. The memory floats up from deep in the past, though why this memory was not triggered at the hotel is strange. Perhaps it was because her focus then was on the resemblance to herself.

This woman disappeared last year in Adelaide and vanished without a trace. There was no conclusive evidence to suggest where she may have gone, but her parents were beside themselves with worry.

Susan read about it in the national newspapers. Looking at the name, Susan is surprised to see it isn't the name she recalls from the papers. This woman is called Fiona. That fits with the smudged 'na' in the Missing Person notice she saw at Barrow Creek. She's nearly sure the name she read in the papers was different, or at least the Christian name. Perhaps she's mistaking this woman for a lookalike? Hardly surprising if she first thought it was a picture of herself.

She wonders if there is a type, people with dark hair and similar features to hers, that Mark goes for. Come to think of it, the French girl's passport photo shares these features; that's why she saw something familiar. She takes out that passport again and compares it to the picture of Fiona, and the similarity is so obvious she wonders how she missed it before. But no time to worry about that now.

She must write down Fiona's details and put these passports back. Susan records these last details, then carefully—making herself move without haste—she replaces all the documents and the tape. It is hard to go so slowly, knowing that Mark might appear at any moment. But she knows she must. She takes a deep breath, trying to force calm into her flustered mind. She feels a slowing of her racing heart.

Her trembling anxiety eases a notch and she relaxes slightly. As she does the box slips from her hand, falling towards the floor. It swings freely, only the end of the tape held between her other finger and thumb suspending it. Hands shaking, she retrieves it and continues.

At last it is done. The box looks the same as when she first took it out of its hiding place, maybe a bit shiny. She finds a dusty rag and tries to create the right patina. It would require extraordinary observation and memory to note there was anything out of place. Before she hops out of the cab she checks once more that Mark isn't in sight. Not seeing him she replaces the box, checks the cabin has no tell-tale marks and walks the short steps back to their camp.

Susan's whole body is trembling. She needs to think. This isn't something she can ignore. Maybe the discovery isn't bad or not what is seems, but she needs to know the meaning.

She could leave now, walk back to the road and wait for someone else to come along. Only she doesn't know where she's going, and she isn't really sure of the way out. It was dark when they arrived last night and, while she could follow the wheel tracks back to the next road, she doesn't know if she can find her way back to the main road. If she runs off, Mark might guess she's found something and start tracking her. She's seen him track animals; he is good; the aborigines have taught him. She knows aborigines can track people almost anywhere.

No, she has to stay, and she has to try to act the same as before. She knows they're driving to Borroloola today. The way she's heard it talked about it between Mark and Vic, who often bases his chopper there, it must be a proper town, with police, shops and schools. That means it will have phone reception, and she'll be able to use and charge her mobile.

She will text her friend Anne in England once they're in Borroloola. Anne is a legal secretary, and she's good at finding things out. Even though it will be the middle of the night there, Anne will get the text the next morning. She can find out who these people are and text Susan back if there's something to worry about. After that she can decide if she needs to leave. So long as Mark doesn't suspect she knows, she doesn't think there's any real danger.

But she must be careful. Mark is smart and a great observer; he'll notice if she suddenly goes cold on him. She'll have to maintain the pretence and be warm and affectionate. But what if he wants to have sex? The thought of being intimate with someone who has hurt others makes her shudder with revulsion. But when she thinks of the way he holds and touches her, she can't really believe he's a monster.

She'll have to turn her behaviour into an acting performance, use the techniques she learnt from the University Dramatic Society. Acting makes all the things you'd never do in real life possible, because it isn't the real you doing them.

This idea is almost exciting. If he wants to make love to her she'll play along, but as another person, a stranger who looks like Susan. Before she knows it, she's fantasising about making love to Mark in the skin of another woman who looks, sounds and acts just like her. She almost wants him to come back right now so she can try it.

But first there are things to do. She stokes up the fire and puts the billy on to boil. She'll make breakfast for them both and put on fresh clothes, her favourite floral summer dress. She'll wash her face, put on her makeup, brush her hair and make herself look good. Then they'll go off together and have another fun day.

The idea has a dreamy, romantic loveliness to it. She fills a basin with warm water from the billy, then finds soap and a washer and sponges herself all over. Teeth cleaned, hair brushed, she can almost feel herself glowing.

She lifts the dress out of her pack. Next to it she sees her most sexy lace knickers. In for a penny in for a pound, she thinks, donning the underwear.

Finally, she finds a pink lipstick, natural but bright. She applies it in front of the cabin mirror. She checks again outside and sees the billy is boiling furiously, bubbling over. She jumps out and runs over to make tea, dropping the lipstick behind her onto the seat as she goes.

She'll tidy up her makeup later. First, she needs to eat; she's starving. She makes toast and covers it with butter and golden syrup. It's delicious, just the pickup she needs. She's starting on a third slice when she hears a distant shout. There is Mark, walking along the edge of the river, a hundred yards away.

Now the play-acting idea seems phoney; she's just plain scared again. Mark will see through her and know. He'll wonder why the change. But it's too late to back out now. She's rolled this dice, and now has to follow the numbers.

She stands and waves. As she does her playful spirit returns, and she skips across to him, putting a bright smile on her face. "Hello, stranger."

Susan doesn't need to ask about his success. Seeing a big grin on his face, she knows that his morning has gone well. "So, victorious hunter, where's the trophy, or the game for the pot?"

As she draws close Mark stops walking and looks straight at her, staring. She suppresses a flash of panic. Has she given something away?

He whistles. "You look gorgeous. Come here."

She walks over to him, more sedate and demure now. She feels a bit like a naughty schoolgirl caught copying from her friend's book. But she can feel her power over him; it's there in the way he's looking at her.

She stops in front of him and looks up, finds herself mesmerised by his eyes. He puts his hands on her shoulders and pulls her in close. His arms come around her back and his hands slide down to her bottom now, feeling it through the flimsy fabric. It feels exquisite. He is hot and hard.

"I was looking forward to breakfast, until I noticed you, now you're all I want." Sweat beads on his forehead. She wants to kiss it away.

She makes herself pull back. "Not so fast, you're all hot and sweaty, and you'll make my dress smell. You'll have to wait until we get back to camp and I can take it off. It's my last good dress, and a girl has got to dress up to go out on the town, particularly a big town like Borroloola. So paws off for now."

She walks alongside him. Every now and then she lets her hand brush against him. She knows he's as acutely aware of her as she is of him. It feels like a jolt of electricity every time their skin touches.

When they're getting close to camp she skips away, picks up her half-eaten slice of toast and slowly and luxuriantly eats it, bite by bite.He looks at her, desperation in his eyes. "I want you so much. Now!"

She flicks back her hair like a playful kitten. "Soon, but not now. Breakfast first, then me. While you're waiting why don't you fix our bed? It needs to be straightened."

She stands, arms crossed, regarding him as he works.

"How's that?" he says, stepping back, with a half smile.

She looks, considering. "More fluffing of pillows I think."

Mark obliges, eyes questioning.

"Yes, that's perfect now."

Susan takes Mark's hands and leads him to one of the camp chairs. Hands on his shoulders, she pushes him down onto it.

She takes two slices of bread and places them over the coals. While they toast she pours two cups of tea. She passes him his and takes a leisurely sip of her own. When the toast is cooked she covers it liberally with butter and syrup and takes it to him.

She stands in front of him, an arm's length back. She tears a piece of toast off the corner. With great delicacy she places it into his mouth, then another, and another. Each time she feeds him she licks her own lips, savouring the taste in her mind.

When all the toast is gone, she passes him the second piece. "Now you can feed yourself. I have other things to do."

Susan steps back two paces. She places her hands on her hips, feeling her own soft roundness. She slowly runs her hands up and down the silky fabric of her dress, accentuating the shape of her body underneath.

She lifts off one shoulder strap and eases her breast free above her bodice. She pauses for a minute to let him feast his eyes, then pushes down the second shoulder strap and lifts out her other breast. She tips back her head, gazing up at the sky. In a quick flick she tips her head forward, hair framing her face.

Susan gazes intently at her nipples. How she aches for him to touch them. She cups each breast and strokes each nipple until it is swollen and cherry red. Dropping her hands to her hips, she eases her dress down to the ground and steps out of it. Now all she's wearing is her lacy knickers. She walks towards him and stops just out of reach. She slowly pushes down her knickers until she's fully exposed, and gently strokes this place with her fingers.

She steps closer, until they're almost touching, and she rubs her nipples against his lips, first one, then the other. She's incredibly aroused; her breasts are in his face and she runs her hands through his hair, feeling her favourite place, that muscular hollow where his hair meets his neck.

"Now you can fuck me," she says.

It's like a dam bursts between them; their mouths are all over each other. Mark stands, lifts her to his waist and carries her to the bed. He kneels and lays her down. He tears off his clothes. With an aching sound in his throat, Mark's body is on top of hers as he pushes into her.

She climaxes as he enters, and he soon makes her come again, then again. It is sex like she's never had it before, totally wild and uninhibited. It goes on and on; when Mark comes in violent shudder he just continues thrusting, as hard as ever, coming again seconds later. Susan feels that he will overwhelm her. Then finally they are both spent.

She lies with her face in his chest. "You know I'm nuts about you. I've never been with anyone like this before. But I need to know who you are."

She instantly knows she's pushed too far, careless in her words. She can almost see the wall crashing down in his eyes.

"Why?" he asks, with anguish. "Isn't this moment enough?"

In that instant she knows there's a terrible secret, but one he cannot share. Compassion wells up in her feelings for him.

"It's all right," she says, "you are who you are. It's not for me to ask you more than you want to share. I'm sorry."

Her words aren't genuine. Deep down, she knows she needs real answers if she's to get to a place where she can be at peace with herself.

Forcing a break in their seriousness, she says, "I think it's time to go. Aren't we expected for morning tea somewhere?"

He laughs. "You know, you so enthralled me I forgot to tell you of my hunting success. I've three fine young porkers down by the river to collect, and I also have something else to show you. The pigs were too heavy to carry, so we'll go in the car."

They dress quickly. He walks to the car and waits for her to follow. As she begins to walk over an image of a girl like her, an image in a passport, flashes into her mind. Could this be how it happened with her, coming to a place like this where she vanished? She represses the thought. She must act normal. She follows him, bringing the bright smile back to her face.

After five minutes of driving, they find the pigs. The place is marked by a flock of birds, some perched around in the trees, others circling overhead, some feeding on the pig innards that Mark discarded earlier. As they approach, the birds reluctantly abandon their feast, squawking and squabbling over the last bits as they fly off.

The pig's bodies are lying on hard sun-baked earth, disguised by a blanket of branches. Mark lifts the pigs up, one by one. Each must weigh around twenty kilograms, but he makes lifting them look easy. He lays them in the cooler, then takes Susan's hand and leads her down the pig track to the river below. In his free hand he carries the intestines of one pig. They pass through a big patch of swamp grass and come to a clear pool of water, tucked into the far bank.

Not a breath of air stirs the water surface, not a single bird call disturbs the silence. She's about to speak, but Mark signals for quiet. He waves her to stop when they're about five steps back from the edge.

Slowly and carefully, he moves forward until he can reach the water. He throws down the pig guts, deliberately causing the water to splash as he places them at the very edge of the pool.

He returns and signals for her to wait quietly. Five minutes pass with nothing; the stillness is absolute, the silence broken only by the sound of a blowfly buzzing at the water's edge. Then, two small bubbles come to the surface, as far out as they stand back from the edge. Stillness again, another minute passes.

Now a small knobbly stick lies on the water where none had been, two slits at the ends of the stick open. Eyes appear two feet behind the stick. They watch her with absolute impassivity. She stares back. Somehow the knowledge she is staring at a huge crocodile has passed into her brain, without any conscious realisation. The eyes move forward in a slow gliding movement.

There is a huge wave as this enormous creature rises out of the water. The crocodile opens its jaws part way, displaying peg after peg of yellow teeth. It swivels sideways, almost delicately, picking up the pig intestine. With a flick of its head, its jaws open wide and snap shut, the pig remains now gone. Gracefully it turns its ponderous body and slides back underneath the pond surface, causing barely a ripple. All is still again, just as before.

Susan's heart is still pounding five minutes later, after they return to the car. She knew that crocodiles were huge, silent, and dangerous, but nothing imagined has prepared her to see, up close, their incredible and silent power, first hidden, seen briefly, then gone as if never there.

When she thinks of those remorseless eyes, watching her, seeing merely another meal, she feels the hair rise on her arms.

Chapter 12 – Borroloola – Day 25

Susan sits alone at a table in the Borroloola Hotel. Mark left a few minutes ago to do some more business, which he says will take an hour or so. He has connections everywhere; always a little deal on the side.

For now, she enjoys the solitude.

This morning has continued to be wonderful. The image of a crazy abductor just does not line up with this man she knows. A small voice in her head says she should be scared to remain with him, that she's in danger and must leave, but the voice is muted. She can't bring herself to believe it, that there's any real threat to her, despite what she's discovered.

But now it's time to decide. Should she try and find the truth, or should she just let it go? If she didn't care about him the choice would be easy. She would take this chance to leave him and follow it up back in England, in safety, far away. But she *does* care. She thinks Mark cares about her too; she's almost certain of it. Commitment, in whatever form, means honesty and truth. That means finding out where following these threads lead. With only five days until her plane departs from Darwin, she needs an answer to her questions before she leaves.

Susan is starting to understand NT geography and get a sense of where they're heading. Today, they're in the Gulf of Carpentaria, east of the bottom of what Mark calls the Top End. Tomorrow they'll head further north, but cross over to the western side of the Northern Territory, something about a big crocodile river, yet more crocodiles. Crocodiles seem a part of what makes Mark, his kindred. After that they'll have a day in Kakadu, right at the top, before a final night in Darwin.

She's unsure if the towns they'll pass through before Darwin will have phone coverage. So, if she wants to find out more, she must do something now, or time and opportunity will be gone.

She's enjoying sitting in the cool soft light after the harsh sun and growing heat of the day. Each day is warmer as they head north. She would happily sit here and sip her lemon, lime and bitters, while she daydreams about a future with Mark.

Can she return and try living in the Aussie outback? Is she prepared to forgo her career in medical technology? Perhaps she could get a job in a hospital lab; Alice, Katherine and Darwin are the main towns and all seem to want skilled staff. Then she and Mark could just see how it goes without the pressure of forcing themselves together all the time.

Shaking her head to rid the daydreams, Susan reluctantly pulls her phone out of her backpack. She turns it on to see that only a quarter of its charge remains. She plugs it in to charge and finds Anne's number.

She'll keep this simple and only ask about the Scottish and American women. They should be easier to track down using English language websites. Have they been reported as missing? Is there anything suspicious? When did it happen?

If she gives each name, current age and town or city from the passport address, it should be enough for Anne to search Mr Google to see if anything about them comes up—a newspaper article, a missing person's notice or anything similar. Once she has the answers she can decide on what to do next.

Her text is to the point:

Anne,
Can you check out the two names below?
Saw notice saying missing in a place I stayed.
Are they home now and OK? Text back soonest.
Will check back next town where phone works.
Having a great time in Oz.
Love and see you soon,
Suz

167

She lists the names of Fiona Rodgers and Amanda Sullivan, along with the age and origin locality for both women. She pushes send and checks the sent box.

The message has gone. It's too late to change her mind.

She thinks about ringing her mum to say hello, but the time difference (3.00 am in London) means it isn't a good time. She'll try to remember one night, when it's morning in England, and if she's in a place with reception. Feeling she's done her duty, she turns the phone off and puts it away.

Susan thinks of Mark and her morning spent with him. It was, it was … well not something she would tell her grandmother. It blows her mind the way they connected with each other, and all the intimate things they did.

That huge crocodile, so silent and so very freaky: one minute, nothing, the next a ton of saurian scales surging from the water with such power and a seemingly weightless, explosive movement. She recalls the delicate way it picked up and swallowed its pig treat, displaying almost quaint relish. After it faded away to nothing again, a silent place. She'd barely breathed as she'd watched it unfold. She shivers now at the thought.

That was followed by their funny morning tea at a place called Seven Emus. It wasn't the grand cattle station she'd imagined, in fact there was not much there at all really, just skinny cattle, broken yards, a range of pets and chickens wandering here and there, in and out of houses. Mark told her it was an extension of the Shadforth clan who had lived in this country for more than one hundred years.

There was something incredibly dynamic about them, their mixed race ancestry, multi-coloured kids running free. It was a place with a blend of old and new; parts of the house and yard looked like they'd come out of the Ark. Alongside piles of junk and broken down cars, scattered around, were shiny new objects:

a TV, a microwave, satellite phone, books, and electronic games. There were also modern cars and boats, even a helicopter that sat to one side—bought to take tourists on scenic flights.

On the way in they'd passed a flash resort, the Seven Emu's Fishing Camp, and turned down a little side track to come to a place by the creek; it was unclear which part of the clan lived there. Mark said there were too many details to explain.

The people who lived there were lovely. They really belonged to this place and successfully managed to straddle the race and class divide with a son studying law at The University of Queensland, a daughter training to be a nurse in Darwin, another who worked as a police trainee in Borroloola. Their parents were so obviously proud of their children's achievements; they spoke of them the same way her mum talked about her and Tim.

Then there was a cousin with a brood of small children, running everywhere, almost naked, snotty nosed, one carrying a pet chook. Their mother screaming at them and waving a stick, but rushing to hug one who fell and hurt his knee, while at the same time she scolded another for eating a piece of bread that fell on the floor.

There was a grizzled old man, perhaps a grandfather, who still had his aboriginal heritage running strong. He told Susan a story of the early spirits of the land, the Emu spirits of his totem. He walked with her to the creek, carrying a fish spear, and showed her where he could spear fish. He told her of going in a small boat into the rough gulf waters to catch dugong and turtle with a harpoon; he told of being a little boy when a white man beat his father. The man accused his father of stealing a cow with no brand. It was on their own land, but this man said he knew this cow by sight and it was his. This man blamed his father for making it run away, so he hit his father with a stick, over and over again, until he lay still in the dirt. His father died soon after.

The old Chinese cook, relationship unknown, was like a second grandfather; he had made Chinese dumplings for their morning tea. He had taken the pig offered, on behalf of the whole family, with gratitude. He had quickly run his hands over it, then hung it from a beam under the verandah. Later he would "smoke-im, real good," but for now, dumplings.

Almost as an afterthought, he sliced off a portion of cheek meat to add to his menu. When it was ready, the dumplings and barbequed pork were served steaming in a spicy sauce. The food was delicious, and Susan ate with her fingers, alongside the others, with uninhibited gusto.

It was such a hotchpotch, and yet so real and alive. Before, Susan had an image of aboriginal culture which she realised now was a stereotype—the noble savage with the spear, living far out and alone, totally at one with the land. Instead, here was a culture that was a living and dynamic fusion, the old and the new all living and drawing off each other, a chaotic harmony, as if blessed by the spirit of this land.

Susan senses this is a new aboriginal and Australian culture and, in maybe fifty years, this culture will evolve yet again, its people changing beyond recognition. Only the landscape will remain the same.

She is roused from her reverie by Mark's hand on her shoulder. "You look like you're having such a lovely dream. Let's walk around the town and down to the river. I'll show you the sights for a bit before we come back for lunch and travel on.

"We have time to relax and enjoy ourselves this afternoon, and I have something special to give you tonight. I want this night to be one you'll remember for the rest of your life."

She feels an instant flash of anxiety at what Mark means. But when she looks at his face, it's open with an affectionate smile towards her.

Her fear vanishes and she slips her arm around his waist.

They walk outside into the bright sunshine of a Borroloola dry season day. Susan soaks up the sun's rays as a warm and gentle breeze caresses her skin. She feels good.

Today is a day to be enjoyed while she waits for the chips to fall. She will not think about her message to Anne until there is something to know.

Chapter 13 – Heartbreak Hotel to VRD – Day 26

On leaving Borroloola, they drive for an hour until they come to a little town called Cape Crawford. Susan thinks 'town' is perhaps too large a word, as the place is only just a roadhouse called Heartbreak Hotel.

There is no mobile reception.

The pub is not much to look at. Mark tells her the room he's rented is basic, not much more than a box with a double bed and an air conditioner, no five-star accommodation here.

But this matters not to Susan. Despite the strangeness of the day, she feels like she's walking on air; this time is theirs alone.

It's lovely to be here with hours of daylight to spare. They check in to escape the heat of the early afternoon. Once in their room, they'd sate their never-ending desire for sex, this time slowly and gently.

As they lie together in the afterglow Mark looks at her with great tenderness. In a low voice he says, "You mean more to me than anything else in the world. I could not bear for anyone to ever hurt you."

He never quite says 'love', but from him these words feel the same. This is the first time he's talked to her in an emotional way. It moves her far beyond anything she has known with any other man. She cups his face in her hands and smothers his eyes, nose and mouth with kisses. "I adore all of you too." Her heart says this man is not a monster.

They lie in a dreamy trance. She sees a small TV on the wall, opposite the bed. Mark tells her it runs from a satellite dish perched on the roof. He encourages her to see what's happening in the rest of the world.

She picks up the remote control and turns it on to see a range of channels, most American, but some local. For a mid-afternoon hour she feasts her desire to connect with the outside

172

world by watching news and channel surfing. It's good to see that somewhere beyond here still exists, but she sees little that has any meaning for her.

After their time in bed they go for a drink in the bar. It's still only just after three. They have a long afternoon yet. Susan orders lemonade and mixes it with a dash of Mark's beer. They perch on high stools at one end of the polished wood bar. There are a few tourists and a tour bus driver in the far corner looking at memorabilia that surrounds the bar, a pair of buffalo horns, a crocodile skull, a photo of stockmen on horses driving a huge mob of cattle across the open grass plains with two helicopters circling above.

Conversation fragments reach them distantly:

"Get a load of that croc's teeth. Hate for him to bite me."

"Maybe not, but I'd sure as hell like to see one that big!"

"How much are the helicopter tours this afternoon?"

"What, they want two hundred dollars each for fifteen minutes. Bit expensive!"

As they empty their glasses, Mark says, "I have something I want to show you. It's just a short drive away."

She smiles. "Another surprise. I love your surprises!"

They drive away from the hotel. In half an hour they turn onto a track with a small sign reading, *Bessy Springs - Falls.*

The waterfall isn't huge, less than a hundred feet high, but it has a steady flow that falls over ochre cliffs into a crystal clear pool that glows in the reflected light. The pool is fringed by a prickly palm, which Mark says is called Pandanus.

They swim in the pool below, then climb to the top of the waterfall and follow the creek back to a series of deep rock pools. On the way they pass through what, to Susan, appears to be a city made of stones.

Mark sees her looking at them. "It's a lost city. Over millennia the weather has eroded the rock in the creek valley into hundreds of stone columns. They kind of look like stone skyscrapers, hey?"

Susan looks at them poking up through the trees. The layers in the stone are building floors. She can almost imagine the inhabitants of these strange buildings. She pictures them sleeping in the daylight, but coming out at dusk, carrying little lights, like fairies, bustling as they come and go. It adds another layer of magic to their own magical reality.

They come to a hollowed out rock pool. It is an almost perfect circle, scoured neat and clean by the thunderous water flow of the wet season. Now, just a gentle trickle runs into this clear water pool, buried deep in the stone, with sand and pebbles at the edges. Susan wades in and discovers that the water is deep and cold. She sees it falls away to the centre where it looks well over her head.

She looks back to Mark at the edge. Are you coming in?

Mark takes off his clothes and comes up to her. He unbuttons her top and slides down her pants, lifting her clear of the water with one arm as he removes the rest of her garments with the other and tosses them ashore.

He holds her body against his in waist deep water. He does not seek sex, just caresses and holds her, and she holds him in return. They gently touch and explore each other's bodies and faces; she touches the big scar on his back that runs across his shoulder. "I think it's a gunshot wound, sustained in a Wild West gunfight," she tells him.

Mark laughs. "I've already told you it was barbed wire from when a buckjumper horse threw me over a fence."

She rolls her eyes and he winks. Even though they both know the true story is something else it doesn't matter; living within ever-shifting truth is fine in the magical land they're in.

A tiny part of her mind wonders if it was like this with the other women he knew, those whose pictures she found this morning, did he wow and caress them before something bad happened. But her mind won't go there, he's too gentle and kind for this thought to persist.

They return to Heartbreak Hotel just as dusk is falling. The western sky is lit by a red sunset, the sun turning from yellow, to orange, to red, to almost purple tinged with black as it descends through the final layers of a distant smoky sky.

Dinner is 'Surf and Turf' in the roadhouse: the menu lists a juicy slab of Barkly Steak, Carpentaria Prawns and Fresh Barramundi. It's delicious for roadhouse food. They wash their meal down with beer, poured into glasses from huge longneck bottles of NT Draught.

Someone strikes up a fiddle. Next minute Irish set dances and jigs start. Roadhouse patrons join in; instructions are easy, little is expected. Thirty to forty people are in the bar but there seems to be no one Mark knows. "It's a tourist crowd," Mark explains. "The locals are busy with mustering and other dry season work. They won't be in until the weekend."

Susan doesn't mind. It means she has Mark all to herself. The night drifts by, a pleasant feeling of her being together with him, sitting side by side, sometimes facing and looking at him, sometimes little touches of hands and thighs. She knows there will be more loving before they go to sleep, but the now is about enjoying his company.

The evening floats on. When Susan starts yawning, Mark takes her by the hand, pulls her to her feet and leads her back to their room. He sits her on the edge of the bed while he opens the small bag that holds his things.

Susan gets the feeling something significant is to happen.

Mark takes an object she can't see out of his bag and zips it back up. He turns and pads softly to sit beside her on the bed. Almost shyly he takes her hand and puts an object in it.

Nestled in the palm of her hand is a blue felt box, the type that holds rings and small jewellery.

She feels a flutter of excitement and looks at Mark, curious.

"Open it," he says.

She opens the lid. Inside is a ring with a milky blue stone the size of her thumbnail. Sitting beside the ring is an almost identical stone, set into a pendant on a necklace of gold links.

"Came from the man I saw today in Borroloola. I got the stones sent off to be made up just after I left Magnetic Island. When I first met you in Cairns I knew they were perfect for the colour of your eyes. After Cairns I hoped I might see you again. I decided that day, after we met on the dive boat, that if I did see you again these would be for you. So, in Townsville, after you left, I arranged to have these made and sent to Borroloola where I could collect them."

She looks up and meets his gaze. It's as though, in this moment, she's drawn within his being, a meeting of spirits. There is such intensity in this connection. At first it was mainly physical, but now she feels a bonding of their souls.

Her gaze flicks down to the gorgeous jewellery, then back at Mark. This is just so wonderful and surprising. Tears prick her eyes. "Oh, Mark, you shouldn't have; they're very beautiful."

Sitting beside her, Mark takes the box, lifts her right hand, which is sitting in his lap, and tries the ring on her third finger.

The ring is a fraction too large, but she loves its elegant cut and the way it sparkles in the light. The stone seems huge, but yet is balanced and perfect.

Mark places the gold chain over her head and lets the second stone fall into place. It sits just at the top of the place where her breasts meet, partly hidden under her top.

"I think I need to see it in uninterrupted view," he says.

She nods, lifts her arms. "Undress me," she whispers.

Mark lifts her top over her head, his fingers grazing her skin and giving her goose bumps. It is thrown somewhere behind. Standing he draws her to her feet and eases off her skirt, discarding this too. He kisses each breast, then the little blue stone, and then each breast again. When he's done he places her under the covers and covers her body with his. It is incredible, the togetherness, as much as the pleasure.

After, she asks, "What made you want to get me this amazing gift?"

He looks at her, quiet for long seconds, then says, "At first it was just your eyes, but now it's all of you. I want you to have something to remember me by, when you return home." He pauses. "Maybe we can find a way to meet and do this all again, be together again."

Sleepily she says, "I hope so, Mark, I really hope so." Half dreamy she murmurs, "Together forever."

After it seems Mark is saying it with her. "Together forever," over and over, or is it a dream?

Later, Susan and Mark lie side by side in their bed in the little box unit room at Heartbreak Hotel, as Susan's dreams slide away and consciousness return. She reaches out and touches his shape in the darkness beside her, so as to know that this is real. It's the middle of the night or, more accurately, early morning. Mark seems to be sleeping soundly, his breathing regular. She is overcome with warmth and tenderness for this man.

She remembers what passed before, of his gift to her. It's amazing he made this decision on the very first day of their meeting, as if he had foreknowledge of what was to follow.

She sees clearly now she's fallen in love with him. She's into this way over her head and cannot conceive of her life without him. Sure, he has odd quirks: he's secretive, defensive, doesn't like questions. But he's hardly had the best start: an abusive father, a mother who gave him little before vanishing. She's sure this is at the root of his emotional wall.

She's in the mood to forgive all. Part of her regrets the text to Anne, digging into the women's identities. There will be a reasonable explanation. After all, the passports are out of date, or at least the Swedish one is. And the Scottish woman's name doesn't seem familiar. She's almost sure the name she remembers from the newspaper is Catherine or Katherine—not Fiona—maybe the surname is the same, but then she isn't really sure. It isn't like Rodgers is an uncommon name.

She's ashamed she's broken Mark's trust by looking for bad secrets. Especially when he's been so kind and gentle, well most of the time.

It has only been once or twice that she's seen a look on his face that's scared her, but then everyone had a dark side sometimes. She's jumping at shadows. She needs to respond to his affection with trust. The memories leave her warm and happy as she drifts back to sleep.

***

It's still dark when Mark shakes her awake. "Hate to disturb your sleep, but we've a long way to go today."

They pack quickly and leave the roadhouse. Nothing is stirring in the tourist parts, but a couple of workers are tidying up out the back. Five minutes later they're on the road and away.

"We're heading for Timber Creek and the Victoria River tonight, passing through Top Springs and the Victoria River District. It's my favourite piece of cattle country. Hopefully we'll get most of the drive out of the way by midday. I'm aiming for us to be in Top Springs for lunch."

"How far is that?" Susan asks.

"Oh, only five hundred kilometres away."

They share the driving. He drives for the first hour while she fully wakes up. Then he gives her the wheel and she drives until they reach the Stuart Highway, two hours later. They stop at the Daly Waters Hotel, just near the junction, where they take on fuel for the car, and two plates of sizzling bacon and eggs for themselves.

After their late breakfast they head south.

Susan is surprised at the direction of their travel, having understood they are to go north. "Why are we heading back towards Alice Springs?"

"We must go south to pick up our road heading west."

Susan can't control an instant flash of trepidation to be heading out into another unknown remote area. She dismisses it with last night's memory. He wouldn't treat her like that if he wanted to harm her.

They reach the road in less than half an hour. The sign reads Buchanan Highway. "The locals call it the Murranji Track," he tells her. "It's an old drover's route. They used to walk cattle to Queensland from the Victoria River District and the Kimberley, far out west.

"It's only two hundred kilometres long, but it was one of the world's toughest droving routes. It has long waterless stretches, poor feed, patches of dense dangerous timber called lancewood, with spear like trunks which impaled men and horses. And they feared creatures in the dark, bad spirits. Cattle would get spooked in the night and rush. Yanks call it a stampede."

Despite the shorter driving distance, this journey to Top Springs feels much longer than their trip to Daly Waters did. They try to talk but, with no roadside scenery, there's little of interest to discuss. The noise of the vehicle bouncing and shaking makes wider conversation difficult.

Susan sits contented anyway, happy to be in Mark's company. She takes the ring from her finger and slips it on the gold chain round her neck. "I don't want it to slide off my finger and get lost," she tells Mark.

She slips the ring inside her shirt, enjoys the feeling of it hidden there, sitting snug between her breasts. It's both intimate and possessive.

At last they leave the scrub behind. The country opens out into wide grassy plains, with creeks cutting down into low hills on the horizon.

"This is the start of the VRD, Victoria River District. It runs from here out to Western Australia and then down to the desert. It's named from its river, which starts in the desert and runs north to the sea.

"For me it's God's own country. The place where God said, after he'd made the rest of the world, 'Now give me space for man and beast, where the grass is good, the water is sweet, the fish are big, and the hills look over.'"

Susan looks at him and smiles. "A man of poetry and many other things."

He grimaces. "Not my strongest talent I admit."

Soon a sign for Top Springs comes into view. A minute later she sees a squat building made of unpainted concrete blocks set on a dry dusty plain. The trees are half stunted, the grass is dead, and there's nothing remarkable from Susan's vantage point. It's hard to see what Mark sees in this country, viewed from here. There's nothing to be seen resembling a spring of water.

They're met by a crusty old bartender, Mick, who clearly knows Mark well. He flicks Mark's hat as he comes inside, grinning at him.

"What no fuel to buy?" he says to Mark.

Mark laughs. "Here! You're joking. You'll rob me blind."

"Must think we're still in old Ma Hawke's days," Mick says.

"Anyone who trained under her must be like her."

"Takes one to know one." It's good-natured banter.

Over lunch endless stories emerge about infamous Ma Hawke. Susan is in fits of laughter, finds it hard to believe most stories, though the old bartender swears to their authenticity.

Mark backs him up. "Not that I knew her myself, but I've talked to too many old-timers who knew her and swear it is all fact, for it all to be made up."

The stories run on and on. "What about the one where she tried to sell a Stock Inspector 300 litres of petrol, from the pump, even though his fuel tank only held 240."

"What about the time when she died and they called the local cops out from Wave Hill. Everyone knew there must be a money stash. Sure enough, the cops said they found ten grand under her bed. Trouble was, next day, after they went back to the Wave Hill Police Station, one of the cop's own dog's dug up money buried in his back yard. A blackfella saw the notes blowing in the wind and thought it was Father Christmas.

"Turned out that cop pocketed another fifteen grand. When he saw the money in the wind he fessed up. But his mate didn't, said he knew nothing about any extra money. He stuck to his story and a search couldn't find it. Even though the first cop said the other had taken his own share he wouldn't cough up the dough. So the honest cop got the boot. A year later the honest one is on the bones of his arse while his mate lives in a new flash house that cost a bomb to build."

After reminiscing for another while, Mark flicks his head towards the bar. "One to carry," he says, ordering another beer for them both.

Mick passes two over, but when Mark goes to pay he shakes his head. "On the house. Tis good to tell tales with one who remembers. I know you came from the city once upon a time, but you're one of us now. Stories are in your blood.

"Old-timers around here say you've got a crocodile spirit. They see it in the dusk, in that last light, when shadows come out to dance."

Goose bumps run down Susan's arms and spine. She can't imagine this hard-bitten old bushie bartender sees ghosts. But something in his tone tells her he can see over the horizon to the other side. She shivers.

Mark breaks the mood. "Well, old fella, thanks mighty for the drinks and yarn. Tell me what's going on out on the VRD?"

"Yair, well, everyone's pretty flat strap as you know. This morning a big lot of trucks came through from Katherine, gone to collect a great shipment of steers to load on the cattle boat from Darwin tomorrow. Hear tell they're putting them together on VRD Station. They say numbers have come up short, and they've cut an expensive deal with Humbert River Station to make up the load. Hear tell they're walking a mob down the Wickham Gorge today."

Susan struggles to understand everything being said, but she gets the general idea that the big station they're heading for is sending lots of trucks of cattle to Darwin to go on a boat, and that they need to buy more cattle from a nearby station to complete the order as promised, which will cost a lot of money.

Mick pauses. "Don't know if you know it, but tis tiger country up there. Lots of scrubbers in dem hills. Reckon tis likely to be trouble. Youse looking for a job?"

Mark winks. "Not today. Hands a bit full, as you can see."

Mick gives Susan a piercing look. "You must be real careful; he's full of charm, but there's a wild place there too. Danger goes with him."

His tone turns serious. "But you'll be right. A guardian angel watches over you, so I know I'll see you again sometime, maybe when his spirit returns to the place of the crocodiles."

There's an edge to his words that makes Susan squirm. But Mark waves him away. "Ah, go way with you, old man. Don't be frightening the lass. I'll take good care of her."

"Sure, and isn't that the nub of the problem," he replies.

It's such a strange conversation that Susan bursts out laughing. "I swear you're all mad Irish here, such superstition as I've never before heard."

The barman winks at her. "Well, isn't me name Michael O'Reilly, as was me dad's afore." Then he doffs his hat. "Will be seein' ye agin."

"Well, I hope so," Susan answers.

As she and Mark walk to the door the man's reply follows her. "To be sure, to be sure, tis written, tis."

Chapter 14 – Out on the VRD – Day 26

As they drive off Mark says, "We're a bit later than I meant. But it's hard to get away when the old man gets to telling stories; he knows them all and at least half are true. The blackfellas around here tell me he's a bit fey and sees spirits. Me, I think the only spirit he sees comes from the inside of a bottle with the name Johnnie Walker written on it."

An hour later Mark and Susan come over a ridge. In front of them the air is full of dust. There are buildings and yards, men on horses, and a couple helicopters working, along with cut down jeeps which Mark tells her are called 'bull catchers' pushing a mob of cattle up a laneway. Over to one side sit six big trucks with double-deck stock crates, each pulling two extra trailers. Another truck is pulled up to a loading ramp, and people are pushing cattle up the ramp into it.

"Well, it is a big day today," Mark says. "All go at the home station. This below is VRD, properly known as Victoria River Downs Station, same name as the district. It was the largest cattle station in the world, before they broke it into four parts. VRD is one of my favourite places, and today is a good day to come, even if it's a bit busy. I thought you might like to see some real cattle station action."

Susan nods, happy to go along.

"A mighty river runs through here, the Victoria River. We're going out on it tomorrow. Pity it's pushing three o'clock. I'd planned a full afternoon here, but I didn't know what was on. Plenty it seems. Let's go and say hello, see if we can lend a hand. The manager here is a good friend of mine."

They park near the yards and walk across to where people are gathered. Most are busy, but a truckie is leaning on the rail, watching as they load cattle onto a truck.

Mark sticks out his hand. "Hi there. I think we met at Anthony's Lagoon last year."

The bloke sticks out his own hand and shakes Mark's. "Bill. Yeah, I remember those big mad bullocks bound for Queensland, fresh out of the swamp. They were a handful."

Mark indicates to the trucks and yard. "Big lift, eh?"

"Yeah. S'posed to go on that flash new cattle boat, the one that takes five thousand in a go, off to Indonesia. It's loading in Darwin tomorrow. VRD promised fifteen hundred, but I hear they might be a couple hundred shy. It's said they came up two hundred short when they mustered the Moolooloo Back Paddock. Still bringing some up from Sanford, as well as a mob of extras from Humbert River. Actually, one truck may have to go over there to load."

Susan remembers the barman saying the same thing earlier.

"Anyway, we're all supposed to load tonight and be in the wharf in Darwin for unloading in the morning. Looks like it'll be a long night of driving. Thank God I'm at the front of the queue. These ones at the back will be lucky to be away by ten tonight. That doesn't leave much time for sleeping. I'm lucky to be looking forward to a good four hours kip at the wharf before the boat loading starts in the morning."

"Mark!" comes a shout from behind them. A strong looking man hurries over. "Bloody glad to see you," he says, shaking Mark's hand.

"You too. How's it goin'?" Mark asks.

"It's been one of those days, cock-up after cock-up. Still, we'll manage somehow. Maybe you came specially to help; God knows I need someone to put a shoulder to the wheel."

Seeming to only just notice Susan, the man turns to her and says, "Well, he always was the last to introduce me to the lovely ladies. Thinks I might pinch them, even though I've got my own missus who's more than enough for me. Buck's the name. I'm trying to run things around here."

Susan shakes his hand. "I'm Susan." She appreciates the man's directness; he reminds her a bit of her father: total focus, no nonsense and straight to the point.

Buck smiles and turns to Mark. "We're short and I cut an expensive deal to get more steers from Humbert. Trouble is they were out in that paddock in the far back corner, and the Humbert stock camp had other work and couldn't muster them.

"It meant I had to send over a stock camp to do the mustering ourselves. All was going well at first; we'd put the mob together and were walking it back. We decided to use the Wickham Gorge way; you know that rough stony track – a tiger trail through the hills that few use. But there's a road for the truck bringing the stores, and there's lots of good fresh feed along the river, so the cattle should have full bellies, going over the weighing scales in Darwin. We had three hundred good sappy steers, just an ideal size. We're short about two hundred, and a hundred as spares is handy.

"Anyway, it was going well until late morning. We had maybe fifteen ks to go till we cleared the gorge and got back into good open country near this end. Then a mongrel scrub bull got in amongst them and stirred them all up."

From the frustration in Buck's voice, Susan figures this was a bad thing. She can't quite follow all the cattle talk, but Buck's expression is easy to read.

"I hear he's the one that busted away when they did the clean up in there last year," Buck says. "A mad horny red bull, with a big scar on his nose. The head stockman tells me you know him well, as you helped with that job."

"Yeah, I should have shot him then, but he'd do above a thousand bucks on the boning room floor, so I let him go. Thought he was next year's pocket money."

"Well, he's got the bullet now, but not before he split the mob. Gone every which way, but at least they're still in the gorge, at least that's what I've been told by the chopper.

"Then, just for good measure, one of the young ringers, trying too hard to put them back together, got spat off his horse and busted his arm, bad break. So we had to pull off the chopper that was putting the mob back together and bring our man out. We called in the Flying Doctor and it's collected him from the homestead just now. So it's all go again, but we're down a good man and the day's near gone.

"The agent in Darwin tells me the boat won't finish loading until the next morning, the day after tomorrow. So, if we can get them steers to the Humbert Station yards and get them loaded by tomorrow afternoon, we should still be okay.

"One good thing is the mob's been left to settle along the river. With a good feed and drink they should be a bit easier to work now. I'm just getting two choppers organised to go and put the steers back together and get them moving again. I would go myself, but I need to stay here to keep the loading of all the trucks on track.

"So, I need a couple spotters to ride with the choppers, if you've got the time. It helps to have a second pair of eyes when the pilot is working in that gorge, as you well know. Since your help with last year's clean up, you know that country better than me. What're your movements anyway?"

"Well, just on my way to Timber Creek, job on the river tomorrow, but my afternoon is free. So now I'm your spotter. Lead me to the chopper. I assume Susan can ride in the other."

"My plan in one," Buck says. "There'll be grub up in the mess when you come back and a bed for the night, if you want it. I'll probably be here till at least nine to get the loading finished. I'll need to find myself a new job tomorrow morning if there's any more stuff ups from here.

"How important is that job on the river tomorrow?" he asks. "Can you put it back? Really need an extra in the stock camp to bring those steers along. They were a bit short before. I should have sent one more. You know how it is, finding enough men for each job when the pressure's on. But now they're down one more, it'll be a real handful to manage the mob, at least till they come out of the river gorge and make the open going."

Buck turns to Susan. "Don't suppose you can ride?"

"A bit," she says.

Buck looks at Mark enquiringly.

"I had a feeling something like this would come along," Mark says. "I should have been here by late lunch. But you know how they get you in with the stories at Top Springs. I reckon we can fit it in. Need to be on my way by lunch tomorrow to get out and have an hour or two on the river before dark.

"And don't worry about Susan. I've seen her. She can ride fine. She just needs a steady horse. I don't want to have to ring her mama, say she got busted up on a mongrel VRD horse."

Buck laughs. "I think we can manage that. There's a real nice four-year-old grey I broke in last year. They've worked him in camp for the year, and they tell me he's real steady now. He has a lovely soft mouth, turns on a pin, runs like the wind. I think that's the one for her.

"When you land tell the head stockman to put him aside. Firefly's his name. Oh, and you can have Bushranger. He's the one that spat Mick today, a big black late-cut colt; you'll know him by the wildness in his eyes. Good horse, if a bit mad. You're just the one to set him straight."

"B'jesus, you are trying to get me killed. Surely there's a real tame packhorse somewhere for me?"

Buck grins. "What, gone chicken in your old age?"

They walk over to the choppers about a hundred yards away, and Buck introduces the pilots. Dick is flying the lead machine, with Mark riding shotgun. Susan is to ride with Tim, who'll work the flanks.

There's no delay. The machines are already fuelled up and ready to fly. They'll need the rest of the day to get the job done. Quick instructions are passed from Tim to Susan as the rotor is spinning up.

"This machine is a Robinson helicopter, designed for two, though it can carry three at a pinch. You need to look out for cattle on your side, and also back behind. Also watch out for the tail rotor and tree branches."

He shows her how to signal him to go in the different directions, and then they're off. They soar into the sky, heading straight and low towards the southwest. The pilot points out as they cross the boundary line between VRD and Humbert River Stations. Flat country is left behind and they fly over scrubby broken hills, rising ever higher as they head west. The ground falls away. Down below them is the Wickham River Gorge.

Susan and Tim spy cattle in small groups scattered along the river, some standing up to their bellies in water. The river itself is mainly a series of rocky pools with a few longer open bits of water. A set of wheel tracks runs along one side of the river.

Parked next to this track is a four-wheel drive with what looks like a mobile kitchen on the back. Four horses are saddled, standing next to the truck. A few more are grazing nearby. There is an open space fifty yards from the truck, and they follow the other helicopter in and land alongside it in this small clearing.

The helicopter engines are left running as Mark gets out and waves Susan over. Both pilots, the head stockman and Mark engage in a brief conversation, and the riders are given instructions: two are to ride ahead a few hundred yards to a place where the valley narrows and there is an open grassy area. They will block the cattle just past that point.

The other two riders are to head up valley where most of the cattle are and work with the choppers to pick up the mobs and put them together, walking them along steadily and not crowding them. As needed, one rider can cut out to help the chopper, while the other stays put at the tail of the mob. They'll bring the mob steadily along towards the block up place, where they will hold them together until the full mob arrives. Then they'll walk them along for a bit to settle them before they stop in the place designated for their night camp.

In another minute they're off again. The two choppers follow opposite valley edges, keeping high to get a good view and not spook the cattle. At first there are lots of cattle in sight, then it's just odd animals in ones and twos, and finally they see no more. They fly on to the next river bend where the valley narrows, a natural choke point.

Here Mark's helicopter lands and Mark gets out. He makes his way across the ground, looking down as if searching for something. "He's checking for tracks to see if any have come back this far," Tim tells her.

They hold a slow search pattern as Mark checks, working out to the valley edges and looking for any sign. Tim explains they need to keep a lookout for any cattle tracks and dung, as well as the beasts. "Sometimes the cattle will camp in a patch of bushes. Then, if you didn't check for their signs, you wouldn't know they were there."

After a couple minutes the call comes, "All clear, carry on." Their chopper works the edges of the gorge, making sweeping searches from side to side, above and behind the first chopper that focuses on the river and valley centre.

Tim points to the other chopper. "He's most likely to come on the cattle in the shade close to the river, but sometimes they'll run up the sides of the valley and try to break back behind the helicopters. It can be hard to see from down there, close to the ground. That's why we sit up here and keep watch. We also check the valley edges where generally cattle are less likely to be found. But, seeing as the afternoon is cooling down now, a few cattle might start to walk up the valley sides to feed."

For the next few minutes there is nothing. Then a call comes over the radio. "First mob, five, in river." The other helicopter drops down amongst the river trees, hovering and moving in lots of directions.

Four cattle burst out of the river, heading straight towards Susan and Tim. In a second Tim has dropped his helicopter to tree top level, zooming in to heel the cattle and turn them down the valley. One last straggler runs out, the other chopper following at his heels. Tim immediately gains altitude, returning to their high side position.

The next two hours are exhilarating. The helicopter is like an extension of Tim's arm, turning faster than she can see or think where to go. Soon Susan and Tim are in sync.

"Two cattle at nine o'clock, fifty yards," she calls out. He breaks left almost before her words are out. "One under tree, twelve o'clock, don't think they've seen him." As instructions are called, Mark's helicopter is instantly changing course.

Now they have a good-sized mob, of maybe a hundred, stringing out in front, and the horse riders have taken position behind them. The head stockman is holding the tail, and his companion works the flanks, coming from side to side, much like what they are doing.

They notice one bull that doesn't belong. It isn't sleek and shiny like the other cattle, instead it's reddish-brown and scruffy.

"Scrub bull," Tim says. "Must have come out of the hills for a drink and doesn't know what's hit him."

The bull paws the ground, looking to charge the outer rider. Some of the other cattle are also starting to drift back and away, seeing a chance to escape with the distraction.

191

Then, like a buzzing fly, Mark's chopper is in the bull's face. The bull snorts, shakes his head and makes a run for the helicopter, which is hovering and advancing just above the ground. A loud boom sounds and it turns tail and gallops back into the mob, moving right into the very centre.

"They won't have any more trouble with him now; there's nothing like a blast of bird shot to put a bull back in its place," Tim tells Susan.

By the time the sun falls below the hills they have the whole mob together on the little grassy flat. The head stockman says the count is about right, maybe one or two missing, but it's good enough for now.

The plan is to walk the mob on through a narrow section of valley until it opens out into another small grassy flat where a second creek runs in. It will take half an hour. There they'll settle the cattle in an overnight camp. In the morning they'll walk the cattle the remaining twelve kilometres to the end of the valley and continue on into the yards from there.

Both helicopters hold position for a few minutes, until it's obvious that all is under control, then the lead helicopter zooms away to the station, with them in hot pursuit, arriving just as the sun is tipping the horizon.

As they touch down Buck runs over to meet them. "That's fantastic. Got a call over the radio. Hear it ran like clockwork."

Mark gives him a friendly punch on the shoulder, "I don't know what you would've done without me. Just needed an old pro on the job. Now all I have to do is give your blokes a riding lesson in the morning on Mr Bushranger. We'll soon see whether he can really buck or is just a great big pussy."

"Why don't you go and have a shower and check into the bunk rooms," Buck says to them both. "I'm afraid it will have to be boys and girls separate tonight, no spare rooms. I'll meet you for some dinner in half an hour. My backup can keep the loading going. It's running well, and the trucks should all be loaded by an hour after dark, touch wood."

Buck arranges for Tim to ferry them to the cattle at first light in the helicopter. "If he takes half a tank of fuel the weight will be okay."

Mark turns to Susan and points towards some buildings a few hundred yards away. "That's the station homestead. It's like a little town. That building to this side," he points to the right, "is the bunk block where we're staying. Why don't you settle in. I need to discuss a couple things with Buck, then I'll collect the truck and drive across." Susan nods and sets out for the building while Mark and Buck walk back to the yard, talking earnestly.

Susan savours the soft evening light. The temperature is perfect, neither hot nor cold. The grass glows golden, and the hills an orange purple as the light ebbs away. A couple of birds wing low across her path. She feels wonderful, so exhilarated from the helicopter dance. She feels a kinship with Mark's love of this area; she understands when he said he thought God created this one place a little better than the rest.

Dinner passes in friendly conversation and banter with a mixture of male and female ringers, other station hands, a governess and the pilots. By the end of the meal she is yawning.

Mark sees and says, "You should go to your bunk. I'm not far off mine either. They'll ring a bell half an hour before it gets light. That's the signal that breakfast's ready."

Susan lingers a minute, lightly resting her hand on his arm. "It feels strange going to a bed without you." And it's true; this will be the first night they've spent apart since Melbourne, many days ago. "I'll miss you, but I'm sure I'll be asleep in five minutes anyway. Thanks for a wonderful day. It's hard to believe that any day can beat yesterday, or the day before, but I can't think of any day better than this."

He touches her cheek. "Me neither, but then yesterday and last night were pretty special too."

He gives her a lascivious look as she rises to leave. She can't help it; her face gets hot as the pleasure of remembering tingles in her body.

All too soon a bell is ringing. There's no daylight yet, just a soft lightening in the window. She was so tired last night she'd collapsed into bed. She couldn't remember sleeping so soundly in a long time.

Mark's in the dining room when she gets there, his plate piled high with bacon and eggs. She joins him, but contents herself with coffee and toast, and thieving pieces of bacon from his plate. He pulls a face.

Soon they're both squashed into the helicopter with Tim at the helm. The air is cold as they take off, and colder still as they climb. Susan tries to hide herself from the temperature by pushing behind Mark; it's good to have his body to shield her.

"Missed you last night," she says in his ear.

He replies without turning back. "No, you didn't. I looked in ten minutes after you left, thinking maybe I should join you, seeing as no one else had come back to the room. But you were sound asleep."

The flight is quick and they're soon on the ground. The other stockmen are already mounted and heading out for the cattle. Susan and Mark's horses, Bushranger and Firefly, are saddled and waiting. Mark holds Firefly's head. Susan swings up and he adjusts the stirrups to fit her.

"Just walk him round a few times and get the feel of him. I'll go and sort out my horse while you do that."

She gently nudges Firefly and he responds, walking out with a fast but smooth step. She pulls the reins. Too hard, she thinks as Firefly stops instantly—she mustn't forget his soft mouth.

He's incredibly sensitive to her commands and is fluid underneath her; Susan and this horse are as one.

Mark leads his horse out into an open area, making sure the ground is flat with no rocks or tree stumps. This is the horse that's been described as a firecracker. It stares at Mark, eyes wild. It's a superb creature, big but perfectly proportioned. There is a touch of madness in its eyes.

Mark pauses and whispers something to it. Whatever it is the horse seems to relax. Almost before Susan can see him move, Mark has put his foot in the stirrup and swung his body over.

She senses Bushranger is as shocked as she is that Mark has mounted so quickly. Bushranger bunches his muscles and then, abruptly, he is flying over the ground, head down, back arched, heels kicking behind: one, two, three, four, five bucks. Despite Bushranger's wild movements, Mark never shifts in his seat; he is grinning from ear to ear. The horse seems perplexed at the confidence of his rider.

Mark sits astride Bushranger, totally relaxed. "Are you finished now? Are you pleased to get that out of your system?"

Bushranger drops his head, as if nodding. Mark wheels him around, and Bushranger walks placidly over to Susan and Firefly. And that's it, a quiet horse and Mark with a big smile.

The morning is a huge thrill. Susan starts at the rear, but once it's obvious she can ride well, she's directed out to the flank to pick up and pull in the wanderers.

Firefly is wonderful; one minute they're at a steady walk, next minute, as a steer pokes out and makes a dash for freedom, Firefly explodes. From a standing start to sudden acceleration in one flowing motion, Firefly stays in perfect balance, and Susan barely moves in the saddle. Then, as he comes alongside the steer, he wheels on a pin, spinning to face the offender if it does not break back. A couple times he uses his body to push the animal. There is nowhere for the cattle to go. After a few seconds they each realise and return to the mob. Susan's directions are minimal; the horse knows his job to perfection and mostly she just goes along for the ride, although, as time passes and her confidence grows, she starts to give fine direction and finesse, her balance complementing the horse's flowing motion. From time to time she waves to Mark, mostly working the other flank, and he waves back, brimming with his own enjoyment.

It seems like no time has passed until the hills are opening, the valley is ending. A twinge of sadness pinches her; her time with Firefly is over too soon.

Half an hour later, they come into a large paddock. Just inside the gate are two vehicles, one station-owned and the other Mark's four-wheel drive. The billy is boiling, there's brownie on a plate, and Buck and another man are walking up to greet them. Susan swings down off her horse, feeling regret at the dismount; she could have stayed at this for hours yet.

"You've made good time," Buck says to her. "It's only eleven. Thought another half hour at least." From the corner of her eye, Susan sees Mark dismount. Bushranger nuzzles him.

"I see Mark has turned Bushranger into model stockhorse. He's one of the best horsemen I've ever seen, you know, a born natural. I've heard rumours he was a handy rodeo rider in his time. I've yet to see a horse beat him, and I swear he enjoys the challenge when they try.

"Anyway, the billy is boiled, tea's brewed. I brought your car out to save an hour of riding back to the station before you could get on your way. I thought I'd like a ride on my old mate, Firefly." He pats the horse's neck. "He's a good horse, isn't he?" he says as a statement of fact.

"The absolute best," Susan agrees.

Chapter 15 – On a Big River with Crocodiles – Day 27

Mark says it's a two hours' drive to Timber Creek, and there they'll meet a small aeroplane to fly them to a station airstrip located out towards the mouth of the Victoria River. Again, this will be a new experience for Susan whose past flying experience is limited to big airliners.

They'd crossed the Victoria River yesterday, near VRD homestead, at a place called Dashwood Crossing. It was a wide river in deep banks, but with only a small flow of fresh water.

Mark explained it was the dry season with no rain for several months. He pointed to a place, high up in the trees, where driftwood was trapped in the branches. "From a big flood a couple years ago, when eight hundred millimetres of rain fell in three days. It was the remains of a cyclone come inland."

"That's almost as much rain as falls in England in a year."

It's hard to conceive so much water flowing down this placid stream. The Northern Territory is a place of hidden surprises, things outside her imagination. Here the unleashed power of nature seems to be an almost everyday part of life.

Today they're heading down the river to a place near where it meets the sea. Before they left VRD Mark showed her a map and explained how, down there, the river is huge, approaching a mile wide. Over the next few hours, the tides in the sea beyond will rise and fall by almost thirty feet. Then, as the water in these vast estuaries adjusts its level, it will become a white-water river, like the ones she's seen in movies running out of mountains and racing through gorges, except here it's huge, brown, full of silt and salt, and the land is flat. It's also full of saltwater crocodiles, built on the same gargantuan scale as their river home.

As they drive, Mark tells her about their plans. It's clear what they have to do, but less clear why, or who they're doing it for. They're going to investigate the downstream reaches of the river, measuring rates of tidal water flow. There is satellite data, and flow modelling, but now they need to cross check the computer predictions against real data from the river at a time when the biggest tides flow. That means being on the river in one of the two days immediately before or after a new or full moon.

"During new moon tides the sun and moon are in a direct line on the same side of the earth, pulling the oceans together," Mark says. "This gives the greatest flows. People call these king tides. New moon is in two days, so either tonight or tomorrow are ideal to collect data. Tonight is best because the time of the tides in relation to daylight will be good. And I don't want this job to interfere with us having a final day in Kakadu and on the Mary River before you have to catch your plane in Darwin."

"What do we actually need to do?"

"We'll measure the flow rates both in and out in the five hours before and after the high tide. It has to be done in a particular stretch of river, near the river mouth. High tide is ten tonight. We need to be on the river from 5.00 pm to 3.00 am.

"We'll take close up photos of various points along the river and write descriptions of bank structure, as well as make depth measurements at various points. That part needs to be done before dark, when the tide isn't too high. Today, low tide is about 4.00 pm, a good time for photographs. Tomorrow's low tide is an hour later, closer to sunset. The longer shadows will make photography more difficult then."

"Do you know who or why they want this data?" Susan asks.

"All very secret but a whisper is heard that the company is in discussion with the Australian Government about construction of a tidal power plant, perhaps a joint project with the Department of Defence, who owns a huge block of land on the north side of the river, land old timers call the Bradshaw Run. It is very hush-hush, 50% speculation and rumour, the way of things with most commercial big businesses.

"I've been told the absolute bare minimum, just where to go and what to do. The work's come to me via a contact in the Middle East, someone I've done pipeline work for in the past. Whoever they are, they need someone they trust to handle the organisation, logistics, collect the data, and not tell others who might leak it, so not a word from you!"

Susan puts a finger to her lips. "Promise given."

I've chartered a flat bottom boat, with two blokes I trust to drive it. It has three great big outboards on the back. It will be stable in the running tide and can be pushed to 40 knots, though 10-15 knots is more comfortable. It also has a pile of high-tech GIS gear on board so we can log our track and record photos and measurements digitally. We also need to take manual measurements, to validate the digital ones and as protection for equipment failure. It's a lot to keep track of, and I need an assistant for that bit."

"It sounds complicated, especially at night, but I am happy to help if you think I'm up to it."

"Last night, after I agreed for us to help out at VRD, I arranged to fly to a nearby local airstrip instead of the original plan, which was to meet mid-morning at Timber Creek, going by boat down the river. Now we'll meet the other two men on the boat out there, close to the investigation site.

"These men are already on their way with the boat, setting things up, waiting for me to arrive. The nearest airstrip is next to the river and an hour's boat trip from the measurement site.

"Tomorrow morning I'll meet a company rep at Timber Creek to give them a verbal report and all the records like measurement sheets, boat logs and an external hard drive holding digital photos and instrument records. Every single thing is to be handed over, nothing kept.

"So, as I was saying, I need a technical assistant tonight, someone to write up measurements on sheets and keep watch over the instruments. I have a friend in Timber Creek on standby, but I wondered if you'd help me instead? Of course, if you just want to come along for the ride, I can ask her to come as well and do that job. What do you think?"

"I'd love to help. And I don't mind just doing a part if you need us both."

"I'm sure you'll manage fine on your own."

Susan has been so immersed in their conversation she's barely noticed their trip. Now they're driving into Timber Creek. It has a hotel, a few houses and a shop. Not much to see at all.

Mark pulls up outside the pub. "Won't stop. I'll just run in and tell Tanya, my stand by assistant, that I don't need her now."

He leaves the engine running and is back in a minute.

"She's pleased you're helping instead of her. Boats and crocodiles at night are not her thing."

Susan's glad to have Mark to herself tonight, but a twinge of anxiety is also present. Perhaps she'd be safer being with another person along. Then she recalls two others will be on the boat with them too, and her mind relaxes.

They leave the town behind them and, five minutes later, they pull into the airport. Really, it's only a shed and a landing strip. A single engine small plane waits out on the tarmac, the pilot standing alongside it checking a map.

In less than five minutes they're taxiing and then soaring into the air, flying alongside a huge river which Susan realises is the Victoria River. She sits in the front, next to the pilot, which gives her an amazing view. Soon the river swings away and they cross range after range of broken hills. After twenty minutes they descend again, coming back down above the river. It's a vast muddy torrent, heading towards a sea seen hazily on the distant horizon.

As they fly along the river Susan spots a crocodile so large it dwarves any she has seen before. It is slowly heading downriver, going with the flow, pushing a bow wave before it, its tail slowly waving behind. She points it out to Mark who nods and says, "That's the mother of all crocodiles. I hope it doesn't want to play with our boat."

Soon they reach their destination and circle for a landing. There are two men and a boat up a tributary a few hundred yards from the river mouth. That's their pickup, waiting to collect them. They make a low sweep over the dirt airstrip checking for obstacles and, a minute later, they're bouncing along it, braking to a fast stop.

A man drives towards them in a utility. "He's the Bulloo River Station head stockman, Bluey," Mark says. "He's caretaking for a month. At a pinch we could have walked the mile to where the boat can collect us, but it's very nice of him to give us a ride."

They exchange brief greetings then the pilot says, "Must be away, tourists for scenic flights in Kununurra, this evening." He taxies out and flies off. They watch him for a minute but soon are driving past the station homestead and following the edge of the Bulloo River towards their boat. In another minute they arrive.

Mark shakes Bluey's hand. "Many thanks, I owe you one. Next time you're in town the shout is on me; just tell Tanya I said so."

"No worries, mate, pleased to help, know you'd do the same in return. How're you getting back from here?"

"Boat will bring us back up the river to Timber Creek when we're done. Should be in town for breakfast or thereabouts."

Their boat moves alongside the bank, and there are just a few feet of shallow brown water between it and them. Mark tosses his gun case to one of the men on board who catches it.

A plank, about a foot wide, is dropped from the boat to the bank, then a metal bracket is dropped over its boat end to lock it in place. "Instant boarding ramp," Mark says.

Susan takes a deep breath and walks across with only a slight wobble, looking straight ahead. Mark takes two quick steps on board. The boat backs up slowly. It's easier than turning around in the shallow river with the tide ebbing out. Near the mouth they have room to turn.

They nose out into the main river channel, and the current catches them. There is a roar as three big motors pour on the power. The boat skips across the surface. One man stands up front, keeping a close lookout, while the other steers.

Mark puts a hand on Susan's shoulder. "How are you travelling? Sorry to rush you so much. I always try to fit too much in. But you seem to take it in your stride. I like that!"

She smiles. "Actually, I'm loving it; you never cease to amaze me. Is there nothing you can't do and do well?"

He laughs, self-effacing. "I'm not always so good at the personal stuff; perhaps you've noticed. We've got another hour's run down the river till we get to where we need to be. We're heading for a place called Entrance Island, where the river narrows and splits into two channels either side. The tide is low now and will be at its lowest in just over an hour, so for now the river is placid. Later it'll be a different, particularly around midnight after full tide. It will get seriously dangerous and be hard to keep control of the boat in the dark with a raging water flow. So, while we have light, we need to run through our course and take photos before we start our measurements. I need to have a good look in the daylight and map out the hazards. It'll be much trickier in the night, so we need to know where not to go.

"Now, apart from getting our recording stuff ready, we should have a spell. It's going to be a long night. There's an Esky with sandwiches and drinks over there; you should eat. There's a bunk in the cabin. It wouldn't hurt to have a lie down; you won't get much sleep tonight."

Susan sits on the deck, eating a sandwich. Mark is busy unpacking and testing things. He suddenly points forward and calls, "See out there, a hundred metres out front at one o'clock, almost dead ahead."

It's a huge crocodile, almost certainly the one they saw from the aeroplane, swimming slowly downstream. Mark directs the boat driver to slow; they drop their speed, the engines barely above an idle.

They take the boat close to the west bank. "We need to stay downwind," Mark whispers. Slowly they ease alongside and then ahead of the crocodile.

It is probably two hundred yards away, maintaining a mid-stream position. In the binoculars it looks huge but, with nothing close by, it's impossible to get any good measure.

When they're two hundred metres past it, Mark directs the boat back to the centre of the channel, directly in front of the crocodile's path.

He signals to cut the engines completely. The boat's motion dies away. Now it just drifts along with the flowing tide. Mark takes the wheel. With deft touches he manages to get just enough steerage to maintain their line.

On and on comes the crocodile, seeming oblivious to their presence. Everyone remains totally silent as the crocodile slowly approaches, never breaking its steady pace, its tail continuing its leisurely wave. Fifty metres, then twenty, then it comes past a bare five metres from their boat. As its head draws level with the bow the tip of its tail is still a good metre behind the stern.

It drifts on by, its swimming continuing unchanged. Suddenly, when it has passed by a boat length, something must give it an alert, perhaps a tiny air eddy or a slight noise, nothing they can sense. An increased tail wave is the only sign it gives as it sinks and fades from view. They wait for a minute but see no further sign of it.

Mark signals to power on again and, in a minute, they've skipped past any place where it might have been.

Susan raises an inquiring eyebrow. "Well?"

"Well, our boat is twenty-four feet, so I put the croc at twenty-seven, maybe twenty-eight feet; I've never seen one quite that big before."

As they sit gliding through the water, Mark says, "There's another secretive crocodile on the Mary River, which is on the way to Kakadu, east of Darwin. It lives in a billabong in a place that only I know about and go to. It's nearly as long and just as wide the one we've just seen. I've only seen it twice. Perhaps we can go there tomorrow.

"You must have the gift of talking to Baru, Ancestor of Crocodiles, to bring this one out today. Perhaps, if you call out to the Mary River crocodile, it too will come out to talk to you, and we'll both get to see it again."

Susan shivers. It's an eerie thing for him to have said.

Chapter 16 – Running the Night Tides – Night 27

They round a bend in the river and see their destination before them, an island at the end of the next river stretch. They stop and anchor the boat while they get ready.

Mark finishes checking the instruments before opening his gun case and taking out a big, stainless steel revolver. He opens the chamber and inserts four heavy bullets, each as thick as her finger. Susan looks enquiringly.

"Just in case a large crocodile should try and come into the boat with us tonight. This is easier than a rifle at close quarters. I leave two chambers empty to ensure no one gets shot by accident." He places the gun in a brown leather holster that he straps to his waist.

Mark brings Susan into the cabin to familiarise her with the instruments. Even though he'll mostly operate them and call out measurements for her to write down, she needs to understand how they work, just in case she also has to take readings.

There's a GPS to log their position, plot their track and keep a record of their real over-ground speed. There's a flow meter, to tell the speed of the water as it passes the boat. There's a depth finder, which runs a continuous record of the depth below them. Finally, there's a side-scan sonar, which gives a reading of the shape of the riverbed.

Mark tells her they'll take up position just before the last big bend south of the island at five o'clock and hold steady for five minutes while they get a reference position fix and zero all their instruments. Then they'll go down the river, passing through the left hand or west channel and returning up the right side through the east channel, passing the island on both sides. As they reach their starting point they'll rerun their course in the reverse direction, going down the east channel, and returning back up the west channel.

When Mark's finished showing her the instruments it's time to start work. They complete a trial pass through both channels alongside the island and, as they go, they take and log photos of the banks and river structures: the islands, shoals, rapids, the places where rocky hillsides run hard along the river, the places of back eddies and the locations where there will be hidden obstacles as the tide rises.

Mark takes the photos and Susan logs the positions. She also practises quickly and neatly capturing the written records they'll later require. It is systematic and demanding work, like keeping track in a laboratory. She's well at home with her task and proud of what Mark says is an important contribution to their work.

She learns how to use the barrage of equipment, along with how to work with the men driving the boat, the hand signals to use to manoeuvre slightly, how to anticipate the drift and Mark's needs as they do their work, the subtleties of the boat, tides and hidden currents.

They return to their starting point, meandering with the currents, waiting to begin their real work in the running tides. They cruise next to the north-eastern bank, in a place where big hills run up against the river.

The afternoon sun sinks slowly towards a horizon of a near cloudless sky. Below it is the thin crescent of a near new moon, a faint shadow in the sky. A fresh water soak trickles out of the hillside, the water glistening as it flows over a narrow strip of sand to the river.

A big boar pig is drinking at the soak. It stands still, head down in the water, slightly back from the river's edge. Susan looks away, watching a flock of low flying geese wend their way upriver, flying a tight vee formation, with strong wing flaps.

Violent squealing rends the air. They all look around. The boar and a huge crocodile are locked in a death struggle. Somehow the crocodile has caught hold of a back leg of the pig and is dragging it towards the water. The pig's screams of terror are pitiful.

Mark watches with a rapt expression on his face. He seems to be communing with the crocodile, oblivious to the pig's suffering. Revolted, Susan turns away. The awful screams go on and on. At last the noise ceases, as the pig and crocodile vanish into the murky river.

Mark's fascination scares her to her core. She can't say why. She recalls the words of the Top Springs bartender, who said it's as if some part of Mark holds a kindred crocodile spirit, a sort of crocodile brotherhood of shared souls.

When the noise ceases the ordinary Mark returns. But in her memory the chilling vision remains, as if some part of his human soul is missing, replaced by that of a crocodile. He calls the carved crocodile he keeps a totem, but it feels more like its crocodile spirit lives inside him.

They get back to work and the hours fly by in a dizzy blur. As daylight disappears they turn on a barrage of spotlights. Now starlight is their only companion outside their pool of brightness.

At first, they run with a rising river; the flow surges ever higher, the shoals hidden, the mud banks gone. Fish flap on the incoming tide, waters flood into side creeks, low banks overflow. It slows and it slows, and little by little this power of water goes slack. Several crocodiles swim along the edges, mouths open, feasting on the in-rushing fish.

At ten o'clock tide and time stand still. They straighten up and walk around the boat for ten minutes in the slack tide. Sandwiches and drinks are passed from hand to hand; they refresh bodies and clear their minds.

Then they begin again. Their first run is relatively gentle, the water in a full but steady flow. It starts to surge as they come back up river. The second run becomes fast and dangerous. The flow through the narrows now sounds like a muted roar as water rushes through the constricted passage. By the time they finish it's past midnight.

The third run downriver is scary. The water thunders through, all sound now blurred and buried below the endless noise assault of cascading white rapids. The boat feels like it's flying. It's hard work to steer safely and keep the boat clear of shallow edges. There is a constant danger of grounding and flipping in the falling tide.

On the return leg, the three motors scream in their effort to maintain speed against thundering water. The helmsman's job is hardest now, trying to hold a steady course against the buffeting flow. At times water surges come bursting through, flinging the boat sideways like a cork. It seems that they must surely be overwhelmed by the raging river. The fourth run is easier; control slowly returns to the boat as the overwhelming power of the river subsides.

By now they're all exhausted, buffeted by the endless movement, eyes gritted with strain. The last run is easy but seems to take forever. Finally, they come back to where they started. They pat each other on the shoulders and backs. Susan doesn't believe any of them thought it would be so hard. But they've done it and are proud of their success.

Mark takes the helm. He tells his two men, who for long hours have alternated between helmsman and spotter, to stand down and each take an hour for sleep. He'll drive the boat and Susan will watch out.

Susan sits in the bow and watches the river flow past. But her work isn't needed now; the river is wide and the passage is easy. She moves to sit alongside Mark. They drive this way until 4.30 am, the darkest and most silent time of night, enjoying the peace as the steady thrum of the motors push them ever on.

The early morning, with the even pulse of the large engines, and the muted rush of the river, seems an ideal space for them to talk in a meaningful way.

Susan chooses not to question Mark's past. Instead, she gives him space to volunteer his own small pieces. He tells a story about an uncle, his mother's brother, who he barely knew, taking him to fish on the Brisbane River; he recounts the thrill of the first fish he caught and of how proud he was when his uncle allowed him to drive the boat.

He tells of a time when a friend from school invited him to their farm in the country, his pleasure riding horses and going rabbit shooting in the fields, two things which have remained great loves ever since.

Susan recounts how her parents bought her and her brother a horse each, which they rode at weekends; she remembers her joy in walking out in the Scottish Highlands alongside her father as he hunted, fished and taught her about the land.

She tells Mark about the first time she killed a deer—the waiting, the nervous anticipation as she held her aim, the instant ecstasy of success, and the poignancy of the moment when she realised what she'd done as this magnificent creature lay dead before her. But then the pride as, with her father, they brought it home and it provided a feast for the whole family, her grandparents and her cousins.

Mark nods as if understanding, then says, "I think most people are hunters at heart, first admiring the prey, but taking pleasure in the kill and enjoying the feast that follows."

Mark describes working as a research assistant in Kakadu, where, for many nights, they had to go out and catch large crocodiles to sample for heavy metals. He tells her about the dangers of pulling a three or four metre crocodile alongside a small dingy to take their samples.

"Weren't you scared catching such big crocodiles from a tiny boat? Couldn't one pull you out into the water or tip the boat?"

"Maybe, but you learn tips from old pros, first tie up their mouth. The muscles that open their jaws are weak. They tire themselves out after a minute and stop fighting. The crocodiles you don't see are the real danger."

"The one you showed me on the Robinson was so freaky. I don't understand how something that big keeps so still and can be so silent. It makes my hair stand up thinking of it."

"You wait until you see, up close, the really big one I've told you about in the Mary River. The first time I saw it was after I caught a big barra. I'd sat there fishing for an hour and seen nothing, not even a bubble. I'd just caught a couple of little fish. Then I caught the barra. It was almost as big as the one Vic caught the other day. It gave a great fight. I only had a light line, and it took ages to land. But, finally I got it in, then killed and cleaned it. It was a female with a belly full of eggs, and I felt sad I'd destroyed all those future baby fish. No point wasting all that fish food though, so I threw the innards into the water close in to the bank where the little fish had the best chance of getting a share. I sat down to watch what came to feed, expecting maybe a hawk or all the tiddlers. It was only a metre from the water's edge, and I was no further back. A tiny ripple made me look up, and I found I was looking right into the eyes of an enormous crocodile that I could nearly reach out and touch. It seemed to be trying to talk to me so I opened my mind to listen.

"The crocodile said, 'You are of my totem; you belong to my tribe. Thank you for your gift.' It surfaced fully, ate the food with one delicate swallow, and slid out of sight back into the watery deep. It could have pulled me off the bank and eaten me as well, but it didn't. Instead I felt as if I'd found a brother, that we shared a common bond.

"I came back many times and never saw it again, although I could feel it was still out there somewhere. Then finally, one day, about a year ago, I shot a small pig, about the size of those from the other day. I decided to offer it to the crocodile and sure enough it came again, much like before. It told me then, 'One day soon you will return to me. And you will bring another too, one who is special to you.'"

"That's a strange thing to say. What's it mean? Is it safe?"

"Of course. I will mind you, and my totem will protect me."

It makes an odd sense to Susan that this crocodile is Mark's kindred spirit, his soul brother. It's weird but not really scary. It never tried to harm him when it could, so that must mean something. Perhaps his totem does really keep him safe. But she feels a part of his life follows in the crocodile's footsteps, sharing its incredibly secretive nature. She senses something in the hidden danger and power of large crocodiles, their remorseless predatory behaviour, has captured Mark's mind, making him impervious to other suffering. That thought makes her anxious, even though she cannot believe he would harm her. Still, a shudder runs through her.

To break the mood she says, "Tell me the name of another woman who was your lover, one you really liked."

She sees hurt deep in his eyes and thinks he won't answer or will tell her a lie, but after a pause his gaze connects with hers. "Her name was Bel."

"What did she look like?"

"She looked like you."

"What happened to her? Where did she go?"

"She went away, to a place where I could not follow."

Susan wants to go further, to ask what he means, but the pain with which he says it is too raw. What is it about those words left unsaid?

If she lets herself think about it, the idea will freak her out. She looks again into his eyes. She sees hurt and remorse, not danger. She believes his eyes speak true. She takes his hand and squeezes it. She wants to take away the suffering she sees.

They sit in silence for a while.

Time rolls by along with the river. Susan begins to yawn and can't stop. Mark calls the men and returns the controls to them. He directs Susan to the bunk, and he lies on the floor. She falls into a deep sleep, only waking when the boat slows to a stop.

It is bright with early daylight. They have returned to Timber Creek. The boat pulls up to the bank just behind the airport where the car is parked. Mark returns the pistol to his gun case, now locked away, unneeded. He packs up the record sheets and computer drives to bring with him, and arranges for all the other high-tech equipment to be stored.

Susan and Mark climb off the boat and follow a path from the river that brings them up to their vehicle. They're both mussy, yawning with tiredness. They barely speak until they reach the car. As they sit inside they agree it was a night to remember, a night of discovery of the river and of themselves.

Chapter 17 – Truth – Day 28

They drive back to Timber Creek in silence, too tired to talk. The night has sucked their vitality. With a night on their feet, and the buffeting river, their bodies are both hungry and exhausted. They need breakfast; their only food since yesterday morning has been sandwiches and a piece of brownie.

"Let's eat breakfast first, and then I'll meet the company representative, pass on the data. After that we can drive towards Katherine a short way and find a place to roll out the swag, under a shady tree until lunch. We both need a good sleep."

Susan nods her agreement. She isn't capable of much more than that.

Mark orders an extra strong coffee with his meal to clear his head for his business dealings.

Susan can't push away an odd anxiousness as she eats her breakfast of eggs and toast. She can't place the source of this as waves of tiredness sweep over her. "I'll wait in the car while you meet the rep," she says.

As she climbs into the car it comes to her. She needs to check her messages, to see if Anne has replied. But she doesn't want to; she's so tired, and it all seems like too much effort.

Fumbling around she finds her phone and switches it on. There's barely a signal, so nothing can get through. She lays her head on the seat. As sleep comes she feels her phone slip from her and drop to the floor.

She barely stirs when she hears Mark return and feels him place a pillow under her head and move her into a more comfortable position. She's only vaguely aware that the car has started and they're driving.

Her mind half registers a phone ping as they drive away.

Susan hears Mark yawn and feels the movement of the car slow to a halt. A shadow passes over her eyes. She hears Mark's door open and close, and shuffling in the back. Then Mark is at her door. Susan feels strong arms lift her body from the seat and lay her down on the swag that he's put out.

She stretches out, aware of the soft comfort of Mark's body next to hers. She cuddles in to him.

It feels near midday when Susan properly opens her eyes. She lies for a minute looking at the green foliage above her, dreamy but waking, feeling refreshed. She notices they're parked under a large shady tree in a green grassy area, which falls away down to the bank of a big river, probably the Victoria.

Mark still breathes deeply beside her. She will let him sleep.

Her mouth is dry, so she goes to the car for a drink. Seeing her door is part open she detours to close it.

The shine of her phone on the floor of the cabin catches her eye. She bends to pick it up. As she touches a button the screen lights up. There's one new message from Anne.

Susan's heart skips a beat, and fear and burning anxiety surge. She doesn't want to know. She climbs into the car and closes the door, needing privacy even though Mark has shown no signs of waking. The message reads:

Dear Suz,
This FREAKS me, what I found:
Those girls came to Australia but are missing.
USA one came 2 years ago, last seen Airlee, Qld, 6 months later.
UK one came last year, last seen Adelaide, SA, 1 month later.
Both listed as missing, but not under current investigation

Investigation summary —
  - Girls may have wanted to disappear
  - Both withdrew most of their cash before they left
  - Both announced they were going on a trip — never seen since left
  - Did not say where were going or with who

- No current links between cases
- Last contacts followed up, no useful information
- Both girls seen meeting unknown man soon before last seen.
- One friend thought man's name Mark — no such person located
- Parents are convinced of abduction or worse
- Re Fiona Rodgers, that was her real name. But everyone called her Kate — her dead sister's name from when a little girl — weird — and she looks a bit like you — double weird!

This all makes me scared — Be Careful!!!
Take extra care if you meet a Mark.
Love Anne

Susan rereads the message three times. Her hands shake; she is totally freaked. The pattern and name match.

Who has she told where she's going? Did she tell anyone about Mark?

No and no!

What is his real name, or even his real car registration?

This is beyond stupid. She has to get away. She might disappear too.

Her mind races; she needs a plan. Can she leave now while he still sleeps?

She looks up. Mark's face is right there at her window.

Susan feels the blood drain from her face; her heart stops; her mind is struck numb with terror.

He's looking at her; he's looking at the phone.

She can't move.

Mark opens the door.

He puts out a hand for the phone. It's not a request.

Susan's hands shake, she pulls the phone away. Too slow.

Mark grasps her hand, prises her fingers away from it. He takes it in his hand. He seems more puzzled than angry. But of course, he doesn't know what she knows.

He looks at the message from Anne, scrolls up and down it.

She watches his face transform, first from puzzled to incredulous, then to something like rage, but far more chilling, and finally to something that looks like anguish or grief.

She can't take her eyes from his face, can't look away.

He stares, fixated, at the phone. He doesn't look at her.

Time passes. Finally, he lifts his head.

Susan quails at his stare. Something incredibly dangerous lurks in the depths of his eyes. Seconds tick by. He just stares and stares and does not speak.

At last a word comes. "Why?"

She hears anguish in his voice but is too terrified to answer.

"Why?" he repeats.

Again, Susan can find no words.

Mark's temper snaps. "Why could you not leave it alone?" He says it roughly. "Why did you need to know so badly? You knew I didn't want to tell you about the bad things in my past." His voice catches. "You promised to stop asking, and now this!"

Susan sits there mute; she tries to look down, anything to break the spell of his hurt eyes.

Mark reaches towards her. Hands like vices grasp both her arms just below the shoulders and lift her from the car. He stands her on the ground, her back to the car. She wobbles; her legs do not work. She holds the car for support.

Marks seems to struggle to master his rage. He pushes his hands to his sides, clenches and opens his fists, muscles corded with emotion. He looks at her face, his eyes boring in.

"Look at me and tell me why?" Mark says between gritted teeth. "And how? Did you search my bags? Did you look through my papers? What?"

His accusations hit like slaps, his anguish like punches.

Maybe he's right. Did she really need to know? Couldn't she have let it be? Why her? Why now? Why him?

In her final question she finds her answer. "Because I need to know; a man has captured me, heart, body and soul. I need to know who he is."

She pauses. "In answer to how, the passports. I found the passports. I didn't set out to find them. I was looking for matches to light a fire. I found a metal box and opened it." Susan's words come quickly. "Four photos of beautiful girls. You had their passports. They'd come to Australia, but their passports had no exit stamps. What was I supposed to think?

"Then the matter of who are you? There's a Mark Butler, a Mark Brown, a Mark Brooks and a Mark Bennet. They all look like you, all have the same initials, all have matching numberplates and licenses. Which one is really you? Are any of them you? Are none of them?"

She laughs bitterly. "Perhaps you're Robert Redford and live in California? Perhaps you're a freak with four name changes or a multi-personality disorder. Tell me. Who are you?"

She doesn't give him a chance to answer.

"I tried to ask you, but you wouldn't tell me. Instead you got so angry. But despite everything I'd found I couldn't believe you were capable of this. No, not you, not the Mark I know, not the Mark I love. He's no monster. But I had to know." She gestures wildly to her phone, which is still in his hand. "That's why I sent this text. I asked someone who'd actually give me answers."

Mark doesn't respond. His chest heaves with feelings she can't interpret.

She drops her voice to a softer tone. "Is it true? Did you know these women? Did they come with you like I have? Did they lay with you just like I have? Did they give you their bodies like I have? I bet they trusted you, the same way I thought I could. And then what, one day, you decided you'd had your fill? You got bored? When you finished with them, did you finish their lives as well? What's wrong with saying goodbye? Couldn't you have let them go? Or did they know something the world couldn't know, just like I now do?

"Did you kill them out of convenience? Or for excitement, the thrill of the hunt? Did you shoot them for sport? Did you tie them up and watch them die? Did you do it with a smile?"

There's no going back now. She can't believe the tidal wave of rage burning in her veins. Her mind sees her anger flaming all around her, her hatred for who he is and what he's done overtakes her reason. His betrayal is overwhelming.

"Are you just a murderer, or a sadistic rapist pig as well?" she spits.

Incredulity sweeps his face along with simple blind rage.

He draws back his arm.

Susan knows he will kill her.

A fist, closed tight, knuckles white, aims straight at her face.

She knows she should move but is rooted in space.

A death wish is present to die in this place.

The fist halts, a bare inch from her face.

Her calm, graceful embracing of her end has stopped him.

Now they both stand staring at each other.

Susan's will to defy him is undiminished.

Her anger is still flaming. She spits in his face.

Outside her body, she sees his other arm swing, palm open.

The blow hits her cheek, knocks her sideways. With hands at her sides she hits the dirt with her face. Leaves fill her mouth.

She lies there for a moment, stunned.

Her anger ebbs away and fear takes its place.

She rises to her knees, facing away from him. She tastes blood in her mouth. She looks back to the car.

Mark is turned away from her. He opens the car door and searches for something.

Susan tries to stand and shuffle away. She stumbles. The numbness in her head makes her brain foggy.

Mark grasps her hands from behind. He forces something around her wrists, pulls her backwards and upwards with rough hands. A hand grasps her hair and pulls, the back of her head is against his chest.

He holds a roll of heavy silver tape in one hand. With his teeth he pulls back the end and rips off a portion. He rolls it over her mouth and around her lips and chin, leaving only her nostrils exposed.

"That will stop that filthy mouth of yours," he spits.

Next, he takes a rope and ties her legs together; she knows she will fall flat if she tries to run.

Then he lifts her bodily into the passenger side of the car and shoves her onto the seat, with her hands jammed behind her back. He winds both windows down slightly, then closes and locks each car door.

She looks out to see what he's doing.

He seems uncertain what to do now; he leans with his head against the driver's side door. It's the first time she's seen him look dejected and uncertain, as if confused by the situation he's found himself in.

Despite her anger and fear, she still feels pity and tenderness towards him. She senses he's in uncharted waters. It's as if, before, whenever he was threatened, he hit out and responded to threats with aggression. But now he needs another way forward.

There's nothing in how he's acted or what he's said that tells her this. But it's the way she makes sense of the little pieces about him that she sees. Like an insight from when the first pieces of a jigsaw start to take a defined shape.

Still, she must find a way to get far away from him.

She doesn't think he'll try and harm her here, so close to where people have seen them this morning. She figures first he'll drive somewhere else. That's when she'll look for an opportunity to escape. She has no plan yet but must wait to see what chance arises and take it.

After a minute of standing there, Mark seems to form a decision and moves away. She can half see him in her side mirror as he rolls the swag up. Then she sees him carrying it and she hears and feels, rather than sees, as he loads it in the back.

After this she cannot hear or see him anymore. She doesn't know if he's moved away or is just sitting quietly, somewhere out of sight. For now, there's is nothing she can do except wait and see what happens.

Chapter 18 – Captivity, Searching to Escape – Day 28

Being tied up and gagged causes an overwhelming rising panic. Susan struggles to breathe; she feels she will suffocate. She wants to retch but is scared she'll choke on her vomit. Then her mind reasserts control and she calms herself. If she takes slow steady breaths through her nose she is fine.

Sitting squashed into the seat, barely able to move, time passes very slowly. She tries to count in her head, but it's hard to think straight and she keeps losing track. She focuses on the dashboard clock. She doesn't know why it comforts her to have a sense of the time, but it does; it gives her a feeling of connection to a wider reality.

As her panic abates she begins to discover how utterly uncomfortable she is. Her face and lip, where Mark hit her, are numb. But feeling is returning, a tingling sting at first, which turns into sharp pain, combined with a headache that throbs from the force of the blow. The way he's taped her mouth shut pushes her cut lip into her teeth, and the tape has hard edges that dig into her face. Together it's like her face is on fire.

What sort of bastard is Mark to treat her like this? Then it comes to her, in an almost funny way, that if this is the worst she has to endure, it's not that bad. She's heard the stories if others who have experienced far worse.

She's never thought about real prisoners and torture victims before; they endure things much worse for weeks or months on end. Susan can't comprehend that scale of pain, after how long these few minutes feel. To fully understand this or worse going on for that long is beyond her.

She tries to wiggle around and reposition herself, but there's no comfortable way to sit. With her hands locked behind her she is pushed forward in the seat, a posture causing her back and shoulders to ache. Her hands and wrists are hurting too, jammed against the seat, the sharp edges of the cuffs poking into them.

The air coming into the cabin from the cracked window means she won't suffocate or get too hot but, with the gag, she is unable to shout out. Mark clearly knows what he's doing, restraining her like this. He must have practised this sort of thing before. She can't reach the door locks with her hands behind her and, with her feet tied, it's almost impossible to move around the cabin sufficiently to get at the door handle. Maybe a contortionist could do something, but it's beyond her. Still, she tries in desperate hope.

After a while it becomes clear it's pointless to waste fruitless energy. She's better served saving her strength until a more promising situation arises. She'll only exhaust herself if she struggles too much. Mark wouldn't go to this much trouble to confine her if he planned to kill her right now.

She tries to figure out what Mark is likely to do and what her realistic options are. It's not likely he'll let her go; she knows far too much, and she has told him so.

She knows at least four of his identities. She has good grounds to believe he's done something to four other women. If she's honest with herself, she thinks he's killed them. The logical extension of this is that Susan is destined to become his next victim. Yet it seems too abstract to grasp that somehow her existence will just cease.

She pushes away her fear so she can try to understand Mark, make some sense of what he might plan for her demise. A truly chilling thought strikes her. It comes like a jolt of insight, the picture in her mind now turning her insides to jelly.

She knows what he'll do. He needs her body to disappear.

If it's found it will prove she is more than just missing. It will prove she's dead. And it will yield evidence that will connect her to Mark. His DNA covers and embeds her.

He has a deep, abiding love of crocodiles and a seeming fascination with watching them kill things. She saw it last night with the pig, and then he explained it further when he told her of his crocodile brother.

Susan shudders, revolted. She doesn't want to acknowledge her mind's picture.

But it makes sense; he'll take her to that place where he knows of an enormous crocodile, somewhere on the Mary River, out near Kakadu. He talked of gifting a pig. It will be her. Her body will fill the belly of this crocodile. She will disappear.

None of her family or friends know where she's travelling or who with. She told her cousins she was going to Alice Springs. But she misled them about her plans from there, indicated she'd catch a bus on. She made no mention of meeting anyone.

If she fails to turn up for her return flight home, it won't be clear for a while that she's really vanished. People will think it's just as likely she's gone another way, perhaps met someone and travelled to another destination, maybe even chosen to vanish.

Her parents might not believe this, but others might. The story will be that she had broken up with her former boyfriend and come to Australia for a change. It's common for people with bad memories to run, to drop out for a few months and then reappear when it suits.

If they investigate and discover her travel in the outback with a man, they'll also discover her affair with David. People will assume she was having a series of liaisons as she travelled across Australia. David, Mark, then whoever came next.

Mark could simply say she left him for the next one; that she went off with another man. Why would anyone doubt him? They were seen to be affectionate together, but relationships between travellers come and go, like the people themselves.

There are so many missing people and, without evidence to lead the way, the police can only investigate a handful.

She thinks about where she's been with Mark and how averse he is to public places, the likes of airports and town centres, places with security cameras. Sure, he met her in the Alice Springs Mall, but he was wearing cowboy clothes with a big, broad brimmed hat, which he has never worn since. With the hat pulled down there would have been little view of his face. Not to mention that his car was parked at the back corner of the car park where CCTV was unlikely.

At Yulara, when they checked in, she'd stood well behind him and had not interacted with any of the hotel staff—her mind had been on getting to their bedroom. Was it even clear she was with him? He hadn't acknowledged her presence; he'd pre-booked with a voucher, and who knows what name he'd given. Once she'd gone to the room she barely came out. They'd eaten breakfast together there, but the restaurant was crowded with tourists, so she was unlikely to be recorded or remembered amongst all the other visitors.

The best chances to connect her with Mark were the handful of station people and miners who'd seen them together, but very few of them were likely to read newspapers in towns, and television watching seemed a rarity. Even if her photo made it to the TV news or newspapers, it seemed unlikely anyone would realise and connect her to Mark, particularly if many weeks or months had elapsed.

She thinks of her phone; that is something to cause him concern. Someone could make a connection there. It ties her to both Timber Creek and Borroloola, and there are good odds someone would remember them together in one of these places.

Has he become careless with her? It seems like Mark was more careful with other victims, making sure to leave no clues. Does that mean something about their relationship is different? Or maybe he's got overconfident. It seems there's a slim chance he could be connected to her, but it's far from certain.

That's why her body needs to disappear, and it's also why it can't happen near here. Somewhere like Mary River makes sense, provided they arrive at night without being seen.

To do that Mark will need to avoid major towns, like Katherine, where the chances of his movements being tracked are much greater. He'll take the back roads and, once they get there they won't stay long, as he won't want to be sighted.

No doubt the next night he'll in Western Australia with a plausible story about how he left her to catch a bus, and then went the other way. No one saw anything bad happen between them; everyone would say they got on well together. If he says he dropped her off to catch a bus, who would doubt it? She'll be just another missing person, gone to ground somewhere in Australia, so many places, cities, and states to choose from.

Her mind is wandering. This endless speculation about how she might be traced won't get her anywhere. That future time, after the event, will be no use to her by then. She needs to turn her mind in more productive directions, think of what she can do here and now. How can she find a way to get away?

An hour passes; she's hot and thirsty. Sweat trickles down her face. If only she'd had a drink *before* checking her phone.

Before she can think anymore, Mark is back. He silently appears at her door and unlocks it.

He looks at her first with what appears to be a combination of tenderness, sadness and confusion. That fades to a blank stare. His anger is no longer visible, but Susan almost wishes it was, rather than the detached coldness he radiates now. He gives a minimal shrug, which seems a small part regretful, like he'd prefer not to harm her, but which also seems to say that now it has come to this, he'll do whatever's needed without remorse. His ability to put emotion aside frightens her. She averts her gaze, determined not to let her mind connect with him.

He starts speaking to her. She's so locked within her own thoughts it takes her a few seconds to realise.

"I'm going to take your gag off, provided you don't start screaming. There's no one to hear, but it'll go straight back on if you do. Do you agree?"

Susan nods, eyes fastened firmly to the floor. She won't meet his gaze, because within any contact lies only madness. She needs to keep her mind locked away from his ability to do harm, so she can stay calm.

He pulls the tape off her mouth. He isn't gentle. There's no kindness in his touch. Maybe he too needs to put distance between them.

She must try and appear calm, not ask for information, not beg, not become dramatic or desperate. It was her calm, after all, that saved her from his fist earlier.

Without the gag her breathing is better. She feels less cut off. She tests moving her mouth around now it's free. Her lip stings but otherwise it seems to work fine. "Are you still angry with me?" she asks.

He grunts, doesn't seem to know what to say, or perhaps he's just choosing not to answer.

She tries something specific. "Could I have a drink please?" Her tone is polite, as if nothing's unusual about her situation.

Mark nods gruffly and turns away. He returns with a pannikin of water. He will have to hold it while she drinks. This is difficult, and the water slops down her front.

"It would be easier if you'd release my hands for a bit or lock them in front."

Mark pulls a key from his pocket, reaches behind her and unlocks one cuff. When she moves her hands to the front he relocks them in place. Susan takes the cup, finishes the water, then hands it back.

Without another word Mark shuts her door, gets into his side of the car and begins driving. After half an hour they cross a big river, following a road crossing that goes through a couple of feet of water. It must be the Victoria River.

He has a map open on the seat between them. It seems as if this route isn't familiar to him as he occasionally gives it a glance.

Surreptitiously Susan looks too.

There are few roads marked in this country, so now, by a process of deduction, she can begin to guess where they must be going. Once she works this out, she starts to follow the topography on the map, where the hills are, where they cross big creeks and rivers. Checking the car's trip metre helps her gauge how far they're travelling.

They'll have to travel along station roads through a no man's land, going around the west, then the northwest of Katherine, in order to avoid the town. It looks like a long, slow drive.

There seems little point in trying to escape in the middle of this nowhere land. She guesses the road they're heading for crosses the Daly River near Pine Creek. It looks like a water crossing, not a bridge, perhaps a causeway. She remembers that the Daly River is famous for barramundi fishing. Maybe there will be fishermen, tourists or some other option at the crossing? From where they are now it looks like about three hundred kilometres until they reach it. It will be late afternoon by then.

Until then, she'll behave as normally as possible, to try and lower his suspicion. Then, if she sees anyone when they arrive at the river crossing, she'll open her door and fling herself out onto the crossing or into the water. Her door isn't locked, and her hands are to her front, so she can quickly work the door latch. Even if the water there is deep she should be able to kick her way to the side.

More importantly, she'll be able to shout for help, as her mouth isn't covered. It's hard to imagine Mark would harm her in front of other people. If the Daly River gives no chance of escape, the next opportunity will be Pine Creek. As it's a proper town she doesn't think Mark will chance reaching it until dark. Still, perhaps if he drives down the main street, she can fling herself out there and be seen.

The afternoon passes slowly. They traverse miles and miles of bush roads. Mostly she can follow where they are on the map, using a combination of distances and features. They make occasional river crossings. A couple of vehicles pass by in a cloud of dust, going in the opposite direction. Each time Mark accelerates and passes at speed, so she realises that, even if she shouts, she won't be heard.

They stop only once for a toilet break. Mark releases the bonds on her hands, but her legs remained tied. She shuffles away and relieves herself. When she returns Mark passes her a cup of water. She gulps it down and he refills it. "Thank you."

Mark nods, a minimal acknowledgement. She presents him with her hands to be cuffed again. He seems surprised by this. Perhaps he would have left them undone. But it's important to her plan that he thinks her well restrained, so he will be less attentive. Him being relaxed will be the only way of getting away, should the chance arise.

They come to the bank of a big river. Based on time and appearance, this must be the Daly River. The light is fading, but it's not yet dark. She can't see right down to the river, but she can make out well-used camping sites.

Mark parks. He gets out and walks to the top of the bank, where the road falls away. He looks back repeatedly, keeping an eye on her. He seems relieved that she stays there, unmoving. He surveys the river, as if assessing whether it's safe to cross. After five minutes he returns to the car. Instead of proceeding across, he drives off-road, following the edge of the riverbank along for a few hundred yards. They sit and wait until darkness fully falls.

Now they return and cross the river. No other people are in sight. The frustration makes Susan want to cry.

Desperation and fear grow inside her. Soon she sees the lights of a town, Pine Creek. But they pass its turnoff without stopping. They never even slow, and there are no signs of any other human life around.

Just as Susan starts to think it's hopeless, Mark slows and pulls over to the road verge. One wheel is making a flapping noise. A flat tyre. They're only a couple miles from the Pine Creek town turnoff.

Now Mark is occupied she has her chance.

She watches him in the mirror. His attention is fully focused on undoing the tyre. She sees headlights appear on the horizon, a vehicle approaching. It crests the rise and heads towards them; its bright lights blazing forward are all she can make out.

The lights and noise of the vehicle's approach are the perfect distraction as she opens her door and jumps out. Like a kangaroo she hops towards the middle of the road.

All at once she realises this is no car, but a huge road train bearing down on her. It's only a hundred yards away, and it shows no signs of braking. The driver hasn't even seen her; she must get off the road. Mark seems unaware.

She tries to hop, but in her need for speed her balance is gone. She pitches forward onto the tar road, just managing to get her hands in front of her to protect her face. She tries to lift herself and crawl, but there's no time. Now the truck driver has seen her, and the brakes are screaming, but it's too late.

Mark's attention is suddenly on her. He moves fast, scoops her up and lifts her aside; then the truck is upon them. As it passes Mark waves and gives a thumbs up. The truckie waves back and powers on.

"You stupid bitch! Are you trying to get yourself killed?".

She sits on the road edge where he dropped her and cries tears of rage and frustration.

"You miserable bastard! Why would you care? By tomorrow it won't matter whether I'm alive or dead with what you're planning. I'd rather let the truck hit me than be your captive."

Mark looks at her with frustrated rage. First, he says nothing, just shakes his head, then he says, "You do my head in. You think I'm crazy. Well, I've got nothing on you."

He picks her up and throws her on the back tray. He climbs up beside her and opens the cooler door, bends in and removes the few items inside. It's almost empty, just a small Esky holding a bag of ice and a couple of bits of food, pushed into the corner of the big cooler. It isn't even cold.

"You won't suffocate in here; there are air holes in the top." He lifts her again and tips her, head first, into the space. A minute later he throws in a pillow and blanket and slams the door shut. She hears the lock click.

Five minutes later the car starts. It spins around, going back the way they've come. They drive on a smooth road for a minute. She feels the car slow and turn. Now they're driving along a rough dirt road to God-knows-where.

Chapter 19 – The Last Night – Night 28

The bouncing goes on and on. At first Susan tries to brace against it and protect herself from being thrown around, but it's impossible; Mark is driving fast and recklessly. He brakes late into corners, bounces over holes or rocks and swerves roughly around apparent objects. Susan supposes she should be grateful for the pillow and blanket he threw in as a seeming afterthought. At least they soften the bumps.

With her hands cuffed in her lap she has only her legs to hold on with and use to manoeuvre. And, as they are tied, that is difficult. Her bare feet get no grip on the smooth fibreglass. She tries to sit up; the roof is a few inches above her sitting head. But the box is too wide to rest her feet on the other side. She finds herself slowly sliding back down.

She manages to turn to sit sideways, using her knees and bottom to brace. But a big bump flings her against the roof, bashing her head and causing her to bite her lip. She tastes blood. A second big swerve and bump slides her along and smashes her into the far end of the box.

She lies on her side, letting herself be flung with the movements. Her head hurts where it hit the roof, her face hurts where Mark hit her, her lip stings, her hands throb from being banged against things and her wrists are painful where the cuffs catch at and chafe the skin. Her whole body aches from being twisted, flung around and being forced into unnatural places and spaces. It seems hopeless.

She lets misery overwhelm her. She cries, almost silently, though she can't stifle an occasional gulping sob. Then she lies in a mute and numb state for long time, seeking to remove herself from this time and place. Her mind goes off to other places—her safe family and friends, her cousins in Sydney, other people she has met.

How could it have come to this? How did she end up as the next victim of a cold, calculating psychopath? Terror twists her insides; Mark's killed four women. What's one more? Any feigned softness is his psychopath's ploy to disarm his victims.

She hates the darkness inside this box. It is utterly pitch black; she can't even see her hands in front of her face. She'd like something, anything, to look at, to help push away the creeping dread rising in her mind, threatening to overwhelm her.

She fears the loss of her sanity. If she lets terror take over she will be a crazy blathering idiot, fit only for a lunatic asylum.

Hatred rises as she thinks of Mark. His friends seem to like him—they mustn't have any idea who he really is. He charms the girls too, but it's a smooth charm outside, and a callous and rotten one inside, like an apple full of worms.

But Susan isn't dead yet, and she's determined not to die as a passive victim, not to make it easy for Mark. She uses her anger to help focus her mind and push away the pain. She may be lying in the dark, but her mind has come alight, teasing at the edges of possibilities, seeking openings she might influence, ideas of how to survive and hopefully stop Mark from ever doing this again. If she isn't destined to live through this, she will try to finish Mark off too. She will be the last victim.

Can she find poison and put it in his food?

Is there some way she can make the car crash? Ideally on a public road where a rescue would be called for?

Susan senses that he wants her body to go to the crocodiles; that he gains perverse pleasure in feeding these monsters, these mindless, remorseless consumers of flesh. It didn't bother him to watch the crocodile grab the squealing pig last night and drag it into the water. She'd watched, both enthralled and revolted, but Mark seemed to gain only sadistic pleasure in letting such violent nature take its course.

If he tries to throw her into the water, perhaps she can pull him in too. There is even a small chance the crocodile will prefer him to her, a long shot, but she will think on it.

She's filled with terror at both the idea of being killed and how he might kill her. Will she scream as the pig did when a crocodile seizes her? Will he smile watching her body get dragged under, or torn apart?

What she really needs is a weapon. If she can injure him in some way—any way—then a chance may come. While she knows her ideas are all improbable, she doesn't care; thinking gives her purpose, and this helps to push away the fear.

She must appear confident and unafraid, maybe act a little cowed to appear unthreatening. She refuses to be a submissive victim, consumed by terror. Slowly it comes to her; she has one weapon over Mark that he can never take away — his sexual attraction to her.

She started to grasp how powerful it was that day at Robinson River. Then, as the initiator, she began to understand the power of her body over him. Even now she can stroke and fuel his desires. Perhaps she can make him act recklessly in a sexual encounter. Maybe it's the opening she needs.

It's a plan of sorts: stroke, seduce, satiate and strike.

Part of her mind, that place she calls morality, is repelled by this thought; a good person wouldn't act like that.

But there is also a perverse satisfaction of thinking about taking revenge through an act that also brings her pleasure. She can't deny that even to think of having sex with him still brings her excitement. A sexual thrill engulfs her as she imagines the hardness of his body within her as she drives her own weapon deep into him.

The car's rough passage smooths, and it feels as if the car's speed has increased. The road surface must have changed to bitumen. Lulled by the regular motion she dozes, waking occasionally. She loses track of time. Is it early or late in the night? Are they driving north, east or west?

She is extremely thirsty and wishes Mark had given her a bottle of water. But, with the thought of water, her bladder begins to ache. She tries to hold on and think of other things, but she can feel it leaking and her underwear becoming damp. The driving goes on and on, and she can sense no likelihood of them stopping anytime soon. She can't hold on much longer, so it's better to relieve herself with some control. It's easier to maintain her balance now the road is smooth. She manages a squat and, with difficulty, pulls her underwear down her thighs. She positions the blanket underneath herself in the hope of avoiding it sloshing around and wetting everything. As it flows out she feels both relief and a sense she has rescued a tiny piece of her own dignity and self-control.

She pulls her clothing back in place and curls up as best she can in the opposite corner, trying to ignore the smell of urine. She wraps her arms around her body. Hugging herself gives her a certain comfort, and she drifts back to sleep.

When she wakes again the car has stopped. What does it mean? Have they stopped in a town? Can she scream for help? Or have they stopped in the middle of the bush where no one will hear and screaming it will only make Mark angry, maybe make him gag her again.

She starts counting to one hundred. If nothing happens by the time she reaches it she'll quietly call out to Mark. If he answers, she'll ask him to let her out. She will ask nicely, even though an undercurrent of anger makes her want to scratch, bite and hurt him.

When that time has passed she calls out. There is no answer. She calls again, as loud as she can. His voice comes back, faint and muffled. "I'll let you out in a minute."

She feels a wave of relief.

Even though it's hard to tell, he doesn't sound angry.

There's a creak as the door opens. He is standing up on the tray with a torch, looking in, face lit by reflection. She tries for a smile and is surprised when he smiles back.

It's cold, but the air coming in is fresh and smells sweet. She hasn't realised how chilled she's become, immobile in this box for hours. She starts to shiver uncontrollably.

"I'm sure you're angry with me," Mark says, not unkindly, "and I hope your trip wasn't too bad. We're here now, at the place I wanted to show you, where the big crocodile lives.

"The locals once called this place Point Stuart Station. It's on the Mary River, east of Darwin, half way to Kakadu. It's a place people rarely come to. I've come through a fence with a gate that keeps the public out. It's getting late, an hour to midnight. There's no one around here for miles, so there's no point screaming."

Mark points some distance away from them. "There's a big billabong full of crocodiles, just over there. I *will* throw you in if you give me trouble. But, if you promise to behave, you can come out. I'll fix some dinner and you can sleep out here."

"Okay," Susan answers meekly.

He reaches in with both hands, grasps her arms and lifts her up. Her legs wobble as she stands, body poking forward out the door. She tries to climb over the doorsill, but without arms to steady her and with legs tied together, she overbalances and almost falls.

Mark grasps her and lifts her clear, setting her down on the tray. There is something almost tender in the way he wraps his arms around her. She is shaking like a leaf, and he seems to hold her tighter, hugging her to him to give her warmth.

Susan tries to push him away, but it's too hard with her arms trapped, and it feels so comforting.

His hands caress and stroke her back gently; it's almost as if he's forgotten what has happened.

She wants to forget too.

She should hate him—she does hate him—but for now, for a minute, she wants to be held and comforted. She cries, tears and little gulps at first, but soon she is sobbing. Mark pushes her face into his shirt and runs his hands through the back of her hair. She just wants to die in this moment of human comfort.

But a fierce independence flares inside her, fed by anger at what he's done. She pushes herself straight and, with all the pride she can find, says, "Thank you for letting me out. You can let me go now."

His hands drop and he steps back. "Okay then." He springs down, agile as a cat, and asks, "Shall I lift you down?"

Susan's dignity returns, and she hold her head up high. "No thank you. Just untie my legs."

He shrugs, bends to loosen the knots, and removes the rope.

Susan walks to the edge of the tray. She reaches out and grasps the side with shackled hands, lifts one foot over, feeling for the side rail. It's precarious, but she should be able to pivot and vault if she uses her hands for balance. Her feet get tangled. She overbalances and pivots forward, falling headfirst towards the ground.

Mark is incredibly quick. As she spears forward, he wraps his arms around her, pulls her to him, and sets her on the ground.

"That was a near thing. I don't want you getting hurt. I know this isn't easy for you, but it's better if we both cooperate."

Suddenly she's laughing. It is so ludicrous and funny, her likely murderer and lover, tender and careful for her safety, while treating her like a wild animal, tied up and confined to a box.

Then he's laughing too; they are both looking at each other and laughing; it can't all be real and true. Their shared laughter is like a circuit breaker. Neither can laugh and hate at the same time. When the laughter subsides, she holds out her hands.

"Unlock me please. Tonight, I'll cooperate; I want this night to be happy. Tomorrow is for crocodiles."

She collapses into another fit of giggles, and Mark starts to laugh again too, but he is restrained this time. It's as if he's only just started to think through the consequences of his actions.

He ignores her outstretched hands and gazes at her, a bitter smile edging at his lips. "Why couldn't you just leave it alone? I didn't want it to come to this. But you do know now and that can't be undone."

She looks at him earnestly. "Please, let's not talk about it right now."

He shrugs. "Well, tomorrow is tomorrow, tonight is now."

There's a sort of fatalistic sadness in his manner, tender, but also incredibly callous. She thinks this is the way he would look at a dog at the vet before the lethal injection was given.

Susan's bravery quails under this reality. But she rejects it.

"Tonight, I'll make a pact with you, which I'll honour. If you let me go I won't try to run away, and I won't try to hurt you. I'll help you cook dinner and I'll be your companion in the same way as before.

"But you, in return, have to tell me your story. Honestly. I want … I *need* the truth. You must tell me of the life you've lived, of what brought us to this place. It's something I must know for my own peace of mind."

Mark looks at her sadly. "I'm not much good at that kind of talk, but I will try."

He releases her hands.

They work side by side. There is something incredibly tender and intimate in this moment. Dinner is simple: bacon, sausages and onions fried up, with a tin of tomatoes mixed through. They eat from the pan, using a spoon. Sometimes they share morsels.

Susan leans against his side; he is solid and strong, like a tree. Without quite realising what she's doing, she puts an arm around his waist and lays her face against his chest. Tears run down her cheeks, and she pushes her face harder into him, feeling little sobs convulse her.

He strokes her hair and kisses her forehead.

She presses her lips against his, tasting tears and salt. "What would you do if we could make this all disappear?" she asks.

"I'd do what I'm going to do you, make love to you." He slides his hand down between her breasts and grasps the ring and locket on the chain. He lifts the chain from her neck and unclips the ring. With the ring in his hand he looks at her with great seriousness. "First, I would ask you to become my wife, if just for this one night."

She holds out her left hand as he slides the ring on it. "Yes!"

They lie together in the dark night. The fire is gone. They make love, and they make love again. When it seems he can give no more, she brings him back to life with her gentle touching and stroking. This time the loving seems to go on forever.

They hold on to each other in silent stillness. There are only a few hours until dawn. He pulls away but keeps his face towards hers. "I must fulfil my part of our bargain. This is my story."

Chapter 20 – Marco's Story – Night 28

"My real name is Vincent Marco Bassingham. Vincent was my father's name. Marco was the name of my mother's brother, who died young. My mother, who was Italian, called me Marco. At school it got shortened to Mark B.

"I liked this name better than Vincent because I hated my father, and I couldn't stand being compared to him. He was a big man, quick with his fists and his temper. Few people could stand against him. Those who tried came out much the worse.

"He would hit my mother, mostly slaps, but at times with a fist or a belt. She was terrified of him. He was a total bully.

"Once, when another man tried to stop him hitting her, my father almost killed him. When a policeman came to ask about it, my father told him to shoot through or he'd do the same to him. The policeman never came back.

"I was seven when my mum ran away; she seemed scared of him all the time and had to find somewhere to escape. My father was so mad at her for doing this. He said it made *him* look bad.

"It was a long time before he found her. When he did find her he beat her so badly she was taken to hospital for several days. She refused to press charges.

"The last time I saw her was the day she was discharged. My father told her she had to come home to look after me or he'd thrash her again, far worse than before.

"The next day she swallowed a whole bottle of pills and died. I only found that out years later. He didn't explain at the time why she wasn't there when I got home from school.

"That's terrible, to lose your mother that way. I'm so sorry. Was your father any better to you after that?"

"He went on with his violent drunken life without a backwards glance. I hated him, but I was frightened of him too. I could fight well enough at school, but with him I had no chance. He was three times my size and hit me with anything he found, belts, walking sticks, a horse whip, a cricket bat.

"Usually he went to the pub after work and got home too drunk to do anything. Sometimes the lady next door gave me dinner, but mostly I had to eat whatever I could find.

"I learned how to look after myself. I would shoplift, pick pockets, steal from store-yards and from people's houses. I almost never got caught. I thought it was really clever the way I could sneak in and out of all those places.

"But, when I was twelve, a policeman saw me stealing a block of chocolate. I was taken to the police station, but as my father was drinking and couldn't be found, a neighbour was called and took me home.

"When my father found out he flew into a rage and whipped me like a dog. My back was bleeding in lots of places. Next day, the police came and took me away. They sent me to remand school where I stayed for over a year.

"I thought my father was a bully. But he had nothing on the guys who ran the remand school. They'd line us up in a row for three hours most evenings. We had to stand still while they sat drinking beer. Every time someone moved they'd belt him with a long cane. They raped the prettier boys; they'd take them to their rooms and often two would have a go together. The boys would come out bleeding and crying. A few boys tried to run away, but they were brought back and beaten, really badly. Some tried to complain, but they got beaten as well, even worse. No one did anything to stop them."

Susan put her hand on his arm. "Did they do that to you?"

Mark put his hand over hers for a brief second then continued. "No, they never got me that way. I was a bit smarter and less good looking, with scars on my face from where my father had hit me. But I knew it was just a matter of time.

"One day I was caught by one of the biggest guys, a warden who I hated. He'd taken to hitting me when I wasn't looking. I was late coming down for school that day. I'd tried to hide away to skip classes but, as I came out of our room, there he was.

"He said it was my lucky day and he had a big surprise for me. When he took off his leather belt and started to unzip his pants, I knew what he was going to do. First thrash me with his belt then, when I was hurting too much to try and get away, he'd take me to his room and fuck me.

"We were right at the top of a big flight of stairs. No one else was around. He grabbed me by the ear, like he was planning to take me downstairs. He liked boys my age. He'd already done this to most others.

"At the top of the stairs he caught his part open pants on the rail. I saw my chance and gave him a big shove. He went flying down the stairs. When I got down to the bottom, he was lying there at a funny angle with his head facing the wrong way and not moving.

"I didn't know he was dead, but I was glad I'd hurt him because he was such a bastard. No one else was there, so I snuck off to school.

"When I came back, after school had finished that afternoon, the police were there asking questions. They wanted to know if anyone had seen what happened. Everyone said no, and they assumed he must have tripped, fallen and broken his neck. It seems they didn't notice his half-undone pants. Perhaps they thought he'd been to the toilet.

"After that I knew how to get rid of people I didn't like.

"Later that year I ran away and got a job working on a sheep station. One job was to help a man fixing windmills. He was a bastard too. He used to hit me with a big piece of hard plastic pipe whenever something went wrong. I was scared he'd knock me off the edge. One day he dropped a spanner from the high windmill tower and said it was my fault. He laid into me with the plastic pipe. I kept my head turned away and hung onto the steel frame for dear life.

"When he paused between swings, I grabbed it and gave it a push away, pushing him out to the edge. He tried to pull himself back as I held the pipe at the other end, but I pushed back harder and let it go as I did.

"He went over the edge, head first. I looked down and saw him lying, dead as a maggot, on the ground down there. Back at the station I told the boss he'd lost his balance and fallen. The boss was happy to believe it. I think he was relieved the bastard was dead too. He was a nasty piece of work.

"By the time I was twenty I'd got rid of three more blokes like him. Nobody asked any questions because each time, deep down, people were happy to see the end of them, and I'd got good at hiding any evidence. One even gave me a new identity; he tried to mug me with a knife and take my money in the car park of a casino in Darwin. I put the knife into him instead. Afterwards I found his car and license. His name was Martin Bennet, and his driver's license photo was pretty like me, so I adopted his identity which I shortened to Mart B. Nobody questioned it. He was scum anyway and was never missed. I even wrote a letter to his sister, copying his handwriting, to get a copy of his birth certificate.

"When I heard there was big money to be made in the Middle East, I got a job there running security for the pipelines.

"We'd get real smartarse robbers, mostly from Egyptian gangs, with no papers. They'd try steal oil and other things to sell. Our job was to make 'em disappear, the more permanently the better. We bumped off a few, dropped their bodies in empty wells, or shafts, places they couldn't be found. Word got around pretty quick to leave us alone. We would catch and kill another one or two every few months to keep things quiet.

"A guy I was working with got me to go to the Congo with him to do security there. There, as well as getting rid of men who caused trouble, the mercenaries could take any women they wanted, force them to have sex. If any got difficult, they were shut up for good. That's where I killed my first woman. She bit me when I was going to have her, so I hit her hard and accidently killed her. We threw her body in the river and it washed away.

Susan visualises a different Mark, a violent sadistic man who takes pleasure in brutally dominating and raping a woman. It hits her like a shock, so discordant from the man who sits beside her. Even when she saw the text from Anne, she never really thought of him like this.

Her words spill out vehemently without thought. "Do you mean you were going to rape her?"

Mark answers gently, almost kindly, "Yes, I suppose so. The other soldiers had taken turns, and now it was my turn. It was what happened to many women in that war. I can't pretend I didn't take part. They usually killed them with a knife when they were finished. I'm glad she died quickly from my fist.

"I've killed maybe thirty people since I was a teenager, mostly blokes, but a few girls. The blokes were bad bastards and bullies, and I reckon the world is better off without them.

"A couple of the women were tarts who tried to touch me up for money or things. One threatened to cry rape if I went to the police. Another took my personal possessions and valuable jewels. Once you've killed one, the rest are easy. Alive one minute, dead the next with a surprised look on their faces.

"Killing people is easy if you know how and don't care. You just need to be smart to make sure no one sees what happens or can identify you. Keep away from CCTV and all that sort of thing. Afterwards you make sure the bodies and personal effects don't turn up. That way they get listed as missing persons, whereabouts unknown.

"With backpackers, when they come out here, they go every which way. They rarely know each other's names, and yet they feel safe in each other's company. Provided they don't know who you really are, or where you're going, it's real hard for anyone to connect you to their disappearance.

"And, of course, lots work illegally and many choose to disappear for their own reasons, so it's always hard for cops to know where to start. I've picked up and made trips with maybe twenty backpackers in the last ten years

"Most have been great fun and we had a blast. Quite a few still send me the odd postcard to one of my alias addresses. A couple even came back for more on the side when husbands and boyfriends didn't know.

People are used to seeing me with women around the traps and, after a while, one girl looks much like another. Some women want to spread it around a bit, try miners and stockmen and the like. I reckon good luck to them and the bloke. When it happens, I leave them with their gear and wave goodbye.

"Only the odd one has been trouble, usually silly things. One demanded I stop the trip in the middle of the Queensland outback and take her back to the Barrier Reef, a thousand kilometres away. I said I was happy enough to let her off at the next town. She said if I tried to do that she'd go straight to the police and cry rape and abduction. I showed her where the road was and told her she could walk instead.

"With most of these girls I use a condom, so they don't get up the duff and try to claim paternity. But this one also said she was on the pill and not to bother. Now she was saying she wasn't really on the pill, she might be pregnant and would get a paternity test to prove it was me.

"I think she thought she could trap me into staying around with her. I would be her sugar daddy, and she could make me do what she wanted.

"I told her to stop being stupid. She spat at me so I belted her across the face with a backhander. Then the silly idiot tried to stick me with a big cooking knife, so I hit her, extra hard, and she didn't get up again.

"I dropped her body down an old mine shaft, then after I dropped a stick of jelly on top to bring down some rocks and make sure she was well covered. I put her gear in another mineshaft a few miles away. No one was likely to find it, but again I used a rock fall to cover it. She's the one in your text called Amanda. I actually did like her and afterwards I wished I'd ignored her whining and taken her back.

"I've got more selective over the last couple years. I really don't want to get into these situations. Now I just take the occasional one I really like for a trip and try to show them a good time. I'm a bit sad to see some go, but then another sweet young thing comes along, full of desire to see the real outback. Usually, by a week, they're ready to head on and I'm ready to be on my own again.

"But then you came along and it's different. The same in parts, the sex is good, you want to see the outback, but different as well; you try to find out who I really am underneath it all. I think, hey, she's starting to fall for me big time, and I am hooked too. You feel like the best person I've been with. I want to make it really special for you, maybe even try and find a way to keep you around for a long, long time.

"But I know it's not going to work because I'm one of those people who aren't good to stay around. Bad things always seem to happen, and I don't want bad things to happen to you.

"In another life, maybe we could have met like ordinary people. I could have got a regular job, and we could have made babies together and lived happily ever after. But this is the only life we've got, and I can't undo my past, and I don't see how we can get to that place from here.

"Deep down I'm one of those selfish people who doesn't want to give up the freedom I've got. I know one day I'll make a mistake and someone will take me down. But I won't let anyone put me away; I'll go on my own terms. I'm not going to spend my life in jail with a whole lot of perverts and bad bastards. A year in reform school was enough; I'm never going back to being locked up again."

Mark's story splits her mind and emotions into two parts. Part of her is horrified at his callous disregard for other people and their lives, while she's also filled with compassion for this man who has never had a real chance to be something other than a monster since he was a child.

She hasn't said a word over the last part as he's talked and talked. She doesn't follow everything he's said, but she gets the general picture; he has killed people, lots of people, including young backpackers.

It doesn't sound like he set out to deliberately do any of what he's said, but when he's in a corner, or angry, killing's the easy way out. His apparent lack of remorse for what he's done is chilling. She can sense a great evil in him. The way he feels a person's life can be so easily extinguished without consequences is shocking. After their death each person is left to one side and his life goes on.

But then, as a kid he never really had a chance, no parents or other role models to give guidance and affection, no love to anchor his life to. If she'd lived a life like that would she be any different?

But alongside this, and despite his difficult childhood, there appears to be a side to Mark that's genuine and decent. It's clear in his affection for his friends in the remote bush camps, his unsolicited gifts of meat and friendship with aboriginal communities. She must connect with the part of Mark where his decency, kindness and compassion live, encourage him to tell her what's special to him, what he loves, what gives him real joy.

"Mark, tell me about a time when you were really happy. Tell me something that makes you smile and feel warm inside."

He thinks for a moment. "When I gave you the ring at Heartbreak Hotel and you asked me to make love to you. When you sat beside me as we drove across the Murranji Track and we barely talked, but you gave me little smiles."

She wants to go down this path with him, but it's not the answer she needs. "I feel warm and happy thinking about those moments with you too. But I mean tell me something from before you met me."

He thinks again for a while and says, "Soon, after I first got to the NT, I got a job at the mine at Gove. The other white mine workers didn't have a lot of time for me because I was just a young wet kid. But there were a couple of black boys who worked there next to me. They came from a local town.

"We became friends, and they invited me to come back with them, to meet their families, their aunts, uncles, brothers and sisters. Soon I became one of the family, going fishing and hunting with them. They taught me how to shoot kangaroos and use a spear to catch fish, how to track animals in the bush.

"But, most of all, they gave me a sense of belonging. Since then I've always felt that the NT was my home, particularly this Top End country, though I love the desert too. Here was somewhere I was always welcome. I never had family in the city who took notice of me. But these aunts and uncles wanted to tell me their stories. Even more, they would sit and listen to my stories. I finally felt I was someone important.

"The most special day came a few months later. These boys, my friends, were having an initiation to become full members of their tribe. Even though I didn't have the knowledge for this, the elders decided that, on that same day, I should get a skin name and a totem to recognise me as part of their clan.

"They gave me their own skin name and gave me their totem, the totem of the crocodile. They told me that, as the crocodile was my totem, I had to look after crocodiles and the places where they live. To help me remember they gave me that carved crocodile spirit you've seen. It's the symbol of my totem.

"So, when I shoot a pig or other animal, I often give it to a crocodile. I kill many animals, but I try not to harm crocodiles, though I'm allowed to kill them if they threaten the people of my tribe or family as, even with crocodiles, there are bad ones.

"That's why I've come here; this place is really special for me. In this billabong, lives the biggest crocodile I've ever seen, until you brought out that one in the Victoria River. It's the one I told you about last night. He's very shy and hides away. But, just occasionally, he comes out. Once before he took a pig I gave him. That was my original plan for this morning, before this all happened, to go shoot a pig for him. Now I can't do that because I'll be leaving here early in the morning. But I'll see him and maybe I'll be with him when I go."

Only an hour has passed, but it seems like a year. Everything Mark has said is such a complex web of good and bad that it's hard to understand where truth and rightness lie.

He's done many awful things; most people would call him a sociopath or psychopath, someone without empathy to restrain his ability to harm. But there is also a good and decent place within him, a part that gives her joy and makes her feel warm.

Susan feels a Jekyll and Hyde split within herself too. There's part of her that loves him without limit, the part that has given him her promise with a full commitment to be his wife. But another part of her hates him with a violent rage for bringing them both to this place, where every choice presages disaster.

Now he's told her his story she must decide what to do. She grasps a moment of clarity. Keeping this love alive is more important. It must rise above hatred. She sees clearly what she must do from here.

She will go away, but she won't harm him unless he first tries to harm her. This will be her pact with the devil. She loves him, despite all he's done. While she must leave him, she will still maintain her promise to him, even when she returns home. His secret will be her secret too; she only needs his promise he won't harm any others from here on. And perhaps, as time goes by, they can try build a real life together out of the ashes of this day.

"It doesn't have to end this way, Mark. I love you and would never do anything to harm you. That's what the promise I made to you tonight with the ring means.

"I know you've done bad things, things I don't like. But it doesn't mean I will tell others. My loyalty to you comes first. I promise to keep your secrets provided you promise me never to harm another.

"So tomorrow I want you to take me to Darwin to catch the plane. I'll go home, but we'll still be friends, maybe even see each other again some time. My promise to you tonight will always stand."

Mark looks at her impassively, giving no sign. She can't tell whether he's in agreement or not. She talks for another five minutes, restating her case, trying to convince him.

Mark listens, silent, next to her.

At last all her words are said, her arguments done. "It's the only way we can go forward together without more betrayal and violence."

He remains silent.

"What do you say? Can we make that work?" she asks.

"I wish so, but no."

Hearing his words is like being slapped.

How can they have lived this night of their pact together, yet he still hasn't moved on, not stepped beyond here into a future which at least gives a possibility they can both continue their lives, even if they can't be together?

"It's easy to say you'll keep my secrets, but you can't un-know what you've found out, or what I've told you. What you now know will become a cancer inside you. It'll eat into you slowly, bit by bit. One day you'll have to speak out or it'll destroy you. It can't end this way.

"I'm going to bind you again for the rest of the night. Tomorrow must be what tomorrow must be."

Susan stands and puts on her clothes. She puts out her hands for him to replace the cuffs. He finds a long chain and padlock. He passes an end between her wrists and attaches the other end to the bull bar of the car.

It can't end like this! How can love grow and die in the space of a single night? Outrage builds inside her.

She doesn't want to beg, but she must implore him. It must come from him, forgiveness and freeing of himself so he can free her too. He's wrong about her, so wrong. She's determined to find the goodness at his core. She can't let it end this way.

Susan grasps Mark's arm to stop him walking away.

He stops and looks at her.

His eyes hold nothing, only chilling emptiness.

She implores with her eyes, not just begging for her own life, but begging for his soul.

He matches her stare, but nothing more comes.

She looks away. A month of her life has just ceased to exist as she knows she will herself when the new day arrives.

Mark walks away.

She is silent, just standing and staring at the endless sky. What is out there? Is there a god who can carry her soul to a place of peace? In the predawn sky there comes a tiny pinprick of light, perhaps a star. She wishes she could hold on to it and that it could help her find her own peace and salvation.

Susan lies on her bedding and rolls to the side to hide her face from this small but penetrating light. She doesn't feel she can stand its scrutiny, the scrutiny of a god looking into her soul.

Away from its light her mind refocuses.

The only one who can save her life is herself. She has no hope in Mark's words or actions, and no deliverance will arrive from the heavens.

Her chafed wrists bother her. She wants a comfortable place for them without the covers touching the raw skin. As she settles on her side, she pushes her hands out from under the covers. They rest in the dirt just past the edge of the bedding. She goes to pull them back to the softness of the bed. As she withdraws, her fingers touch something in the dirt; it's cold and metallic. She feels for it again. It's a piece of flat metal, six or seven inches long and an inch or two wide. It comes to a sharp point at one end. The other end is blunt and slightly rounded, like the inset of a knife into its handle.

That's what it feels like, the blade of an old fishing knife, dropped in the dirt long ago. Its handle has disappeared, perhaps burnt in a fire. She gets her fingers under it and picks it up. The point and edges are sharp, though jagged, as if pitted with age.

She's been seeking a way out. Now here it is. That cold bastard couldn't return her love, despite her begging. Now it's time for her to fashion her own destiny.

Mark's two different faces flash across her mind, one tender and loving, putting a ring on her finger, caressing her body, and the other with empty eyes that neither give nor receive anything.

One she cannot conceive harming, the other has no life force she can reach or touch. It's just a hollow shell.

Chapter 21 – Crocodile Destiny – Day 29

Susan doesn't know when she fell asleep, but she wakes in the early dawn light. Her dreams have been of otherworldly places, a collage of aboriginal dreamtime places, some warm and friendly like in meetings of these people she's been to with Mark, others dark and terrifying, filled with ancient predatory beings with the faces of crocodiles and huge vulture like birds that tear at flesh and feast on people. And somehow Mark lives in both worlds, two parts of the same whole.

Amazingly she feels refreshed, despite her limited time asleep, the awful dreams and the discomfort of the handcuffs and chain.

As her awareness returns, a deep knot of terror grips her in the pit of her stomach. How can this man, who has loved her so tenderly in the night, now be her executioner today?

Is this what it's like to be a prisoner on death row, knowing that only an hour or two of precious life remain, and there is an inexorable path forward to the end? Do other prisoners still have hope at this point?

She knows he'll kill her sometime this morning; she just doesn't know when. He'll want to pack camp and be away early, before others may be around. Will he feed her breakfast? She doubts her bubbling terror would let her eat.

Mark squats by the edge of the water looking out, his body almost motionless, but with a manner of intense concentration. It's like he's communing with the crocodiles of this place before he offers her as a sacrifice, following an ancient ritual to placate the spirit beings.

Should she pretend sleep, try to delay the moment? Her terror rises high, almost overwhelming her with panic. She needs to retreat to a place of calm, but she wants cry. Why couldn't she die quietly in her sleep.

There is something so utterly horrid in dying the way he plans for her. He really is a callous and hateful bastard. He could have hit her on the head while she was asleep and she wouldn't have to endure this.

Anger surges through her, and with it comes a ruthless coolness, allowing her to keep her mind in a calm place. While her nerve holds she must try to finish this. She must try to create a chance. She rolls her body over and feels to her side.

There it is, that piece of sharp metal, the old blade of a knife. It gives her a thread of hope.

She slides the knife into her knickers, laying it flat on her belly with the point facing down, sitting over her pubis. She just hopes he doesn't want to give her a last bang before he gets rid of her, one last quickie for good measure. She doesn't think it's likely. She senses that his mind and body have already moved on to another place, one where she, the living breathing Susan, no longer exists.

She makes herself sit up and rattle her chain. Mark looks her way. He seems agitated; perhaps he's surprised she's awake so soon. Perhaps he's not ready for her and the day, when dawn has barely come.

She tries to smile. A quick plan comes to mind.

She'll ask him to release her so she can relieve herself, and when he releases her she'll keep her back turned but remain in view. Then, still wearing her track bottoms and T-shirt, she'll say she wants to clean up and ask him to remove the cuffs so she can wash herself. She'll ask him for a bowl of water and a cloth.

She'll remove her T-shirt and track pants, putting the knife under her clothes pile, and start to clean herself, making sure to give Mark a good view of her naked buttocks as she washes.

She knows he'll watch her, and she will make sure it turns him on. She'll call him over, saying she needs his help to wash her back, and pass him the cloth over her shoulder. As he begins to wash her back she'll pick up the knife and turn towards him, keeping in close so he can't see it. She wants her breasts to be in front of his face, to have his eyes focus on her nipples.

This will be her only chance. When he's distracted, she'll drive the knife into his belly, upwards, just below the ribs, into that soft unprotected skin.

She needs a second weapon close at hand, in case the knife isn't enough. What can she use? She surveys the site and sees a piece of wood, a short piece of broken branch about a foot and a half long and three inches thick. If she stands next to this she'll have a chance to pick it up and use it, if needed.

She knows she must create real lust in her own mind to play her part convincingly. She mustn't rush the scene. She needs his desire to build and make him careless.

As she makes her plan it's as if she detaches from her mind and moves outside her body. She observes herself, as if from a great distance. She is a second Susan, one who watches and waits. Far away, her body double, is acting out her part.

Her plan seems surprisingly simple to set in motion, seen from afar.

Mark releases the other Susan from the chain when she asks. This other being walks away and relieves herself, looking out at the water.

"I need to wash myself," the other Susan says. "Could I ask you to bring me a basin of water, a washer and soap, please?"

Mark unlocks the other Susan's hands. He gives her a washer and soap. This Susan walks away, stops alongside the broken branch. Mark pours warm water into a basin and carries it over to where she stands.

She watches this Susan take the basin, hold it steady and place it in front of herself.

Mark steps back a few paces. She sees him watch this Susan closely as she takes off her clothes and gets ready to wash. She watches her double hide any view of the knife with her body as she takes it out and lies it on her pants, then covers it with her top, leaving just the tip of the handle visible.

As she begins to wash a sudden wrench pulls her mind back into her body. Now it's only her and him. She's really scared again. She knows she must do this all by herself; she can no longer hide from the reality of the actions she's about to take.

Mark seems distracted but, once Susan starts her wash herself, she can feel his eyes on her. She thinks of their lovemaking on that other river, the Robinson River. She lets it arouse her body, all the while keeping her mind locked away in a place of cold rage.

She spares a glance over her shoulder. Mark watches her intently, and she can see his arousal is growing.

She waves the washer and calls out, "Could you wash my back please?" Her voice is husky, as if throaty with arousal. It blends with her fear, giving a tremulous quality.

Mark approaches. She passes him the soaped washer then rinses her hands for a good grip. She takes the metal blade in her stronger right hand, knowing her body hides it from his view. Her hand has a tremor as she tightens her grip on the knife. She forces her mind to become calm and her hand steadies.

She feels the washing cloth, his firm but gentle strokes, working down and lingering on her buttocks. He reaches around with his free hand and fondles a nipple. God that feels good.

With her mind in a totally detached place she turns slowly towards him, her breasts almost brushing him as she faces him, keeping the hand holding the knife out of sight.

Mark's free hand stays on her breast; she can feel his panting lust. His eyes are totally on her erect nipples. His second hand now caresses her bottom.

She brings her elbow in under his arm. It's now or never. She focuses all her attention on the one movement she must make. With eyes turned down she looks at her target, that piece of soft skin a hand-width below the left side of his rib cage.

She takes a deep breath and brings her second hand to support her grip. With all her force she drives the blade in.

It's harder than she expects. Her wrists twist and buckle with the impact. But she sees the knife go in, almost all the way.

She feels a huge flinch of his body as he arcs back, bringing his hands up in shock. It seems to happen in slow motion, a slow silent movie without sound. His hands grasp for the knife handle. It's then she knows she must do more.

She ducks below his arms, looks to the side to locate the broken branch. Grasping it with her left hand, she turns and starts to swing, then adds her right hand for more power.

If he was quicker he could have blocked her. But both his hands are grasping the short protruding butt end of the blade, as if to pull it out. In the last second, he looks up. He sees what's coming. He moves to throw up a hand but is too late.

A look of puzzlement is on his face; it seems he can't comprehend how it's come to this. A trace of an admiring smile creases his eyes. His lips start to move, but the word dies unsaid.

The wood hits the side of his head with a dull crunch. It sounds like a thing has broken, but whether within the wood or in his head she doesn't know.

Mark falls backwards, hits the ground, doesn't move.

Susan looks down at this man; she feels awash with awful horror at what she's done. She doesn't know if his injuries are terminal, whether she has killed him.

But it can't end like this. She won't just leave his body lying here for someone to find, perhaps even rescue.

In a flash it comes to her. He'll take her place with the crocodiles. Perhaps his crocodile spirit will bring the big one out of hiding and his body will be its feast. It's awful to contemplate, yet fitting. Susan looks at him again; he hasn't moved.

There's a trickle of blood from his head and ear, and more blood around the knife end, but not much. Is he still alive? She doesn't know; she hasn't seen him breathe, but he's still pink.

She's feels she's carrying the weight of four dead women on her shoulders, acting on their behalves, as well as her own, as she lifts Mark's feet in her hands and tries to drag him to the water's edge without success.

It's less than ten metres away, but he's too heavy to pull, and her hands keep losing their grip on his thick ankles.

Susan moves to his head and lifts him to a half sitting position. She's terrified he'll wake up and grab her. Should she hit him again to be sure? No, that seems too horrible.

She passes her arms under his shoulders. Knotting her fingers together on his chest, with his head lolling against her, she uses her legs and pushes herself backwards, moving them both a few inches, then a few more, dragging him slowly. In a minute or two she's within a metre of the edge. She twists and rolls his body until his legs are in the water, then she pushes his head and shoulders with her feet until two thirds of him are in the water, his head and shoulders still on the bank.

In her panting efforts she's almost forgotten the danger that crocodiles might pose to her, so near the water's edge.

She looks up. There, no more than ten metres away, two nostrils poke out of the water, and a little further back a pair of eyes watch. The creature is clearly interested.

Susan backs up to the place where she stabbed Mark. She looks at the crocodile, then at Mark. Is it her imagination, or did his chest just rise and fall? There was a definite movement in the water where he lies.

But it's too late to worry. The crocodile is swimming purposefully over to investigate. It nudges its nose alongside Mark. It is big, around five metres, not quite as big as the one on the Robinson River, but a good half tonne. The crocodile bites at and shakes Mark's legs a couple times, then moves farther up the bank until it is standing over his body on raised forelegs.

It twists slightly sideways and grasps Mark around the belly, pulls him into the water. Now Mark is floating free, his limbs lolling about. The crocodile changes grip and moves its body in the water, turning Mark parallel to the bank. It opens its huge mouth and closes it down over his chest.

Snap, then crunch as ribs give way.

With almost leisurely ease the crocodile swims away trailing the upper body to one side and the legs to the other. It is half way back to where it started when there comes a sudden swirl. Another large crocodile, similarly sized, has come alongside and grabbed Mark's head.

They are now tearing at his body, pulling in opposite directions. Blood stains spread in the water as Mark is torn open.

Just when it seems neither can win, a huge splash and swirl comes crashing into both their bodies. A new crocodile grabs Mark's protruding torso and flings him in the air, half lifting the two other crocodiles from the water as they hang on.

Now tearing and ripping noises mix with the splashing. Body fragments and blood swirl around a thrashing cauldron. None gives ground but the weight is with the biggest one.

Susan knows this is the one Mark talked about. It dwarfs the other crocodiles, it is half their length again and double their combined weight. It's clear who will win.

A leg is pulled free, and one crocodile swims away with its spoils. Then there's a mighty tearing contest around Mark's head and upper body. First the head disappears, now there remains only a mangled torso, which the two crocodiles tear at.

With another loud rip, an arm and shoulder come free. The second crocodile abandons the contest, departing with its prize.

The remaining crocodile, contest winner, cruises around the floating remains, pushing them a bit this way and that. Then, with the upper torso just in front of its nose, it opens its mouth, grasps and flips the body into the air. It tips its head back, mouth wide. The body is gone in a single huge swallow.

The crocodile does a leisurely circuit of the area, a victory lap, then it submerges and vanishes from view.

The water is still.

For a few seconds a fine mist drifts over its surface, a last relic of the remains. Susan breathes it in, feels the tendrils invade her, and shudders.

Chapter 22 – Hiding the Shame – Day 29

The crocodiles are gone. She no longer sees blood and body parts in the water.

Susan's sensation of mind-numbing horror recedes a notch. Rising to meet it is an overpowering feeling of shame. She had thought, when she came to this country, that she was too smart for the backpacker abduction trick, she wasn't one of those silly girls who took lifts with strangers or put herself into vulnerable positions. Yet she knows, with absolute certainty that, if she hadn't found that old blade, she too would have joined that list of ugly statistics.

She's disgusted with herself. She has indulged in an orgy of sexual pleasure even after she had good grounds for suspicion about this man. Not to mention that she could have escaped on at least two occasions but still did nothing.

Then there's the matter of her conspiring to conceal evidence. From the time she found the passports she had the option of taking them to the police. She could have done that at Borroloola and brought an end to the uncertainty about the fate of these women for four sets of anguished parents.

Yet she did nothing, preferring to hope for an alternative truth about the man who captured her mind as much as her body. Only when her own life was a millimetre from extinction had she acted. But that was self-preservation, not real courage.

She looks at the morality inside herself and finds it wanting. She remembers talk of others, those who looked askance at the Germans during Hitler's time, the ones who saw nothing, did nothing and said nothing, despite the evidence right in front of their eyes. She's no better; when the test of her moral core came, she failed it, utterly.

Now she's reaping this whirlwind of her own actions. Despite Mark's awful deeds, was she entitled to be both his judge and executioner?

She can justify using the metal blade to escape; perhaps hitting him was also defensible. But as he lay on the ground, she knew neither whether he was alive or dead.

How can she justify pushing his body into the water for the crocodiles to finish? In her heart of hearts, she knows he might have lived. She could have taken the car, gone for help, or called the police if she didn't want to return here again.

She knows the real reason she didn't is because she simply does not want to face reliving her part in this. She doesn't want to be part of a police investigation into this hideous man.

In her heart and soul, she wanted him dead.

Partly it was to pay him back for her humiliation, partly to let it end, a small bit about what he did to others, but mostly it was because she doesn't want to give evidence, to describe his exploitation of her naivety, then to tell of her sexual and physical entrapment, which she actively aided and abetted.

She wants this whole ugly story to vanish; she doesn't want to have to tell her parents or friends of her cowardice and foolishness, nor to have testimony splashed over the tabloids, Australian and British, words like *British Slut, Murderer, Killer Feeds Man to Crocodile*.

She has cold bloodedly given this man his death-wish with crocodiles. She imagines his eyes opening, awareness returning, in those final seconds, as the crocodiles tore his body apart.

The worst part is that, despite the shame that tears at her soul, she's mostly glad for what she's done; she judged he was not fit to live and she acted on it. She remembers his words at Barrow Creek on the taking of personal vengeance when others do harm. It feels like a perverse moral rightness to use his own spoken words as justification for her deeds.

Susan's mind twists in another direction, one of relief and rationalisation. She's alive. Only she knows what's transpired. There is no need for anyone else to know. Nothing is served by telling the mothers, fathers, sisters or brothers of the other missing women of their fate, destroying any remnants of hope.

Her mind sees a way out. Her aeroplane doesn't leave until tomorrow morning. She can make the whole thing vanish. No one has seen her and Mark here. She knows he drove here in the night, coming from the other side of Katherine, with no stops. That was to avoid anyone seeing him, connecting him to her disappearance or to this place. It can work to her advantage. She's even more unknown than him.

The chance of his body being discovered, after the crocodiles finish, is remote. They've eaten the main parts. The fish will finish off any remaining last scraps.

Now she needs to move Mark's car to somewhere where it can't be connected with this place. All the residual contents of their trip together need to vanish into the bottom of one or more billabongs.

She understands about DNA and forensic evidence. She knows how to make detection difficult, if not impossible. The lab she works for does that sort of work. And, without a basis for suspicion, who will even look?

All she needs is a few hours with no one else in sight and she can pull this off. Even if someone arrives right now, there's almost nothing to see, nothing to arouse suspicion, and there's plenty more she can do to hide any traces.

What she needs is a careful plan to follow. Renewed energy from the need to do something decisive pushes her shock and lethargy aside.

She finds a notebook and starts to write out a list of all the things she needs to do. She tries to think of any sources of future problems and their solutions.

The campground—she needs to remove the traces of blood from the edge of the water and the ground where she struck him. She must ensure no items that can be connected with either her or Mark are left lying around. She'll do her best to get rid of footprints, tyre tracks, soil on or in the car or other things that may link her to the vehicle and this place.

The car—it needs to be abandoned somewhere else, somewhere with no connection to here. Perhaps it can take her to Darwin and be dumped there.

His personal effects—the clothes, food and personal items can be burned. The heavy items, firearms, camping gear and tools can go to the bottom of a billabong. Not right here, but if she takes them and spreads them out, up and down the river, the likelihood of anyone finding them or connecting them seems remote. As the guns have serial numbers that might be traceable to him, they should be dumped elsewhere.

Her own things—she realises her backpack and clothes have his DNA all over them. It will be hard to ensure it all vanishes. All but a handful of her things must go, either burned or thrown into the rubbish in various places. The things she needs to take home can be dealt with once she's back in England.

The car will have to be thoroughly cleaned to remove all traces of her presence and all other identification, either of her or the other girls. Then there will just be an empty car. She can't get rid of the cage or cooler box, but a good clean should see most traces gone. The cooler box will have to be cleaned extremely thoroughly, considering her time in there. No doubt particles of her skin, hair, blood, urine and more will be present.

And she'll need to clean the car a second time at her destination to ensure her DNA from the final trip is removed.

Once she nears Darwin, she can find a shop selling garbage bags, cleaning gear and unworn clothes to change into for her final leg home.

263

While she'll have to play some of this by ear, each extra step is another level of separation and security. Susan is determined to remove every last trace of Mark from her life.

First, before she does anything else, she needs to make it difficult to recognise or identify the vehicle in case anyone turns up while she's here. She retrieves mud from the river bank and smears it on and around the number plates, confusing threes, eights and other numbers with strategic dabs of mud. For extra cover she splashes the number plates with water and extra dirt to make them as near to illegible as possible. Then she takes the swag cover and a ground sheet, drapes them over the cooler box and cage on the back, to make these less visible and identifiable.

She also needs to make her own identity less obvious. She puts on a long-sleeved shirt and a pair of long pants. She ties her hair up tightly with a rubber band and finds a hat to wear to hide her hair colour. She mixes mud and soot from the fire with water and smears it over her face and hands to give her visible skin a darker colour. If someone turns up here and only glances at her this might help hide her identity.

With her plan made Susan starts her work. She adds branches to the smouldering coals of last night's campfire to create a big hot fire, one with plenty of flames to completely destroy all the things that will burn.

She does a thorough walk around the site, picking up all loose items, along with any rubbish, and piling them next to the fire, then she uses a shovel and digs up the bloodstained soil, which she puts in a bucket.

Keeping a careful watch for crocodiles, she walks towards the water, her heart hammering in her chest. She shudders as she comes close, determined not to be the next victim. There is no sign of life in the water, but she stands back a couple steps as she throws the bloodied dirt from the bucket in.

She goes back and levels off the dug-up patch then covers it with loose dirt and leaves. She scrapes at the place she dragged him over and then spreads more leaves over this faint track, until it's no longer clear. If someone looks hard they might see a few disturbed areas, but they are't obvious. She's happy that this deals with the most immediate evidence.

Next, she considers her own things. It's easier to begin with these. She removes all her possessions from her pack and separates what she knows she needs for her trip home.

She sees her packet of contraceptive pills and realises she's missed yesterday's dose. The thought of having a baby with that man revolts her. She takes a double dose of the pills. Surely, it'll be fine. A slight risk, yes. A missed pill means the effectiveness falls below 99%, but, surely, she wouldn't be that unlucky.

She puts the things she needs to keep in her small overnight bag, then one by one, she places all her other clothes on the fire and watches them burn to ash. It's cathartic to destroy links to this trip and this place.

She goes through the cabin of the car and empties out all the compartments, under and behind seats, and all the other places and spaces. She makes two piles: what can be burned and what can't. Piece by piece everything that will burn goes into the fire. She keeps adding wood and stirring the fire with a stick, to ensure no charred pieces remain.

Next come Mark's things. Revulsion ripples through her at the thought of touching them, but it must be done. First his clothes. Each thing she finds returns her mind the time and place where she saw him wear it.

There's a cap she doesn't recall seeing him wear, yet it seems strangely familiar. Somewhere, deep in her brain, it rings a bell of association, though she can't think why. It has a picture of a soaring wedge-tail eagle on the front, but the connection is out of reach. She throws it in the fire.

Sadness take hold of her when she picks up the cowboy gear that he wore on the day he met her in Alice Springs: a holiday that held such promise. Those good times are gone. She makes herself stop this remembering.

There's his leather satchel of papers. She feels obliged to open it, to check what's inside. It's still locked with a combination lock, and she has no idea what the number is. She finds a big screwdriver and a hammer in his tools and smashes the lock open.

She lifts out the pile of papers and goes through them one by one. Mostly bills and receipts relating to work; she sees the two names, Bennet and Butler, but not the others. After a quick glance she consigns each sheet to the fire. The main part of the satchel is empty, and she's about to consign it to the fire as well.

In a side pocket she feels something. She finds a pouch and a book. She removes the pouch. It's not large, just filling her hand, but it's heavy. She opens it. The contents spill into her palm. She gasps as she sees a pile of coloured stones of many types, sizes and shapes. She doesn't know much about precious stones but recognises that this is what she's looking at. There are probably fifty to seventy stones, ranging from a few millimetres in size to some as large as a man's thumbnail. She recognises the reds and blues of rubies and sapphires, and a golden one, perhaps a topaz. Some of the smaller glassy ones may be diamonds, and some flecked white and blue stones are probably opals. She recognises two milky blue stones, cousins to the ones Mark gave her. She takes the chain and ring from her neck and places these with the other stones. They all belong together.

Susan deliberates on throwing them away. They're clearly valuable, up to at least tens of thousands of pounds, she imagines. Some might belong to other people who've hired Mark to sell them. If so, they may represent the life savings of miners she met. While she doesn't want Mark's ill-gotten gains, she feels loathe to destroy the property of others. She'll keep these precious stones for now. She refills the pouch and sets it aside.

There's a second object in the satchel, what looks like a diary. Instant revulsion rises at the prospect of seeing Mark's deeper self as told through his own eyes. She holds the book in her hand, arm bent, ready to cast it into the fire. But, perhaps, there's something in here about her and why he chose her.

She flips quickly through the pages and sees lots of small entries containing dates, places and items relating to transactions. She sees the names Kate and Cathy a few times. Both names seem to be the same person. She realises with shock that these must be notes about the Scottish girl, Kate Rodgers. The other women are probably listed too. It seems awful to burn the last record of their lives.

She can imagine her body destroyed and hidden in a remote place, then someone finding this last record and casually discarding it, denying all future opportunity to those who knew her to learn of this last part of her life. While she doesn't want anyone else to see this and read of her shame, it's an ultimate disrespect to others to destroy a last remnant of their lives in this way. She will keep the book and hide it away.

Flipping to the last page, she sees her name. It must have been written within the last two days, perhaps last night.

> *Susan has really got to me. There's something so brave and beautiful about her. Why could she not leave alone? I don't want to do this, but now I must make the choice between me and her. What should I do? I must end it. It will be quick.*
>
> *Perhaps I should let her go, trust her, see what she does—can I take this chance? I fear her knowing will destroy us both. I think it is best for it to finish now, to let it be over, but my mind jumps both ways.*

She reads it, rereads it, and then she reads it again. Had he really meant to let her go, or did he just have doubts that he overcame?

Emotions of love and hate well up. She remembers his serious but gentle eyes. His ruthless psychopathic heart. Tears prick her eyes. She hates him beyond all thinking, yet she misses his smile. What a mess.

Susan looks around. Should she take this diary to the police and tell them she's made an awful mistake? If she does perhaps this mess could all be unscrambled. The diary is a record that tells anyone reading it of who he was and what he's done. With this to read no one will blame her.

But then, if she does, they'll confiscate the diary, use it as evidence, and she'll never get to see it again, except perhaps in court. She needs to have this for herself, whether to read it or not; perhaps there may be something in here to help her find herself again. She'll put it somewhere out of all reach, in a bank vault perhaps, maybe left there until she dies. It holds a story she can't casually destroy—that much she knows. Susan finds a handkerchief and wraps it around the diary, to separate it from the rest of her life yet treat it with respect. She places it in the bottom of her overnight bag, along with the bag of gems, and covers them with her clothes. The rest of his personal effects go in the fire: toothbrush, razor and shampoo.

She starts on the back of the car. Fortunately, the cooler box is almost empty. The inside smells awful. She takes out and burns the blanket and pillow she used last night. She carries a couple buckets of water and empties them into the cooler box; the cleaning part can wait.

Susan lifts each box off the back of the car and opens it. She creates a pile of non-flammables to add to the small pile from the cabin. Those items are all destined for the bottom of the billabong: knives, tools, metal boxes and cooking things. Steadily the pile grows. She fills a bucket with the contents from the pile and walks almost a hundred yards along the waterhole. She throws the items out in different directions. She repeats this five more times, each in a different place.

Now only the guns and heavy tools remain. They can go somewhere else, perhaps in a different billabong, somewhere along her route to Darwin.

One of the last things to do is to destroy the food. She's has left it for near last, knowing she may need to eat. She's probably been working for four hours, slowly and methodically, hunger forgotten. It must be past midday. She must make herself eat; she's starting to feel light-headed, with all her early morning energy long gone.

The thought of food brings Mark's face into her mind; they shared this food together so many times over the days before now. It was a part of their own private ritual, an intimate enjoyment of togetherness.

She can't let herself think of those good times. All that's left is the image of his face, devoid of emotion. She pictures his eyes looking at her in that way. If he'd killed her, she knows there would have been no recognition of her life force gone, no anguish, just cool dispassion as he discarded her from his mind and moved on to the next task.

She pictures the large crocodile carrying Mark's body in its mouth. That awful ripping and tearing, as all three crocodiles pulled and tugged, causing body parts to separate, the dismemberment of what had been a living breathing person.

A wave of bile rises insides; she retches.

Susan finds a cup of water and rinses her mouth. She has to keep going. She starts burning food. The smell is bad, but she pushes on. She empties metal tins and glass jars, the plastic she burns on the fire.

Only a quarter packet of broken biscuits remain, crushed in travel. She takes a piece. Her mouth is dry; she chews slightly then gulps it down with a mouthful of water. She repeats this with another fragment. Occasionally her stomach threatens to rebel, but each time she pauses, breathes deeply, calms herself, and takes another piece.

She realises she's totally forgotten about the most important thing, the thing that started this path to madness: the metal box with the women's passports and Mark's multiple IDs. Like the diary, she cannot burn the passports. That would be like killing the women a second time.

Susan thinks of throwing the box in the water and burning his IDs, then just bringing the passports away with her. But she knows that's a crazy risk. What if she's searched at airport security? Four passports, all of which don't belong to her, would spell disaster for her. There'd be no possible way of explaining them. By a process of elimination, she realises her only real choice is to hide them.

She carefully examines the area around her, looking for landmarks. There's nothing distinctive close by, only a big waterhole with a partly cleared area along its banks, perhaps where people have camped and fished. A few hundred yards away a rocky knoll rises above the ground. She takes a spade and the box and walks towards it.

The hill itself is bigger than she first thought, ten or fifteen feet high and about twenty yards wide across the base. It's also rocky and hard to dig. There are no obvious cracks or crevices to use as hiding places.

On the other side is a big flat rock, squarish and about a metre across. It sits low on the ground, just beyond the start of the rise, with clear dirt beyond it. She tests the ground there with her spade. It's hard but not rocky. She chips away at the surface. Her hands are blistered and sore, and it's hard going at first. But once she's down a few inches the ground is softer, a dark sandy loam. She digs down about a foot, hard up against the side of the big rock, which keeps going beneath the earth.

She places the box in the bottom of the hole and then sees another piece of flat rock, about twice the box's size, lying nearby. She lays it flat over the top of the metal box. It will reduce the risk of rust or water damage. She backfills the hole, pushing the dirt down firmly with her feet, and then scatters the remaining dirt around the area.

Not too bad, but a bit obvious if someone comes looking here soon. She puts another flat sheet of rock on top to hide the freshly turned dirt. With leaves to make it look natural, she defies anyone to know something's buried here. So long as she can find the campsite again, she can find this place again too.

It's mid-afternoon as she walks back to the car. Only two tasks remain. The first is to burn their bedding, the last remains of their life together. It's too personal; she doesn't want to burn these things, the objects of their lovemaking, but she can't stop now. She lifts the mattress and throws it onto the fire; it smoulders and smells awful, but eventually the foam burns through. She pushes the ends together until only a pile of sticky burning goo remains. The pillows, quilt and sheets follow.

As she picks up the bottom sheet her lace knickers fall to the ground. They're a symbol of their passionate lovemaking, even when trust was lost.

At the sight of the white lace, Susan's starts to shake and cry, the tears silently dripping down her cheeks.

She cries for herself and her loss of innocence. She cries for him too, the loss of his life and for her lost belief in his goodness. She tried so hard to believe he was good, could do no wrong. Now it's time to let that idea go. Eventually the crying passes, leaving her feeling utterly drained.

She picks up the knickers, looks at them one last time, and consigns them to burn.

The light is fading as the sun falls behind the trees. She's so tired she wants to lie down, but there's one last task to complete. She has to wash the car, inside and out.

She washes the hateful cooler box first. Five times she carries water, sloshes it around, empties and wipes the box out. Her arms are shaking with fatigue as she lifts each bucket, and her legs wobble with exhaustion as she walks back and forth.

She repeats the procedure with the cabin. Then she does the tray and cage, then finally, the outside of the cabin. She scrapes and washes the wheel arches and the underbody as best she can.

Now the daylight has faded to a red-pink glow. It's hard to see in the guttering firelight. She piles the fire up one more time. The groundsheet and canvass swag cover go on the fire, the oily plastic coating blazing brightly.

As she watches it burn, she strips off her clothes, throws them in the fire, and uses some water from the water tank, a bottle of detergent she saved from Mark's things, and a cup to rinse the grime and dirt from her body. She shivers in the cold night air, naked and vulnerable. Quickly she puts on the clean shorts and T-shirt she's kept aside.

Finally, Susan dowses the fire. In the dark she needs to be careful near the water. Cautiously she scoops a bucket of water out, but there are no signs of crocodiles. She represses a shudder as she thinks they won't need to eat again so soon; they have already feasted today.

She picks up the ends of the burning sticks and throws them in the water. Then she throws her bucket of water on the coals. It explodes with a great hissing. She repeats this several further times until little heat remains. She takes the shovel and uses it to carry piles of ash, along with any other fragments, to the water's edge, where she throws them in. When she's finished, only a slightly hollowed out depression remains where the fire has been. She throws several handfuls of leaves over this.

With the fire gone the mosquitoes are thick. She swats them away, but it's futile. She wishes she'd kept the insect repellent. There are noises of animal movements in the night. She desperately wants to be gone far from this place, but she makes herself do one last check around with the torch she kept. Nothing remains. She tears a branch from a tree and walks around, brushing dirt in all the places where she thinks they may have walked, trying to hide obvious tracks. She tosses the branch into the water, satisfied she can do no more.

As she looks across the water she sees a faint cloud of something sitting over its surface, mist like, but not quite. It eddies towards her despite the non-existent breeze. Involuntarily she finds herself breathing it in. It feels as if there's more in it than water laden air, as if a familiar presence is in the air attached to this place. It gives her a fleeting sense of Mark's grinning face merged with that of a crocodile. This air at the water's edge feels like a spider's web, sticky tendrils of nothingness catching hold of her skin.

She shudders and forces this awareness out of her mind, determined to let no residue of this place remain with her. She stumbles as she turns away, engulfed by weariness, driven in these last hours by need alone. She forces herself to stand straight. She must summon the strength to leave this place.

Chapter 23 – Escape – Day 29-30

Susan walks away from the billabong in the dark. It seems like the longest day in her life, and her body shakes with exhaustion. She hasn't eaten all day except for those few biscuit fragments. Now her work is finished she wants to crawl into a bed, lie under a warm quilt, curl into a foetal position and sleep.

She climbs into the driver's seat and puts the key in the ignition. Thankfully, Mark had left the key lying on the driver's seat. The last time she sat in this seat was only yesterday, but it feels like an unfathomable age before in another life.

Susan knows she must start the car and drive away, but waves of nausea and exhaustion flow over her. She will rest, just for a minute. She lays her head back in the corner of the cabin, against the headrest, and closes her eyes.

The horror of the ripping crocodiles swims before her eyes. With extreme effort she pushes the image away. She stays there, immobile, her mind numb, beyond thinking. She dozes and wakes with her head slumped sideways, her neck aching. Her hands sting from the chafing of the restraints and the hours spent cleaning, scouring and re-cleaning to remove all the evidence of herself from the car.

She sits up straight. Her head feels a bit clearer, and the fatigue seems to have faded. She must get going while her reserves last. She starts the car. The diesel engine roars to life. She lets it run for a minute to warm up as she checks the gauges.

Everything seems okay. She looks at the fuel levels. The main tank is down to not much, barely an eighth above empty, but the reserve tank still has over a third, and the light is on, indicating it's in use.

She finds the light switch. With headlights on she feels she can escape the darkness for a few hours. She hates this whole place but feels better within the solid mass of the car, engine throbbing and lights bright, as she sits locked in her cocoon.

She finds and engages the gears, lets out the clutch and heads away. She remembers now all the water she used to wash the car. It comes to her there may be tire tracks or footprints in the wet ground. With supreme effort she forces herself to stop, get out and go and look with the torch. Sure enough there are several clear footprints and a set of obvious tyre tracks for about five yards, until they reached dry ground. She scrapes at these with the spade until they're indistinct, then throws fresh dirt and leaves over them.

Now she really is finished. She knows there's nothing more she can do here. She drives off and picks up a track leading away from the clearing. She drives slowly, staying in first gear for a while, until she feels she has reasonable control. She changes up to second and feels the vehicle move more freely. Sometimes the track turns sharply, and she struggles to pick the direction in the headlights and veers to the edge of the road. Once she thinks she'll scrape the passenger door on a tree at the edge of a sharp corner, but she avoids doing so with a last minute swerve.

She has only a vague idea of where she is, but hopes she'll be able to follow signs to take her back to the highway, then on to Darwin. For the first couple miles there is a single track, which ends at a closed gate. It has a padlock on it, which hangs in place but isn't locked, and she's able to open it, drive through, and close it behind her. On the other side of the gate is a big sign saying: 'Private Property - Keep Out'. This fits with Mark's description of a private place. So far so good!

Now there are tracks going everywhere. It's hard to tell the actual road from yet another camping track. A couple times she picks the wrong route and ends up in a camping area alongside a billabong. At times she sees distant lights illuminating tents and turns away. She's starting to feel like she's in a maze, and the feeling frays away at her fragile sense of purpose.

Then a bit of luck runs her way; she's now on a main road going somewhere. After about fifteen minutes of driving she comes to a big gate on the road. She's terrified it will be locked, but it's not. She pulls the gate open and drives through. She's tempted to drive on and leave it swinging, but she forces herself to stop, get out, and close it properly. She leaves the engine running; the thought of stopping the car and being unable to start it again causes a wave of panic.

She drives on. The road is wide now, well formed, and almost dead straight. But after another quarter of an hour it ends suddenly in a T-intersection. The new crossroad seems to be an important road, but less so than the one she's already on. She has no idea which way to choose.

For no particular reason she turns left. The road goes on for a few hundred yards. Then, after some side-tracks come off it, it deteriorates into a track. Susan follows this, living in hope it goes somewhere but, after another couple hundred yards, the road comes to the edge of a vast open plain. No further road is in sight, just a large expanse of grass, which seems to run out to a river, miles away.

It's profoundly depressing to know she has to back track, but she's soon back at the main junction. She tosses up whether to return along the main road or try the other direction. In the end her need to be thorough overrides her desire for the ease of the big highway. She follows the other road going right. She's relieved when, a few hundred yards later, it ends in another gate. This time there is a lock she cannot get through.

She finds a place to turn around and heads back. Back at the gate on the main road she' sure this is the way out, so she drives on with renewed confidence. The road continues on past a series of minor turn-offs, heading in a consistently straight direction.

If she comes to another dead end, she'll want to cry, then lie down and die. But the road keeps going, on and on, as if forever. She checks her distance. She's driven twenty-five kilometres since the last gate. That means she must be going somewhere. Still the road goes on, further and further, seemingly endless.

At last there's a sign for an approaching T-intersection. Susan slows, almost to a crawl, as she reaches what she thinks is the intersection. Please God, let there be a sign. Desperation rises when she sees nothing in sight. Then the road rounds a final bend, and, gleaming in the headlights is a big shiny sign, pointing to Darwin to the right and Kakadu to the left. This new road is bitumen. The sign reads *Arnhem Highway*.

She nearly cries with relief. As she heads along this new road she sees another sign that tells her Darwin is 135 kilometres away. Tension flows out of her muscles, and a huge wave of relief and happiness rises within her. She's as good as made it. After another hour and a half or so of driving she'll find a place to rest before going to the airport to catch her plane home.

The road is straight and easy to drive. She passes a lit-up roadhouse called the Bark Hut Inn. She's tempted to stop, just to buy a drink, but knows she shouldn't let anyone see her around here in this car. She comes to a big river with the sign *Mary River* written on the bridge. She drives across it, watching a large expanse of clear dark water pass below. There are no headlights in sight and no signs of people nearby.

This river will make a good final resting place for the guns and other remaining heavy things. She stops at the far edge of the bridge, climbs out and looks around. Then she stands quietly and listens. Just bush sounds. This will do.

She picks up the box that holds tools, and one by one she drops them into the water. As she's carrying the last things headlights light up the eastern horizon. She quickly drops the remaining tools over and runs back to the car. She hops back in and starts the engine, ready to drive away if the vehicle shows signs of stopping. But it roars past and drives into the night, heading towards Darwin, seemingly impatient to be home.

Once it's gone, she takes out the gun case and false number plates. The gun case falls straight down like a spear, entering the water with a hollow splash. Next, she flings the six unattached number plates in different directions. It's like casting the remnants of Mark's identity to the four winds.

She drives on, happy she's taken a big first step towards removing this month from her life.

She concentrates on driving steadily, not too fast or slow. She passes a couple cars going the other way. The first time she forgets to dip her headlights, until angry flashes made her aware. After this she drives with the lights on low beam. It's easier than trying to remember, another thing for her tired brain to do.

The landscape starts to change, with signs of fencing and farms, indicating she's almost back to civilisation. As her anxiety fades the fatigue really begins to hit her. She finds herself yawning. What she most needs is a super strong cup of coffee. She pinches her face, moves her shoulders and jiggles her legs, anything to keep brain and body awake. She sees lights in the distance and then she's in a little town with a sign that proclaims *Humpty Doo*. She thinks of Humpty Dumpty, broken man, a character not unlike herself and grimaces. She forces herself on.

The next big intersection has traffic lights and a sign for Stuart Highway and Darwin to the right. She lets out a breath of relief—she actually knows where she is—the Stuart Highway is the main road from Alice Springs to Darwin. With Darwin barely thirty kilometres away, she decides she'll only drive for a little longer before she finds a place to pull over and rest. Although it feels like the middle of the night the clock on the dashboard reads 9.30 pm.

Soon she sees a big sign for a roadhouse and supermarket coming up. She pulls into the supermarket car park. It still has occasional shoppers—perhaps the place stays open until late.

She looks at her face in the mirror. Considering what she feels like inside, her face looks remarkably normal, a bit puffy under the eyes and hair a bit wild. She gropes in her bag and finds a comb, fixes her hair and checks her clothes for obvious marks. She takes a last glance around—no one is close. She steps out, careful to make sure she appears casual.

As she approaches the shopping centre doors they automatically slide apart. She steps into an overly bright, modern, fluorescent lit world. The air-conditioning is unexpectedly cold, and she shivers.

No one seems interested in her. She has about eighty-five dollars in her purse. That should be enough to buy some food, a drink, some cleaning gear and maybe some new clothes.

She picks up a basket and works her way around. She selects a small block of cheese, dip and biscuits, and a bottle of Coke. Next, she collects a plastic bucket, detergent, methylated spirits, cleaning cloths, disposable household gloves and a packet of garbage bags. She also buys two cheap sets of clothes consisting of track suit, T-shirt and socks.

There's a map of Darwin for sale. She opens it, memorises the directions to the airport and puts it back. It seems simple and she expects there will be signs.

She pays, returns to the car and drives on. After another few miles she sees a rest stop and toilet sign on the left, exactly what she's been looking for. Its only other occupants are a couple of large trucks; there is no sign of their drivers. They're likely asleep in the cabins.

After washing her face Susan sits at a little table outside with her cheese, dip, cracker biscuits and Coke. It's the first real food she's eaten in almost twenty-four hours. While part of her craves food, nausea still lurks just below the surface. She eats slowly, one biscuit at a time, with a smear of dip and a piece of cheese, chewing each with steady deliberation, and following each with a mouthful of Coke. A couple times her stomach threatens to rebel as nausea rises. But she calms herself with deep breaths.

After she's had her fill, she climbs back into the car, pulls the new tracksuit over her other clothes and curls up on the seat. What blessed relief it is to close her eyes and let it all go.

When she wakes up the cabin clock reads 3.13 am.

Time to get active again.

She opens the cabin and shivers in the chill air. Reluctantly, she removes her new clothes, so she's back to her old T-shirt and shorts. She takes out her overnight bag and places it, with her food and cleaning things, on the nearby table.

She sets to work, starting with a bucket of water and detergent. She washes every inside surface of the cabin. Then she climbs on the back and does the same for the cooler box, washing it first, then wiping off the excess with a second cloth. Next, she swabs all the surfaces with a cloth covered with methylated spirits. Then she does the same for the rest of the tray. Finally, she washes the rest of the outside of the cabin as best she can. Without a high-pressure spray she can't really do the underbody, but she doesn't think it's very important.

She surveys her work; she thinks she's done enough. There's little chance of anyone recovering her DNA, should someone check the vehicle. It's important to her that there be no trace of her left in the car.

She takes her remaining clothes and divides them into two sets. One set, including the clothes she slept in, goes into her small overnight bag, along with her passport, ticket and her other personal effects. She leaves a pair of sandals on the back tray. She puts her overnight bag and its contents inside a garbage bag; this is what she needs for the return leg on the plane. She double bags it and rests it on the back tray.

In a second bag she places the rest of the cleaning gear, which she also sits on the tray. Then she washes herself off again, pulls off her clothes from before, and puts them, along with her other discarded clothes, in another garbage bag. She ties this up and puts it into a garbage bin nearby.

Susan is naked in the dark. She quickly dresses in the final set of new clothes using disposable gloves. When she's dressed, she puts new disposable gloves on her hands and walks over to the car. She lays a garbage bag on the floor and sits inside, careful not to touch anything else. She slides her feet into her new socks.

Then she starts the car and drives away, following the signs for the airport. It is just 5.00 am when she reaches the airport concourse. There are a few people around, early morning cleaners and the like. She drives past the car park and looks at it.

Should she park there? Probably not. It's too likely to have CCTV to capture her image as she exits the car. She wants no direct link between the vehicle and her. She's already noted that the airport is only a kilometre or two from the main road, and on the other side of this road are housing estates. If she parks on the street in front of one of these, it's unlikely anyone will notice a common four-wheel drive. It's likely to be weeks before anyone wonders whose car it is and investigates.

So, she drives back out and parks on the side of the service road opposite some two-storey houses. There is not a soul in sight as she climbs out.

She puts on her sandals, lifts the other things off the tray, then she gives the parts of the cabin she's used, and the back tray where her things rested, a final wipe. She locks the doors.

She opens the garbage bag that holds her overnight bag, removes it from inside and sits it on the pavement. She puts all the cleaning gear and other unwanted objects back in its own garbage bag. With this garbage bag in one hand, the overnight bag in the other and the car keys in her pocket, Susan walks towards the airport, following alongside a cycleway.

She passes a bin at a bus stop and throws the garbage bag of cleaning things inside. She turns onto the airport access road. A few hundred yards along this road she crosses a creek and tosses the car keys into it. Susan can feel dawn approaching, though there isn't any light in the sky yet. Her spirits lift. It's a new day, and her ordeal is almost over. Her freedom, back in her beloved England, is close at hand. She notices that her speed has picked up and her step has become jaunty. She consciously pulls herself back to a more regular walk. She can't afford to get too cocky now; there are only a few more steps to go.

Her flight is due to depart at 10.00 am. It's only just after six, according to the massive clock inside the terminal. She's perhaps a bit early, but at least it means she has time for a shower and breakfast before she needs to check in.

Susan heads straight for the shower sign. She luxuriates in the hot water and steam for a good ten minutes, determined to wash every trace of the outback from her body. Washing it out of her soul might not be so easy, but she'll try. Breakfast is a bacon and egg muffin and coffee. She buys a magazine from a newsagent, wanting something to occupy her.

The lady at the check-in counter raises a snooty eyebrow when Susan declares she only has carry-on luggage. But Susan isn't concerned; it's her own business. She's anxious as she passes through airport security, particularly about the little pouch of stones. But there's nothing in her bag that draws their attention. Then she goes on through passport checking and stamping. As she opens her passport for checking a slip of folded paper falls out and onto the floor. "You dropped this," the man behind her says helpfully, passing her the paper.

"Many thanks," she says, accepting it from him. She doesn't recognise it, but she places it in her ticket wallet; she can look properly at it later.

Then she is through and sitting in the departure lounge.

The minutes tick by very slowly. She tries to read her magazine, but beautiful girls in beautiful clothes aren't a good enough distraction. She tries to relax and pretend she's enjoying herself, but she's wound up like a spring. She keeps expecting someone to call her name out.

When boarding is called, Susan doesn't rush. Inside the plane a pretty stewardess, with long blond hair, directs her away from the entry door along the row her seat is in. A second stewardess, part way down her aisle, is directing passengers to their own seats, speaking with a broad Cockney twang. Susan is comforted by the voice.

"Hello," Susan says to the stewardess.

The woman recognises her as English. She turns to Susan with a bright smile and says, "Another English visitor. I hope you enjoyed your trip to Australia."

Susan forces a return smile; she can't bring herself to nod.

At last the plane is taxiing out and soaring up into the sky. As it levels out Susan realises she's still clutching her passport. She goes to put it away, and it flips open to where it's just been stamped: *Australian Visitor Visa - Departure.*

That's it. That's what she was. She was merely a visitor.

Chapter 24 – Devil Spawn – One month later

Returning to work is relatively easy; it's almost as if she's never been away. Some people haven't even noticed her absence, and this suits her.

She's still staying with her mum and dad, though getting her own place is high on her list of priorities. What happened in Australia has a surreal quality, it's as though it happened to another person and, all the while, the real Susan stayed at home and worked in England.

A week after her return home a letter arrives, postmarked Australia. She flips it over and sees David's name and address on the back. She puts it aside, unopened.

She and Anne are still good friends, but their relationship seems to have suffered from how little she tells Anne about Australia, particularly about her text message. She gives her a half-baked, boring story about it, explaining it away as curiosity about something she read in an old paper. Perhaps Anne believes her, perhaps not, but it slides away. Instead she tells her little bits about the things she did in Sydney and Melbourne. This seems to satisfy Anne's need for an Australian story.

Susan only half keeps track of her periods; she had one in Sydney. She expects the next one will be a couple weeks after her return home. After she's back for three weeks she has a definite feeling of unease. She remembers how she missed the pill one day, that awful day. As her work is busy that memory is pushed aside. Then, one Saturday morning, still in bed, it hits her that she's been back for over four weeks. It's past six weeks since her last period.

It can't be true. Her mind fills with growing panic and disbelief at the possibility of having his child inside her.

She looks in the mirror at her naked body. Why has she not noticed before? Her breasts and nipples are starting to change, her breasts softening, nipples enlarging and changing colour. Her eyes can't deny what her mind is refusing to believe.

It's true. She's infected with Devil's Spawn.

She carries Mark's child!

This horror movie refuses to end. She is trapped inside it.

She has tried to excise it from her mind.

Now it possesses her body instead.

About the Author

Graham Wilson lives in Sydney Australia. He's written 13 books which include 12 novels and a family memoir as follows:

1. The Old Balmain House Series – 3 novels
2. Crocodile Dreaming Series – 5 novels and 2 book prequel

He has also written two stand-alone novels, *Risk Free*, *Mysteries*.

The *Old Balmain House Series* starts with the novel, *Little Lost Girl*, which was previously titled, *The Old Balmain House*. Its setting is an old weatherboard cottage, in Sydney, where the author lived for seven years. Here a photo was discovered of a small girl who lived and died about 100 years ago. The book imagines the story of her life and family, based in the real Balmain, an early inner Sydney suburb, with its locations and historical events providing part of the story background. The second novel in this series, *Lizzie's Tale*, builds on the Balmain house setting. It is the story of a working class teenage girl who lives in this same house in the 1950s and 1960s. It tells of how, when pregnant, she is determined not to surrender her baby for adoption, and of her struggle to survive in this unforgiving society. The third novel in this series, *Devil's Choice*, follows the next generation of the family in *Lizzie's Tale*. Lizzie's daughter is faced with the awful choice of whether to seek the help of one of her mother's rapists' in trying to save the life of her own daughter who is inflicted with an incurable disease.

The *Crocodile Dreaming Series* is based in Outback Australia. It starts with this first novel, *Visitor*, which tells the story of an English backpacker, Susan, who visits the Northern Territory and becomes captivated and in great danger from a man who loves crocodiles. The second book in the series, *Victim*, follows the consequences of the first book based around the discovery of this man's remains and his diary and Susan being placed on trial for murder. The third book, *Void*, is about Susan's struggle to retain her sanity in jail while her family and friends desperately try to find out what really happened on that fateful day before it is too late. In Book 4, *Vanished*, Susan disappears too. It tells the story of the search for her and four other lost women, whose passports were found in the possession of the man she killed. The final book in the series, *Invisible*, is the story of a woman who appears in a remote aboriginal community in North Queensland, without any memory except for a name. It tells how she rebuilds her life from an empty shell and how, as past fragments return, with them come dark shadows that threaten to overwhelm her.

The two books in the Prequel, collectively titled Vengeance, are the story of Mark, the boy becoming a man, at first seeking to walk in the footsteps of his childhood hero, Breaker Morant, but who, over time, becomes a monster and is ultimately destroyed, as the vengeance he seeks turns upon himself.

The books in the Crocodile Dreaming Series were previously published as ebooks in an earlier edition. They have now been extensively edited, with reader input. The improved versions are now being released in print format, over the next 2 years.

Risk Free is a tale of corporate greed and corruption in Sydney. *Mysteries* is a story set in Sydney about a mother and child who disappeared without trace 30 years ago and an old house with hidden secrets.

The book *Arnhem's Kaleidoscope Children* is the story of the author's life in the Northern Territory: his childhood in an aboriginal community in remote Arnhem Land, in Australia's Northern Territory, of the people, danger and beauty of this place, and of its transformation over the last half century with the coming of aboriginal rights and the discovery of uranium. It also tells of him surviving an attack by a large crocodile and of his work over two decades in the outback of the NT.

In writing these books Graham has drawn extensively on his experiences growing up in an aboriginal community, with many childhood aboriginal friends, and his identity as part of the aboriginal community of Oenpelli (now Gunbalanya). He proudly acknowledges his aboriginal skin name. His everyday name of Ngaginka (crocodile leg) reflects his own crocodile scar. It is widely used by others in the community as they talk to him.

As an adult working in the NT he had many close aboriginal friends spread across the NT, from whom aspects of book characters are drawn. While he has not sought specific approval for parts of this story that reference aboriginal customs, he is satisfied he has told this story in a way that fits with cultural ideas of those people he knows who have given him these insights.

He is also in the early stages of planning a memoir about his family's connections with Ireland called *Memories Only Remain* and is seeking ideas for books about the early NT cattle industry, its people and history. He is also compiling stories of people who worked for the NSW National Parks and Wildlife Service.

Graham writes for the creative pleasure it brings him. He is particularly gratified each time an unknown person chooses to download and read something he has written and write a review, good or bad, as this gives him an insight into what readers enjoy and helps him make ongoing improvements to his writing.

In his other life Graham is a veterinarian working in wildlife conservation and for rural landholders. He has lived a large part of his life in the Northern Territory. His books reflect this experience and give an authentic background to many stories.

More information about Graham and his books and writing is available from the following sites:

Graham Wilson – Australian Author on Facebook
Graham Wilson's Webpage:
http://grahamwilsonbooks.com

If you want to contact Graham directly please email:
grahamwilsonbooks@gmail.com

www.ingramcontent.com/pod-product-compliance
Lightning Source LLC
Chambersburg PA
CBHW020910130726
47904CB00006BA/1807

* 9 7 8 0 6 4 8 3 1 1 2 7 0 *